BRAKING FOR BODIES

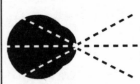

This Large Print Book carries the
Seal of Approval of N.A.V.H.

A CYCLE PATH MYSTERY

BRAKING FOR BODIES

DUFFY BROWN

WHEELER PUBLISHING
A part of Gale, Cengage Learning

GALE
CENGAGE Learning·

Farmington Hills, Mich • San Francisco • New York • Waterville, Maine
Meriden, Conn • Mason, Ohio • Chicago

GALE
CENGAGE Learning®

LIBRARY OF CONGRESS CATALOGING-IN-PUBLICATION DATA

Names: Brown, Duffy, author.
Title: Braking for bodies / by Duffy Brown.
Description: Large print edition. | Waterville, Maine : Wheeler Publishing, 2017. | Series: A cycle path mystery | Series: Wheeler Publishing large print cozy mystery
Identifiers: LCCN 2016046418| ISBN 9781410494993 (softcover) | ISBN 1410494993 (softcover)
Subjects: LCSH: Large type books. | GSAFD: Mystery fiction.
Classification: LCC PS3602.R6958 B73 2017 | DDC 813/.6—dc23
LC record available at https://lccn.loc.gov/2016046418

Published in 2017 by arrangement with The Berkley Publishing Group, an imprint of Penguin Publishing Group, a division of Penguin Random House LLC

Printed in the United States of America
1 2 3 4 5 6 7 21 20 19 18 17

To Nate and Jack
who brighten my life every day.

To Barry Aldemeyer
best poet and friend.
Life is so much fun with you in it.

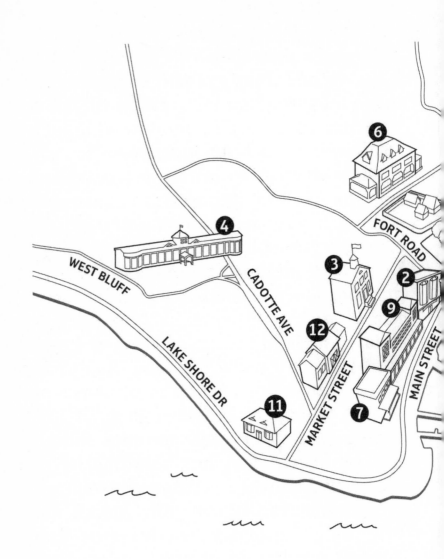

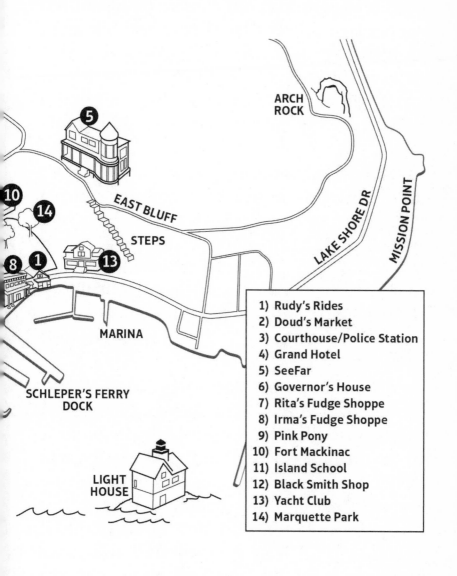

ARCH ROCK

EAST BLUFF

STEPS

MARINA

SCHLEPER'S FERRY DOCK

LAKE SHORE DR

MISSION POINT

LIGHT HOUSE

1) Rudy's Rides
2) Doud's Market
3) Courthouse/Police Station
4) Grand Hotel
5) SeeFar
6) Governor's House
7) Rita's Fudge Shoppe
8) Irma's Fudge Shoppe
9) Pink Pony
10) Fort Mackinac
11) Island School
12) Black Smith Shop
13) Yacht Club
14) Marquette Park

1

"What's with the garlic and bottle of olive oil?" I asked Fiona when I bumped into her, the two of us heading down the Shepler's Ferry dock, which was crowded with tourists. "Spaghetti for dinner and I'm invited?"

It was June on Mackinac Island and a perfect evening with small swells on Lake Huron and clear skies overhead. Those of us brave enough — or stupid enough, the jury was still out on that one — to tough out the winter from hell on the island so deserved an evening like this. A year ago I lived in Chicago and thought I knew all about snow, winter and ice. Yeah, right.

"It's the devil himself in three-inch lifts on that ferry." Fiona gripped the yellow *I ♡ the Town Crier* tote bag I gave her for Christmas and stared at the big white ferryboat gliding up to the dock. "Irish Donna said garlic and holy oil got rid of evil. I figured olive oil marked *extra virgin* was about as holy as I could get on short notice around here, not that the *extra* part made much sense. I mean either you're a virgin or you're not, but since that ship sailed for me a long time ago, who am I to judge?"

The setting sun sparkled against the purple sequins of Fiona's paperboy hat fitting her present position as reporter/editor/chief cook and bottle washer of the *Town Crier* as the ferry engines growled in reverse, bringing the big boat to a gentle stop. "I'm guessing we're not talking devil as in horns, pointy tail, red suit here."

"More like bleached teeth, smarmy attitude, and the hair implants hide the horns."

"Politician?"

"Peephole Perry, editor and creep of the *Inside Scoop,* that tell-all rag I worked at back in L.A." The dockworkers in orange vests scurried about securing the lines as Fiona added, "I can't imagine why he'd leave the land of fake and famous for a remote island. Either he's on the run and needing a place to hide out 'cause someone's had enough of his lies, or he's shaking someone down for a sizable chunk of cash."

Day visitors to the island queued up to board the ferry to the mainland as those on the ferry disembarked, stepping carefully from the bobbing boat to the pier. Fiona's jaw clenched as she searched the crowd. "I thought when I left L.A. last year I'd never see Peep's little bloodshot rodent eyes again." She gave me a sideways glance. "And I know why you're here; my brother sent you to keep me from shoving that Hollywood jackass in the lake, didn't he?"

I zipped my jacket against the evening breeze and went with the laid-back innocent approach to fibbing. "I'm just here to pick up Irma's wedding dress, figuring it's the least I can do with being her maid of honor. Can't believe she's getting married in four days. The Butterfly Conservatory is the perfect venue, and Reverend Lovejoy who wrote that *Senior Moments* book is actually coming in to perform the ceremony, and the Happily Ever After string quartet is playing as the happy couple walks down the aisle, and Irma and Rudy are writing their own vows —"

"And you're babbling." Fiona gave me a squinty-eyed look. "That means you're lying. Spill it or I'm putting it in the *Crier* under local interest that you haven't had a date in six months."

"Hey, neither have you." I sighed. "And maybe your dear brother mentioned there could be a situation, and since I was headed

11

here and he was headed for a blacksmith convention, I should keep an eye out." I hitched my chin toward a blond version of Charlie Sheen the nonsober years, judging by the silver flask in his left hand and inability to walk in a straight line. "I'm thinking the situation is coming our way right now."

"Hey, you." Fiona held up the olive oil and stomped her way toward the short blond. "Go away. There's nothing for you on this island; it's small, it has bad cell phone service, the Wi-Fi sucks and we eat fudge instead of avocados. Mess up somebody else's life, okay, and leave me the heck alone."

The guy smiled, kissed Fiona on the cheek and flopped his skinny arm across Fiona's shoulders. "Is that any way to greet the Peepster?" He hiccupped, pulled her close, cut his eyes side to side and lowered his voice. "Call me Perry, just Perry, got it? I have to blend in around here."

"Blend?" Fiona pointed. "You're wearing turquoise pants, three gold chains and a gold Rolex."

"Great, huh? It's my down-low look."

A guy in a navy Detroit Tigers ball cap with dark eyes and built like Adonis looked at Peep like he was nuts. I looked at Adonis like I wanted him for dinner. I wasn't proud of my gawking, but I truly couldn't help it after a long, cold, male-deprived winter.

Porters piled luggage twice their height into bike baskets sagging under the weight as Peep stumbled up the pier crowded with visitors for the annual Lilac Festival. The Peepster was zonked, not on Fiona's BFF list and I hated leaving her alone with him. Not that she was in any danger, but truth be told I didn't want to miss anything. This was drama, really good drama, and I had a front-row seat . . . but I had a dress to pick up.

"Hey," I said to the dockhand in an orange vest helping people off the ferry as it rode the swells. "Got a package for Irma Sutter in there?"

He helped a lady in a yellow fleece jacket. With one hand he shoved a clipboard at me and with the other grabbed a woman who was swallowed up in duffels and garment bags and nearly tripping into the lake. I signed the clipboard, snagged the white box tied with a big pink bow that he thrust at me and hustled my way back to Fiona.

"I'm here, so get used to it," the Peepster growled to Fiona as I drew up. He slid a gold cell phone into his pocket, then hissed at me, "This is none of your business; get lost."

"It's an island, dude, there is no lost."

"Wanna bet? There's all kinds of lost, even around here." The Peepster scowled, then turned back to Fiona. "Look, kid, you owe me. I gave you your first reporting job and let you sleep in the office when you didn't have a roof over your head." He eyed the woman with the luggage who was nearly fish food back at the boat. I could see her face now, forty-something in a cherry-red pencil skirt that matched the highlights in her hair.

"Zo here lent you clothes when someone stole all your stuff," Peepster added. "We were just one big happy family back in L.A., remember?"

Fiona's face turned the color of her hat. "What I remember is that I had no money and gave Zo my gold bracelet so she'd let me borrow her clothes."

"You mean this bracelet?" Zo stuck out her arm with an adorable turtle charm suspended from fine gold links braided together. "I just love it to pieces and get compliments on it all the time."

"You're probably the one who stole my stuff in the first place to get it," Fiona steamed, yanking her arm away from Peepster. She jabbed her finger in his direction.

14

"And I worked for you for almost nothing when I was too stupid and desperate to know what I was getting into."

"And, like, what are we getting into, Peep honey?" Zo yelped. She stopped dead, tilting to starboard from the weight of the bags, her eyes widening as she took in Main Street. "Like, there's a real live horse on the street. Like, a really big live horse? And there's another horse and OMG three more? Like, are they shooting a film or something, and, like, what's with all the bikes?"

Fiona pointed toward the town. "No cars, no pollution, no gridlock on the 405. And . . ." Fiona wagged her brows at Zo. "Not one Kardashian to tweet about. How are you going to live with that, huh? The ferry's loading up right now and I bet there's a red-eye to L.A. If you hurry, you can make it."

The Peepster's lips thinned to a straight line. "We got business here, important stuff." He faced Zo. "We're staying the week. Deal with it. Now get the luggage on one of these horse wagons going to the Grand Hotel. You said it was a decent place to stay on this hunk of rock, but I didn't figure on needing an animal to get there."

Peep heaved himself onto the maroon carriage with driver in black top hat and red jacket. Zo handed off the luggage. "Like, this is kind of romantic, Peep?" she cooed as she slid in beside him on the bench seat. "Like, just the two of us? We can come here when we get married?"

"Perry, it's just Perry," Perry mumbled. "And I'm already married, so keep it down, will ya?"

"But you're not going to be like married for long now, are you, Peep honey. You got me." She snuggled closer and gazed around. "This place is really, like, you know, a movie set or something with the cute shops and the big lake out there and everyone on bikes and stuff just pedaling along? Maybe tomorrow we can, like, get one of those double bike thingies? Maybe we can get married in that little gazebo in that park over there. Wouldn't that be, like, scrumptious?"

Peepster ignored Zo and glared down at Fiona. "You and me, we need to meet. We got things to talk about. Bring your checkbook. See you in twenty."

"Not if I see you first." The carriage lumbered off and Fiona heaved a garlic bulb, missing her target by a mile. "See what being extra virgin gets you? Nothing in more ways than one! Talk about being overrated."

She dropped the bottle back in the yellow bag next to a stack of yellow papers. "And to top it all off, Peepster and Zo are staying at the Grand Hotel. The place has been here for over a hundred and twenty-five years. It survived storms, prohibition, fires and now it's never going to be the same. In a week Zo will have them all saying *like,* ending everything in a question and doing avocado facials."

She studied the box in my hand. "At least you got Irma's dress except . . . except . . ." She snagged the package. "Idle Summers? The address is for up at the Grand Hotel. Didn't you read the label?"

"Label?" I studied the front of the box and swallowed a groan. "You were alone with the Peepster and I was worried."

"You were worried you'd miss some juicy gossip after a winter of being cooped up at the bike shop and talking to cats. Now you got the wrong wedding dress. I think this takes maid of honor to a new low. What are you going to do?"

There was one long blast from Shepler's Ferry, meaning the boat was sailing off. My hair stood straight up and I tore back down the dock, Fiona running right behind me, the two of us snaking our way around tourists and workers. We pulled up at the end of

17

the pier, nearly careening off into the dark water as the big ferry drifted out into the lake.

"Irma's going to kill me," I panted, taking the box from Fiona's hand. "Like in door-nail dead."

"If you say *like* one more time I'm shoving you in the lake myself."

I leaned against one of the posts supporting the pier to catch my breath, the last rays of sun casting gray shadows across the water. Fiona and I were on the lighter side of thirty-five and island besties. She grew up on Mackinac, worked the paper with her family, then hightailed it to L.A. to be a reporter in the big league. She came back here a few months before I landed on these sunny shores and took over running the *Crier.* She didn't talk much about L.A., but she didn't seem to miss it . . . except for In-N-Out Burger. Those must be some crazy-good hamburgers.

"So what's the 411 on this Peepster guy?" I asked Fiona before she could ask me what I was going to do about the missing dress.

"Long story short, he's a total jerk." She raked her short blonde hair.

"And?"

"Skunk, dweeb, pond scum, total piece of crap." Fiona worked her bottom lip as we started back to Main Street. "He's trouble, Evie. He knows stuff about . . ." She took a deep breath. "Well, he just knows stuff."

"About you?"

"Me?" Fiona's eyes shot wide open. "Of course not. Not me. Never me." She forced a smile that didn't reach her green eyes. "But they don't call him Peephole Perry for nothing. He looks through peepholes, finds out everyone's secrets then holds it over their heads and they dance to his tune or he'll put it in that crappy rag of his, the *Inside Scoop,* or threaten to tell their producer, their agent, the director of the film they're working on." She took a breath and added in a quiet voice, "their dad."

"No one really believes what's in the tabloids, do they? I mean really. UFOs, I had Elvis's baby, Oprah goes bald isn't exactly Wikipedia type of reporting."

"It gets people thinking the worst, and . . ." Fiona gazed out at the ferry now zooming past Round Island Lighthouse and the harbor light blinking green to mark the entrance. "Never in a million did I expect Peephole Perry to show up here. Heck, I didn't think he knew where Michigan was."

"My guess he still doesn't, but I got a bad feeling about him."

Fiona smiled and it was genuine this time,

her green eyes bright with a hint of devil like usual. "That bad feeling is 'cause you left Irma's wedding dress on that boat and now you have to fess up. Do you think it's part of that black cloud thing you brought with you from Chicago last September?"

I shook my head. "No way. There is no black cloud. It's gone . . . all gone. I got Rudy off that murder charge, didn't I? I'm cured of all cloudness. I'm officially cloud free. I had all winter to get rid of it. Heck, it probably froze to death just being here. The wedding dress fiasco is an easy fix. I'll get the right box on the next run. The ferry will be back in an hour and all will be right with the world."

I handed the box over to Fiona. "Take this to Idle when you go up to the Grand Hotel. If you don't meet with Peep, he'll come looking for you, and what did you mean about Peep telling your dad? Tell him what? Why should you bring your checkbook? Fiona, what's going on and what the heck happened out in L.A.?"

2

"Nothing happened out in L.A.," Fiona added in a rush as she grabbed the Brides and Bliss dress box from my hands. "It's just that Dad wouldn't much like Peep. Heck, nobody likes Peep."

"Except Zo," I chimed in. "Zo really likes the guy, and from what I can see they deserve each other."

"There is that." Fiona tucked the dress box under her arm and hitched the *Crier* bag onto her other shoulder. "I have flyers in here about the lilac festivities that need to be dropped off at the Grand, and I need to meet with Peep." She rubbed her forehead. "Just when I thought my past was behind me, it rears its ugly head and bites me in the butt. Wish I could think of a way to bite it back."

Fiona plucked out a yellow flyer and shoved it at me. "Do you see any typos? Everything needs to run smooth at the newspaper while the parents are visiting here for the wedding. The *Crier* was their baby for twenty-five years till they handed it off to me and escaped to sunny Arizona. They're eating hummus, drinking smoothies, doing tai chi and they listen to Yanni. All that sun's fried their brains."

"The flyer looks good to me," I said, scanning the sheet. "But then I was in advertising for eight years where they spell catsup with a *K*."

Fiona took off for Market Street. The *Town Crier* was on the bottom floor of the white clapboard shop; Fiona lived on the top. My name wasn't Sherlock but even I could tell that something had her jumpy, and Fiona wasn't a jumpy kind of person. Fact was, she was the one who stuck with me through thick and thin — and things got thin as tissue paper a few times — to prove Rudy innocent. We learned to pick locks together, outsmart motion detectors and scale porch railings with a single bound. Okay, that part was a lie. More like flop over railings and land in bushes.

With the lilacs in full bloom the island smelled like a giant florist shop, but the chill in the air was a reminder that winter hadn't left the island all that long ago. Vintage streetlights and twinkle lights nestling in the trees came to life as I headed in the other direction for the bike shop. Rudy had agreed to hold down the fort while I picked up the dress, so now I just had to make up an excuse why I didn't have it. I fell in step with a brew crawl making their way from bar to bar and probably heading for the Ice House, which actually was once an icehouse. After this last winter I didn't care if I ever saw ice again. I flipped up the collar on my jacket and looked like one of the gang as we ambled past Irma's fudge shop with lights ablaze and customers at the counter, then to my bike shop. Well, the sign said Rudy's Rides, but it was half mine.

When I met up with Rudy last year, the place was on the skids, Rudy had a busted leg and he got accused of murder. Since I worked for his daughter back in Chicago, my job there was in serious jeopardy with the *accused of murder* part happening when I was supposed to be here helping Rudy and not making things worse. Rudy and I hit it off, so I quit my design job that I totally sucked at, depleted my 401(k) and was now half owner of Rudy's Rides. We'd carved out a niche market of renting theme bikes painted with golf clubs, cooking, music, flowers and the like. If we had a good season the shop would be in the black. If not, Rudy and I would be riding our bikes to the unemployment office.

I took the ramp we'd added to the front porch and sang out, "Honey, I'm home" to the black cat and the calico sitting on the windowsill. They responded with a *so what, it's only you* look as I slipped through the open front door. I congratulated myself on a job well done in avoiding Irma and sticky questions and —

"Okay, okay, where is it, where is it?" Irma chanted as she danced her way to the front of the shop from the living area in the back that I now called home. Rudy and Irma cohabitated at the fudge shop, and with cat fur and fudge not being a match made in heaven, I tri-habitated with Bambino and Cleveland.

Irma twirled her way past the old wicker rocker and the pool table that I'd inherited along with the cats namely because black cat Bambino slept in the left side pocket. Irma might be a card-carrying member of AARP for some years, but she was the perfect blushing bride. And as her maid of honor, I was sworn to keep her that way and not blab about the missing dress!

"Uh, where's Rudy?" I needed to say something before guilt won out and I blurted the ugly truth. "I thought he was watching the shop."

Irma tossed her hair and did another twirl. "He's over at the Good Stuff stirring up a new fudge recipe. Brandy Bonanza is his latest brainstorm for the adult crowd, so I came over here to fill in. I rented out that Wizard of Oz bike for two weeks," Irma said as she pirouetted around the rows of bikes. "And the Tiger Woods bike and Spring Has Sprung that you just finished up and the Martha Stewart bike. Love the little plate of chocolate chip cookies you painted on the fender of that one. Okay, so enough about business, where's my white dress box from Brides and Bliss?"

"Uh . . ."

"You hung the dress up over at the fudge shop for me so it wouldn't wrinkle."

"Well . . ."

Looking starry-eyed, Irma framed her face with her hands. "Don't you love the pink blush color and the jacket with the beads, and remember how it took me months to find that dress. I just love my wedding dress and can't wait to try it on again."

"I . . . I gave it to Fiona to take to her place. You don't want Rudy to see it, that would be all kinds of bad luck." I was going straight to hell for this whopper of a lie, but I'd have to chance it. I couldn't very well have the bride in jail for murder, namely mine.

Irma's lips pursed to a pout. "Well, I guess I can go visit my lovely dress at the *Crier* just to make sure it fits."

Think, Evie, think! "Except . . . Fiona's working on that article about the Pattersons' anniversary, and you know how the Pattersons are about getting details right. Maybe you should wait till tomorrow, and I really need to pick up paint over at Doud's Market to finish the fly-fishing bike I'm working on. Can you watch the shop for maybe twenty minutes? Gee, thanks, I really appreciate it." I escaped out of the shop, not giving Irma a chance to say no and giving me the chance to meet the next ferry and get the dress.

Cones of light dotted the Shepler's Ferry pier, the last of the day tourists lining up, as Sheldon — my know-it-all iPhone — buzzed my butt. Not only was the Shepler's Ferry dock good for docking ferryboats and delivering passengers safe and sound to the island, but it was one of the few hotspots for getting decent cell phone reception. Sheldon had a text from Abigail, my old boss and Rudy's daughter back in Chicago, wanting to know how I was doing with the wedding plans. When I worked for Abigail, it took her two years to remember my name; I was never one of her fave people and I was definitely not about to tell her that I'd lost the dress.

The ferry pulled in and that was good. The bad part was that Nate Sutter, Irma's son and the local law enforcement officer, stood on the dock, hands on hips, looking pissed. I'd pretty much learned to live with the pissed part because Sutter used to be a cop in Detroit. I figured the Detroit gig was enough to make anyone pissy.

Sutter was easy to spot in his Windbreaker with a yellow *I AM THE POLICE* patch on the sleeve. And maybe his shoulders were a little broader than most guys' and his brown wavy hair always needed a trim and there was a faded scar on his chin, his body more gym than couch potato, and he favored his right leg when tired, like now. Most of the island female population considered Sutter a real biscuit, but personally I never noticed much about the guy at all.

"What are you doing here?" I asked Sutter as I drew up next to him and the ferryboat kissed the dock. "Some drunk-as-a-skunk fudgie onboard causing a problem?" *Fudgie* was the nickname the locals used for the tourists and the tons of fudge they gobbled down each year.

"You're half right," Sutter groused, his brow furrowing as a woman in fuchsia pink capris and gold shoes and blazer bellowed to one of the ferry workers, "Take your hands off me, you bully."

The other passengers waiting to disembark gave Miss Loudmouth a wide berth as she ranted on: "That two-timing no-good husband of mine said he was going away on business. Yeah, it's business all right, funny business with that bimbo of his. Well, I wasn't born yesterday. I've followed them all the way from L.A. and I know they're here and I'm going to find them or die trying."

"Ma'am," Sutter offered, "I have no idea where your husband is." He helped the woman off the boat. "And you need to calm down, you're causing a scene."

"A scene! A scene! Ha!" The woman yanked her arm away from Sutter and threw her overnight bag on the dock, her bleached-blonde hair flopping over her forehead. "You haven't seen anything yet," she snarled. "I'm going to catch that little weasel and that gold-digging secretary of his and toss her in the lake myself and divorce his scrawny butt right on the spot."

"Turquoise pants and gold Rolex?" I added. "He's at Mission Point Resort." Sutter gave me a *what the heck are you doing* look as I pointed up to Main Street. "One of the horse taxis will take you there."

"Horse?" Miss Loudmouth froze, her eyes arced to her hairline. "Do I look like a woman who rides a horse, for God's sake?"

"If you just think of this town as an extension of Warner Brothers Studios, you'll be fine."

Sutter folded his arms. "Thanks a lot," he said to me, as the two of us watched the woman drag her luggage up the dock. "Now she'll cause trouble at the Point and I'll have to go there."

"Except her husband is up at the Grand and maybe she'll decompress by the time she finally figures it out, or she'll be too tired to care."

Sutter arched his left brow. "So this is you doing me a favor?"

"Uh, sure. Why not?" Actually I did it to buy Fiona time with Peep so she wouldn't be caught in the middle of a domestic-triangle mess. Fiona had enough mess to deal with . . . whatever it was.

"Why are you here at this hour?" Sutter wanted to know, breaking into my thoughts on Fiona.

"Doing my duty as maid of honor and picking up your mother's wedding dress."

29

Mentally chanting, *Please be there, please be there, please be there,* I skirted around the boarding procession of tourists. "Do you have a delivery for Irma Sutter from Brides and Bliss?" I asked the same ferry worker I talked to before.

He scowled down at me. "Lady, you just picked it up on the last run."

"It was the wrong box," I said, dropping my voice so Sutter wouldn't hear. "Can you check again? Please? And hurry?"

Mumbling, the guy disappeared back inside the ferry as Sutter came up beside me.

"All I got," the worker said as he re-appeared, "is this box for Idle Summers up at the Grand." He shoved the Brides and Bliss white box with pink bow at me.

"But . . . but that's who the other box was for."

The guy hunched his shoulders. "Hey, I just deliver 'em. My guess is this Bliss place sent two packages to Mackinac and one of them is yours. They just both went to the same person. It happens."

I signed the clipboard *again* and glanced back to Sutter, who had a devil smile on his lips. He stuffed his hands in his jeans pockets and rocked back on his heels. "You lost my mother's wedding dress?"

"And I found it. This is probably it right here, just going to the wrong person, is all," I declared with a lot more conviction than I felt. I said a quick prayer to Saint Jude, the patron saint of hopeless causes. I slid the bow off the box and pulled back the tissue. "It's . . . it's chiffon with yellow rhinestones."

"Maybe I can get you into some kind of protection program so Mom doesn't find you."

I did a full-blown smile to confirm my innocence. "It's like the guy said, the other box up at the Grand has got to be Irma's dress."

"Isn't there something about you and a black cloud?"

I jutted my chin. "There is no cloud." *Maybe.* "I'll meet Idle and straighten things out." I gave Sutter a hard look and tried to retie the pink bow so it didn't look like a teething two-year-old did it. "I just saved you from the L.A. crazy woman, so you owe me. Promise you'll keep this . . ."

"Fiasco?"

"Incident to yourself."

"You want me to lie to my mother?"

"Just don't say anything, okay, and don't come anywhere near the Grand because that will cause attention and she'll find out because no one around here can keep their mouth shut."

Sutter made a cross over his heart and added, "I bet it's the cloud." He retied the pink bow to perfection, then took off. When I got back to the bike shop, I stashed the second Brides and Bliss box around back, slapped a perky innocent-as-a-lamb smile on my face and went inside to face Irma.

"Where have you been?" she wanted to know. "And where are the paint cans?"

Holy freaking cow! The paint. "Wrong color."

"I tell you, the whole island is going to hell in a handbasket." Irma shoved a paper at me. "The Sherlock bike needs to be delivered to Heaven Sent up on the East Bluff. They want it tonight for an early ride tomorrow. What's with fudgies and early biking? Didn't they ever hear of vacation? I need to get back to the shop to help Rudy close up. He's swamped, Brandy Bonanza's a big hit." She gave me the squinty-eyed look. "What's going on with you? Your left eye's twitching."

I walked to the door, herding Irma in that direction. "Tell Rudy I said hi, thanks for holding down the place, see you later. Gee, your hair looks shiny, you'll make a lovely bride." Then I closed the door, leaving Irma on the outside.

"What?" I said to Bambino and Cleveland, perched side by side in the middle of the pool table, paws on hips, giving me the *you big fat liar* look. Okay, they didn't really have their paws on their hips, but they would if they could and the look was for real, I swear. They were sweet and darling felines to the rest of the world, and to me they were judgment on steroids, like that little cricket in Pinocchio who never let him get away with anything. "So I told Irma a little fib." I fessed up. "It's for her own good so she doesn't have a meltdown."

Cleveland twitched his tail.

"It's the truth."

Bambino curled his lip.

"All right, all right. You win, I lose. I didn't tell Irma what was going on because I didn't want her to be disappointed in me, and how about some tuna and we forget the whole thing." The fur balls might be very judgmental, but tuna as a diversion won out every time.

I dished out tuna; tied the white box to the basket of the Sherlock bike, which was painted up in tweed hats, pipes, magnifying glasses and book titles; and wobbled off down Main. Shops were closing for the night, and the Lilac Festival crowds were heading for dinner or the bars or a stroll through Marquette Park. Until I came to the island the only thing I'd ever ridden was mass transit, and considering my present biking ability, everyone around here would be safer if I'd kept it that way.

There were two directions on the island, up and down, and from Main Street everything went up. Huffing and puffing and sweating like a roasting pig at a barbecue, because I sat on my butt all winter and painted bikes instead of getting to the gym, I struggled onto Cadotte. Streetlights glowed like pinpoints of bright in the night; the Grand Hotel in the distance was bathed in moonlight. Strollers and bikers in fleece jackets enjoyed the evening, and was that Zo on the other side of the street in shiny red biking shorts and jacket, huffing and puffing on a red bike? No one would ever question Zo's favorite color, but it was nice to have some company in the huffing and puffing department.

My great plan was to switch the dresses with Idle before I had an ulcer from messing this up, and then I'd drop off the bike at Heaven Sent. There were no addresses on the island, just names of shops and the behemoth Victorian cottages like Edgewood, Lakecliff, and Over-the-Glen that suited Daddy Warbucks way more than Goldilocks.

The white porch of the Grand Hotel was a Ripley's Believe It or Not two football fields long and lined with twenty-five hundred of the biggest, reddest geraniums on earth. Tonight the air was still a bit chilly for socializing outside, so most of the action was inside. "Saint Louis Blues" wafted from the open French doors, and carriages crowded the main entrance with people coming and going. I pedaled around back of the hotel to find a less congested path to park, struggled past the recycle and trash bins, then held tight to the handlebars and started down the other side.

God bless down! Shadowy bushes and plants whizzed by as I flew around toward the front of the hotel, the only light shining down from the porch above. Lilacs and more geraniums lined the path on one side, the hotel shops on the lower level were now closed on the other side of me and . . . and something big and dark and sort of blue was smack in front of me. A garbage bag? A big garbage bag! The Grand Hotel did not put their garbage out front. What the —

Brakes! Holy criminy, brakes! I jammed the pedals into reverse, front tire skidding, back tire fishtailing, as the momentum carried me forward and flipped me over the handlebars. I slammed into the Brides and Bliss box; it sailed off into the night and I landed with a solid *oomph* on top of the bag. Sherlock tumbled onto my back, a pedal wedged where no pedal had any right to be. I lay there for a second, my tongue counting teeth, the little bones in my spine realigning.

Landing on garbage was not a high point in my life, I'll give you that, but the squishiness kept me from looking like skinned roadkill. The bag smelled like salad . . . Italian? Personally I thought it needed more oregano. I blinked open one eye and spotted the Brides and Bliss box to one side, the yellow rhinestone dress dangling from a lilac bush.

I blinked open the other eye and stared at the Peepster, his face inches from mine. His eyes were open too, but they weren't staring back at me. They weren't anything. They were cold, vacant and dead.

3

Dead? No! I blinked a few times and refocused. The Peepster had a deep gash across his forehead and there was blood.

Yes, dead! Yikes! Forgetting teeth and bones, I shoved Sherlock off into the grass and scrambled to my feet, trying really hard not to scream. Bloomfields did not scream. A whimper now and then if things got a bit hairy, but that was it. I stumbled backward and slipped and fell on my butt. Life was not improving. I pulled Sheldon from my back pocket, prayed my landing hadn't smashed him to smithereens and hit speed dial.

"Got the dress?" Sutter said from the other end.

"Got a problem." *Breathe, Evie, breathe.* "Path on west side of the Grand. Meet me." I disconnected and gulped in air. I focused on the lilac bushes instead of the Peepster and came face to face with . . . "Fiona?"

Eyes wide and scared, she gave a little wave.

"What are you doing here!"

"Meeting Peep like he said."

"Define *meet.*"

She crawled between the bushes. "I saw him in the lobby and we talked, and then I went off to clear my head, then got a text from him to meet up here." She pointed a shaky finger. "He was like this when I showed up, and I hid when I saw your bike coming 'cause I didn't know it was you, and before you ask I didn't have any part of this but on the inside I am kind of yelling yippee and doing a happy dance."

"Fiona!"

Fiona stood and helped me up. "Were you just talking to Sutter?"

"Yeah, and you've got to get out of here. Anyone on that dock this evening knows you and Peep were not bosom buddies, and he's staring at the stars and not thinking *Gee, is that the Milky Way?*"

Fiona nudged Peep's arm with the toe of her gym shoe and gave me a little shove. "Check for his cell phone."

"Me?"

"I'm not going to touch him. I didn't like the guy when he was sucking air, much less now when he's cold and creepy. You didn't know him."

"I knew enough, and why do you want his cell phone?"

"Hey, Bloomfield," came a voice from above. "What's going on down there?" For a second I considered the possibility I'd died in that fall and this was God wanting an accounting since I was here with a dead guy. I rolled my eyes up to Sutter leaning over the railing. Okay, not God, but at times he thought he was. Sutter clicked on a flashlight and Fiona dove back into the bushes.

"You . . . you got here really fast," I stage-whispered. "Why are you on the porch?" Nate Sutter was not a Grand Hotel kind of guy; he was more a beer at the Mustang Lounge with a side order of fried green beans kind of guy, most of the time not bothering to order his own and swiping mine.

"That L.A. wife caught up with the L.A. secretary." Sutter leaned over the edge. "The hotel staff called me to deal with the fallout. I sent the secretary in one direction, the wife in the other, and the duel's at dawn. Why'd you call?"

From her hiding place in the lilacs, Fiona made the *shh* sign with her finger over her lips and added the pleading puppydog look of *don't give me away.* I knew she wasn't a killer; at the moment it just looked that way.

"You have the L.A. wife and secretary and I have the L.A. husband/boss and he's . . ." *Dead as a rat in a trap* wasn't exactly the thing to be yelling out at the Grand Hotel. "He's fallen off the porch," I said instead, and from the amount of alcohol consumed here on any given night, a header seemed perfectly reasonable.

"Is he hurt?"

"Sure, let's go with hurt. But not 911 kind of hurt."

"Then he's okay?"

"Well, he's not in pain."

Sutter disappeared back over the top and Fiona scurried out to Peep. She hunkered down, pulled her sleeve over her hand and started digging through his pockets . . . wallet, keys, flask. "His phone isn't here. Where's the darn phone? I've got to find the blasted phone."

I didn't know about the phone problem, but in my shaky condition the flask had definite appeal. I picked it up with the edge of my fleece before Fiona could stuff it back in Peep's pocket with all the rest of the stuff. I unscrewed the top, prayed the alcohol gods were smiling in my direction and took a swig.

"Vodka, good vodka," I said, the booze warming my insides. "What is that gooey stuff on your sweater?"

Fiona took the flask, gulped and swiped the back of her hand across her lips. "Peep always did have excellent hooch, his one good quality." She passed back the flask. "It's slippery. Everything's coated in olive oil. Don't mention to Sutter that I was here, and keep him busy; I need a few minutes to look around. I'm desperate."

"Desperate about what?" But I might as well have been talking to myself because Fiona was nowhere in sight and Sutter was hustling up the main drive in front of the hotel. Olive oil meant there was an olive oil bottle, and since I didn't believe in co-incidences on an eight-mile island I figured extra virgin was the culprit. I watched Sutter as he dodged horses and carriages and chatted with a few of the drivers, and I tried to catch a glint of light reflecting off broken glass. There! Using my jacket, which was already a mess from playing slip-and-slide with the Peepster and the olive oil, I picked up the broken bottleneck and wiped around the edge to get rid of fingerprints.

Here's the thing. Fiona didn't do in Peep, but her fingerprints would be on the bottle since she bought it. The real killer's prints

41

might be there too, but I couldn't take the chance of the only prints being Fiona's. Sutter turned onto the path where I was, his black Windbreaker and dark features fading into the surroundings. I casually dropped the chunk of bottle next to the body and stepped away as Sutter clicked on his flashlight. He drew up next to Peep, bent down and felt for a pulse.

"You call this hurt? The guy's toast."

"Yeah, but I got the *no pain* part right. I was going fast and couldn't stop, so he really was hurt, he was just sort of dead first. Not that I could be yelling that in front of the Grand Hotel. Talk about bad for business."

"Have you been drinking?"

Not nearly enough, I thought as Sutter looked closer and said, "The front gash is flat and looks like he might have fallen off the porch. Then there's another cut on back of his head. The first blow didn't kill him. Someone finished him off from down here, or they hit him on the porch and fell over from the blow. This happened at eight ten; he smashed his watch in the fall."

I figured words like *gash* and *cut* warranted another helping . . . or two . . . of vodka. I took a swig; Sutter caught me in the act.

"Does that belong to . . . ?" Sutter glanced back to Peepster. "You're kidding."

I took another swig. "He didn't have any use for it, and this is all really stressful and . . . and it's his fault so he owes me."

Sutter muttered something that would do HBO proud, pulled on gloves, pried the flask out of my hand and put it beside the body.

"If I have a breakdown it's all your fault."

"Fake Rolex, not even a good fake," Sutter said, not caring about my mental state enough to give me back the booze. He picked up the chunk of broken bottle and held it to the porch light. "Extra virgin olive oil, and from the looks of the pieces probably the murder weapon, meaning he was finished off down here."

"Or . . . or maybe he fell with the olive oil bottle in his hand?"

"Right. And then he hit himself over the head. What do you know about this?" he asked me. "And you know something. Your left eye's twitching."

"I was nose-to-nose with a dead guy; I get to twitch. Anybody would, just ask, and there are lots of people to ask right now, and . . . and . . ." *Oh boy.* "You know, I think we should go with the *fell off the porch* story and forget the murdered part, and before

43

you blow a gasket, hear me out. The falling story is easy and uncomplicated and will give us time to find the real killer without throwing everyone into a panic. He or she won't know we're on to him or her, and we won't be upsetting the fudgies with tales of murder and mayhem at the Grand Hotel."

"Are you out of your mind? We can't act like nothing's happened. What do we do, just toss some mulch over the guy, plant a geranium and have a beer?"

Okay, Sutter would find out about Fiona, the olive oil and Peep soon enough, but Fiona was looking for something she didn't want out there, and if I could buy her time I would. But Fiona wasn't my only concern. Selfish as it was, I needed to come up with a way to not upset the fudgies who were here spending money on bicycle rentals and more fudgies coming the whole summer who would spend more money. One hint of murder and bye-bye bike shop.

"Think of it not as forgetting about the murder," I pushed on, "so much as postponing things till we can find the killer. Then it reads *Man killed by jealous lover* instead of *Man killed and no one knows who the heck did it.* There's nothing to be gained by going inside the Grand Hotel right now at the height of the dinner hour and yelling *Mur-*

derer on the loose, run for the hills. We haul the guy to the medical center like he's had an accident."

"We got a crime scene here, Chicago? The wife and secretary just might want to take the body back to L.A., and the yellow tape across the path could, just maybe, be a giveaway to one and all that something's up, ya think?"

"What's to tape off? You got the murder weapon and time of death, and Doc's in Traverse City. Unless you want to leave a body on the path for the next three days till he gets back. With all that olive oil and in the hot summer sun, the Peepster will . . . marinate."

"Peepster? You know him?"

"And Doc's not there to examine the body and release it, so the secretary and/or wife can't have the body till he signs off on it, and that buys us time. We've got to figure this out for all our sakes."

Sutter's eyes narrowed. "This is about money, isn't it?"

"It's about good business for the island. Warren Buffett would take the guy to the medical center."

"Do I look like Warren Buffett?"

"What's going on?" a guy called down from the porch. "Is somebody down there?

45

Did somebody fall?"

Sutter and I exchanged *uh-oh* looks and a woman on the porch squealed, "Oh my goodness! It's a body! This is fantastic! I know what this is. It's one of those murder mystery weekends right here at the Grand. The victim's right down there, I can see him all sprawled out there on the ground. Oh, this is so much fun."

"Look, lady," Sutter shot back. "This is no mystery weekend party. This is a real crime scene here."

"Of course it is," she squealed again. "You all are great actors, this is amazing. What a fantastic surprise at the Grand Hotel." She got out her iPhone and started clicking pictures. "I've been to these before; they're a hoot and for it to come out of the blue like this unannounced and just happening is so real."

"It *is* real," Sutter growled.

"And you even have a smashed bike, I wonder what clue that is, and I bet there's a murder weapon down there and I think I see blood. They never have blood." She clicked more pictures as a string of onlookers lined up on the porch doing the same; more iPhones clicked and someone pulled out a flashlight.

"I see the weapon," the guy said next to

46

her as he pointed over the railing. "It looks like a green bottle of some kind. Bet he was hit over the head."

"I think he was hit over the head after he fell off the porch," a lady in a blue evening gown chimed in. "If I were setting up a murder, that's what I would do. A little shove here, a little whack there . . . perfect. I wonder who are the suspects."

"We're all suspects," the squealing woman squealed again. "That's what makes this so cool. And we all get to find the killer. I've read every Sherlock Holmes story and I'm really good at finding the killer. I'm going down there for a closer look." She hooked her arm in the air to the others. "Come on, everybody, let's go. The game is afoot."

The clatter of hotel guests stampeded across the porch, and Sutter waved his arms in the air as if trying to land a 747. "No! What the . . . This is crazy. Holy crap!"

"Give me your jacket," I said to Sutter. I tossed it over Peep's head and shoulders. "Call Molly, I bet she's still at the police station. Tell her to bring crime scene tape and a body bag and then get one of these carriages to haul Peep to the medical center. We can make use of that new refrigeration unit Doc insisted get put in."

"That refrigeration is thanks to you and

the last body you found that got stashed where no body should ever get stashed. Do you see a pattern here, Chicago? You? Bodies? Two murders in ten months where there hasn't been a single murder in ten years?"

Sutter ran his hand around the back of his neck and let out a deep sigh. "I'm a cop, I can't go along with this. The carriage driver's going to know we've got a real body and this isn't some stupid game."

"He'll keep his mouth shut or this time next week the only thing he'll drive is himself to the unemployment office back on the mainland 'cause there will be no one staying at this hotel or anyplace else on this island."

I grabbed Sutter by the front of his T-shirt. "Listen to me. If you don't go along with this, you'll have an island full of hysterical fudgies because there's no way off this chunk of rock till morning. It's murder and mayhem week at the Grand Hotel, so put on your deerstalker hat and get used to it."

The sun wasn't up yet as I sat at the chipped yellow Formica table in the kitchen at the back of the bike shop. The mess with Peepster and Fiona as prime suspect had me drawing hangman nooses on the Hello Kitty notepad I'd just bought at Island Stationery. A smiling cat with a cute pink bow deserved better, but today I was tired to the bone and had a lot more questions than answers.

I poured coffee and made another pot. It was going to be a two-pot day; I could feel it in my bones. I never did find that Idle Summers gal to get Irma's dress, but the hotel crowd loved the yellow rhinestone dress in the bushes and thought for sure it was a clue. Who knew murder could be so much fun? But if the real Peep story got out, every business on the island was toast.

I gazed out across the deck to the sky brightening from grays to blues with morning streaks of pink and white. Mother's new law office, still under construction, sat to the left with the postcard-perfect harbor dotted with boats just beyond. Of course in winter that lovely harbor froze solid as granite, snowdrifts reached my butt and the temp got so low around here it busted my outdoor thermometer.

I dumped cereal, added milk, then scooped Cocoa Puffs out of one side of a pink bowl I'd picked up at a yard sale as Bambino and Cleveland lapped milk out of the other side. Man and beast in perfect harmony. Actually it was girl and felines, but close enough.

"Blessed be Saint Patrick," Irish Donna said as she sashayed in the back door. "Ye be setting yourself up for a bad case of cat cooties, sharing food like you are."

"Now that I think about it, my hearing's improved and I can see better in the dark." I took another scoop of cereal and said around a mouthful, "And I can jump higher."

"And any day now ye be a-sprouting whiskers, chasing mice and using a litter box; best be keeping that in mind, Miss Smarty Pants."

Irish Donna owned the Blarney Scone up on Market Street with her husband, Shamus. That he was pushing seventy didn't deter his wandering eyes and hands one bit. Donna also helped out at the *Town Crier* and was the resident island sage. She said I had a black cloud surrounding me that attracted bad luck like a lightning rod. I didn't want to believe the cloud idea, but it sure explained a lot about getting left at the altar by Tim the Terrible and the finding-dead-bodies thing I had going on. I refused to think that the missing wedding dress was part of the cloud. That was just a fluke, right?

Donna poured Mr. Coffee, added a shake of cinnamon from the cabinet, then took the seat across from me. "So when is your ma coming back here for the summer?"

I studied the little Cape Cod about ten feet off to the side. "Her plan is to practice law in Chicago in the winter and here in the summer. I'm thinking she'll show up next week. With her office not finished here, my guess is she'll move in with me at the bike shop. Attorney-a-Go-Go, Wills on Wheels, Bikes and Briefs."

Last summer the parents went to Paris. Father left Mother for a fan dancer and took up drinking French wine and painting nudes on the Left Bank. Mother came to the island to recuperate, told everyone her name was Carman, switched her Ann Taylor attire for Mae West and dated a retired mob boss. Bloomfields never did anything half-assed, and best I could tell this was midlife crisis gone loopy.

"And why are you here at six thirty?" I asked Irish Donna.

She slid her gold shamrock necklace across the table to me. "Ye be needing this sooner than later, I suspect. I had breakfast at the Village Inn and heard about what you had going on up at the Grand. A murder mystery weekend is a fine idea, me dear, or the Blarney Scone, Rudy's Rides, the Pink Pony, Horns and every other establishment

51

would be belly-up by August."

Donna pushed the shamrock closer still, with a dusting of flour on her sleeve from making the best scones on the planet. "Maybe this be helping with finding the killer before the fudgies catch on. Down at the VI we be calling it the Peep Show so as not to give away what's really happening when discussing the murder situation out in public like we do. I voted for Bo Peep myself, but some of the boys are feeling a mite randy after the long winter around here, so the Peep Show 'tis. And then there be Irma and her wedding dress not being over there at Fiona's like you said?"

I stopped my spoonful of Cocoa Puffs in midair. "It's six thirty. Who in the heck looks for a dress at this hour of the morning?"

"Ever been a bride, me dear?"

"Not successfully."

"Well, this one's a mite attached to the dress and heading this way in a huff."

I dropped the spoon in the bowl, splashing milk across the table; Bambino and Cleveland didn't miss a lap. I slipped the gold chain with the shamrock over my head. "Is your buggy parked outside? I need to get to the Grand Hotel quick." I grabbed the battered white box leaning against the wall and hustled for the door.

"That be Irma's dress?" Donna asked.

"Not exactly. There was a little mix-up."

Donna arched her brow, her coffee mug stopped halfway to her lips. "Mix-up? And ye being the maid of honor like you are? 'Tis the cloud for sure."

I pulled myself up into Donna's horse cart, which had a Saint Christopher medal where a cup holder should be and no place to plug in Sheldon to get recharged. I'd always miss having a car and how fast it got me from place to place, but Paddy had pretty brown eyes, got ten miles to the bag of oats, and didn't have to get his oil changed.

The crisp air made my cheeks tingle and turned my nose pink. I had on an old jacket from Target and Donna had a terrific long green coat that set off her red hair, giving me an attack of coat envy. She spread a plaid blanket across our laps and picked up the reins, and we clip-clopped off down Main Street. I figured it was a safe bet that Donna could have said *Grand Hotel* and Paddy would take us there via horsey autopilot.

"Guess this is as fast as Paddy goes?" I started biting my fingernails as a few morning bikers and strollers passed us up.

"Ye can be getting out and pushing to help

Paddy along if you got a mind to, me dear. Or ye can be telling me about the dress catastrophe in case I need to tell your ma why your poor dead body's rotting at the bottom of the lake."

By the time we pulled around back of the Grand where the nonguests parked, I had Irish Donna up to speed on wedding problems and my stomach was tied in knots. We headed for the door, stepping around two refrigerators and a stack of bundled cardboard waiting for the recycle dray. Getting rid of trash on an island was a constant battle and cost the earth to ship out.

"This way," Irish Donna directed as I turned right instead of left. "The Grand might be all modern on the surface, but there still be old rooms and stairways so the staff can move about. There even be gambling rooms tucked away. The way I hear it, an old woman sat at the door looking all innocent like with embroidering hotel pillowcases and keeping an eye out so only the right folk got in. In Prohibition they went and smuggled hooch across the lake from Canada and brought it into the hotel in baby buggies, of all things. When things got slow the owners called the police in town to come raid the place. It made the papers from coast to coast, and then everyone knew gambling and booze was going on at the Grand and headed right for it. Mighty good for business, it was."

"That is the best ad campaign ever, and it was free."

Donna waved to one of the porters hauling boxes into a freight elevator; everyone at the hotel knew her from working at the *Crier* and making blueberry scones to die for.

"We should have brought along the latest edition of the *Crier,*" I said to Donna as we headed for the back stairs. "It would have saved Fiona a trip up here."

"Fiona's da is doing the deliveries these days. He's visiting with his old friends for a bit, and Fiona's ma is taking a hand with writing the news. If ye ask me, they both be missing the paper more than they be letting on. We can ask at the front desk about this Idle Summers person and where she might be this fine morning. Kind of a funny name if you're asking me."

"Uh, I think we found Idle," I said, pointing across the hotel lobby.

4

"Well, blessed be Saint Patrick," Irish Donna said to me as we stared at a show placard proclaiming Idle Summers as a famous singer and appearing nightly up in the Cupola Bar. "That explains the stage name she be givin' herself."

"And the yellow rhinestone dress from Brides and Bliss." I tapped the box under my arm.

Donna and I crossed the lobby with its pink geranium carpet that stretched from one end to the other. Green couches and brocade chairs formed intimate conversation areas with sparkling chandeliers overhead and white French doors leading out to the massive porch. If there was a lobby in heaven where you waited your turn to talk to Saint Pete, this was what it looked like.

The hotel was just starting to come alive with early-morning guests, and was that yelling coming from the small game room at the back? A waiter and two hotel clerks in maroon uniforms stood by the closed doors looking anxious and wringing their hands, as guests gathered around.

"I get it," came Sutter's voice from inside the room. "I get that you both loved the Tweep."

"Like, his name was Peep," Zo bellowed with a sob. I recognized her voice. "He was *my* Peep. Like, how could he be dead? How could this happen? We came here to be alone together!"

"He was not your Peep, you skanky floozy," came the wife's voice; the crowd by the closed doors was growing. "I was married to him for twenty loving years. Mrs. Madonna Perry. He was *my* Peep."

"Like, ya think there was any love in being married to the ice princess, and like what kind of a nut job changes her name to Madonna?"

"Someone who can sing just like her, that's who."

Irish Donna turned to me. " 'Tis a pity we didn't bring popcorn. A mighty fine show they're putting on for us, it is."

A woman in khaki shorts and pink sweater standing behind Donna tapped her on the shoulder. "This is all part of the mystery weekend the Grand is putting on for us. It started last night with the body in the bushes. You should have seen it, it was terrific. The body bag got carted off in a horse carriage, and that to-die-for handsome police officer put up the crime scene tape. Let me tell you, that guy can tape my scene anytime he's got a mind to."

The women in the crowd nodded at the to-die-for part; a few of them were fanning themselves and looked a little faint. Another woman in capris and a yellow straw hat said, "And now the fun starts with us trying to find the killer." She nodded to the closed doors. "I mean to tell you they are amazing actors. I've been to mystery weekends down in Atlanta, but this takes the cake."

A man in jeans and brown Docksiders scribbled in a notebook. "Right now the two women in that room are tops on my suspect list. One's the mistress/secretary who had to be ticked off that this Peep guy didn't marry her, and then we've got the wife who wanted Peep dead for cheating on her. They both have motive and they both were here at the Grand, so they have opportunity. But how does this olive oil thing fit in? Why olive oil?"

"Well, I'm headed down to that market in town to see who bought a green bottle of the stuff." The pink sweater lady hiked her purse onto her shoulder. "That bottle was the murder weapon. It was right next to the body and oil all over the place."

The capris lady let out a dreamy sigh. "Well, I'm waiting right here to talk with that hot policeman in the room and see what he thinks. There had to be fingerprints on the bottle." She giggled. "Actually I don't much care what he thinks or if there were prints or not, I just want a little eye candy to start off my day."

I handed the mangled Brides and Bliss box to Donna and lowered my voice. "Find Idle and see if she has Irma's wedding dress. I'll catch up with you later."

I started off and Donna grabbed my arm, her lips in a pout. "A fine thing it is when ye be leaving a friend in the dark like ye are and not be on the level with what you have going on."

I hated to get Donna involved in a murder; if someone had killed once, they'd have no problem killing again. But Donna was Fiona's friend, and she also had a knack for zeroing in on good gossip. She'd be a big help and besides, she'd bug the crap out of me till I gave in and took her along. "Fiona's connected to the Peep Show, and I think the little creep had something on her. I want to look around in his room."

"You think there was some hoochy-coochy

going on between the two of 'em?"

"No way would Fiona hoochy Peep. Ugh. I'm thinking more like blackmail and I can't imagine what it's about." I pulled desk clerk Penelope off to the side; at least that was what her name tag said. "You realize this is no game and so do I. Do you know the women in there for real?" I nodded to the game room, where the crowd was getting bigger.

Penelope was late twenties, pretty, petite with blue eyes and dark hair. "Know them? Are you kidding, there's been nothing but trouble since that d-e-a-d man and the red-haired woman who says *like* every other word got here. And then the wife, Madonna, shows up. Madonna? Seriously? And now everyone thinks this is a freaking mystery game and things have just gone downhill from there. Cook burned the morning popovers, we ran out of towels on the second floor, the *Town Crier* promised us Lilac Festival flyers with all the activities that never showed up and now everyone is asking me what's going on."

She pushed back her curly bangs. "Do I have *Google* written across my forehead? How should I know what's going with that blasted festival? There are flowers, they bloom, get over it."

Penelope closed her eyes and pulled in a deep breath. "The place is a zoo, I tell you. We're all going to lose our jobs. I'll be back in Dallas this summer asking *Do you want fries with that?* Do you know what summer is like in Dallas? Heat and dust and cowboy hats as far as the eye can see. I hate cowboy hats."

"What if we find the killer?" I cooed. "Then it'll look like part of the game and everyone wins. The police get their guy, we keep our jobs, and the fudgies have fun. Even when it hits the papers, the fudgies will think it's part of the game." I hooked my finger, drawing Penelope closer, with the three of us in a huddle. "I need to take a look in the dead guy's room to figure out who did him in. He was shacked up with that Zo gal in the game room."

"You're a cop?" Penelope whispered back. "You two sure don't look like cops."

"We be knowing a cop," Donna tossed in. "Fact is I used to babysit him. Rambunctious little tyke."

"I can't let just anyone in a guest's room," Penelope grumbled, still keeping her voice low. "What kind of a hotel do you think this is? My boss will skin me alive."

From the game room came Zo's screeching. "Like, you really think I'm riding to any police station with you? Like, you must be nuts?"

"I'm not riding with you either, you tramp."

"Like, you want a black eye?"

"You'd look great with a fat lip."

The clerk grabbed my arm. "Follow me."

Peep's room was on the second floor toward the back of the hotel. "Remember," Penelope said as we stepped around a housekeeping cart piled with towels, soaps, shampoos and bed linens, then slid in her key card. "I had nothing to do with any of this."

Donna did the cross-her-heart thing and we stepped inside. "Great day in the morning," Donna said as we took in the unmade bed, the pink-and-green-flowered bedspread in a heap on the floor. Zo's clothes were scattered like a tornado had torn through the place, pink towels were flung across a chair and a half-finished bottle of Gray Goose vodka was parked next to an ice bucket. "Top-shelf booze and a cheap room, like something out of a dime novel it is."

"If you consider three fifty a night for a room as being cheap."

Donna pushed aside the curtains and filtered sunlight crept into the room. "We're pretty high up here, and look off into the trees, but it's still a view of the back road way down there below. Far cry it is from the Jacqueline Kennedy suite or the Victorian suite way up there on the top floor where you can see clear across the lake." Donna peered out the window. "It overlooks the service road, but it's pretty high up here so you don't see it all that much." She dropped the mangled white box on the bed and opened a dresser drawer. "So what it be that we're looking for, love?"

I opened another drawer. "Fiona knew Peep and Zo back in L.A., and best I can tell is that Peep had something on her and he keeps the info on his cell phone."

Donna gasped. "Ye not be thinking our Fiona did the big lout in?"

"Of course not," I answered in a rush.

"Course not," Donna echoed, pulling on another drawer. "Was a slip of the tongue is all . . . still . . . sometimes a body can be pushed just far and they snap like an old twig and . . ."

I gave Donna a hard look.

"Right, Fiona would never be doing such a thing. But 'tis a good bet that if the Peep had Fiona in a desperate way, he was doing it to others. Who else was he knowing on this here island?"

"You think maybe he came here just to

see Fiona," I added, rifling through drawers — shirts, pants, lingerie. "But if he was blackmailing her, she doesn't have enough money to make it worth the trip, and why come all the way out here? He could blackmail her from L.A."

I held up a skimpy white uniform with a red cross on the front. "I sure wouldn't have taken Zo as a nurse."

"With a see-through top and panties, and is that a pith helmet and a rope right there in the drawer? Are those fur-lined . . ." Donna picked up handcuffs, a glint in her eyes. "Been a while since I had . . . Well, never you mind."

I dropped the nurse's outfit back in the drawer as if it were on fire, tossed in the handcuffs and kicked the drawer shut with my foot. "Ick!"

"Don't be getting your bloomers in a bind, me dear. It is L.A. they be coming from, and they do things a mite different out there on the coast than we be doing here in the heartland. Why, I do remember a trip me Shamus and I took to Hollywood. There was this heart-shaped bed and —"

"And let's try the closet," I added in a hurry. "But if there's a Superman outfit or something involving whips, we're out of here, and no more L.A. stories, okay?"

"Suit yourself, but they be some mighty fine stories if I do say so myself. I'll be looking in the bathroom behind the toilet. In the movies they always be hiding stuff behind the toilet."

Donna started off as the brass knob on the main door turned, grabbing our attention. The lock clicked open; Donna's eyes were the size of golf balls. There was no dust ruffle, so we couldn't hide under the bed. Since when did dust ruffles go out of style?

Donna snagged the wedding dress box and yanked me toward the bathroom as the door swung open. We tiptoed into the tub and Donna gently pulled the pink-and-white-striped shower curtain across. The door in the bedroom closed; the plush carpeting muffled the footsteps. My heart hammered in my ears as Donna squeezed my hand tight enough to cut off circulation. If it were the maid, she'd be bustling around cleaning and calling Zo a slob. It could be Zo, but from the conversation we overheard in the game room, she was on her way to the police station to give a statement and have one last look at old Peep belly-up on a slab.

It could be the killer looking for that cell phone, and since he'd knocked off Peep, two more dead like Donna and me wouldn't make any difference. I held my breath. Sweat slithered down my back; our only weapons were a loofah and two mini bottles of the Grand Hotel's geranium-scented shampoo. We could spa the killer to death.

Footsteps came into the bathroom. A cabinet opened, then closed, and Donna squeezed my hand tighter. A man's silhouette moved around the room, then retreated. Donna let go of my hand and we exchanged smug *we got away with it* smiles until the shower curtain flew open. We both jumped, I screamed, "Help!" and swung the loofah and Donna flung shampoo bottles.

"Bloomfield!"

"Sutter!" He rubbed a spot over his eye where Irish Donna had nailed him, and I hit him again with the loofah. "You scared us to death! What are you doing here?"

He held up a room key card. "I have a search warrant. What's your excuse? And I'm betting it has something to do with Fiona, a bottle of olive oil and the dead guy."

"Sounds like the beginning to a bad joke."

"This is no joke." He looked at us in the tub armed with bathing equipment, a half smile at the corner of his mouth. "Well, maybe a little." He held out his hand to Irish Donna. She took it and stepped out of the tub, and our little parade headed into the bedroom.

"Well, it's been really nice catching up like this," I offered in a cheery *aren't I cute for hiding in a tub* voice. "I guess Donna and I should go. You know how it is, places to be, things to do —"

"Sit," Sutter ordered in his Detroit cop voice that was not cheery at all. He pointed a stiff finger at the bed.

Donna and I sat with the white box sandwiched between us, and Sutter pulled out a desk chair. I'd never been in a room at the Grand Hotel, and this was not exactly how I'd planned the event of enjoying a lovely feather bed, pink lilac drapes that matched the bedspread, fringed shades on the glass lamps and a purple sequined hat wedged between the side of the bed and the nightstand. What the heck?

"Talk," Sutter grumbled; the spot over his eye was red and forming a big knot.

"Well, now, me darling boy, there be nothing much to talk about this fine lovely morning," Donna volunteered with a charming Irish lilt in her voice that could disarm the devil himself. "We're here trying to find the killer, is all, just like you are."

"So we can all keep our jobs," I added, taking a discreet look back at the hat to make sure I wasn't hallucinating. No hallucinating; it was Fiona's hat all right. Now I needed a distraction so I could get the darn thing. Sutter would find it for sure, and if Peep's cell phone was in this room too with incriminating stuff on Fiona, her goose was cooked.

"Let me get you some ice for your eye," I offered.

"My eye's fine. Tell me about Fiona and this Peep guy, and you know plenty because you were on the dock when he and Zo landed."

Here was the tricky part. I had to tell Sutter something and it had to sound convincing, contain an element of truth so Sutter wouldn't wring my neck later on, and most important what I said could not implicate Fiona. There was enough info out there to do that deed. "Peep, Zo and Fiona all knew each other in L.A., and I guess they missed each other and —"

"They be doing the reunion thing," Irish Donna added. "You know, where you be catching up and getting those T-shirts that look alike and taking pictures."

Sutter leaned back in the little chair and folded his arms. "According to the porters down at the ferry dock, this nostalgic reunion had Fiona throwing garlic at Peep as he rode off into the sunset. And for some

68

reason she had a bottle of olive oil that she dropped in her yellow *Crier* tote bag. Some coincidence that a bottle just like it winds up as the murder weapon over at the Grand."

"A lot of people buy olive oil," I ventured. "And there weren't any fingerprints."

"How do you know there weren't fingerprints?"

Well, crap. Some people did great under pressure. Then there was me. "Just a guess, and you really need something for that eye, and if you ask me Zo probably did in Peep." I stood up, looking for a distraction. I needed something to get Sutter's attention so I could snag the hat and get his mind off the fingerprint blunder. Where was a mouse running across the floor when you really needed one?

"Think about it," I went on. "Zo had to be pissed at Peep when wifey Madonna came along. Or it could have been Madonna doing the whacking when she caught up with Peep. Having him here shacked up with Zo had to toast her cookies, and oh look, there's an ice bucket. You need ice for that eye." Before Sutter could stop me I reached for the bucket, praying for anything but empty. I pulled off the lid and knocked the bucket with my hand, sending cold water into Sutter's lap. Not a mouse, but not bad.

Sutter jumped up, and I scooted back and snagged the hat from beside the bed. Donna caught me, her eyes huge as she spied the hat.

"Blessed saints, 'tis a mess you are, you'll be needing something to dry off with. Here," Donna said, tossing Sutter a pink towel that landed over his head and down his face, giving me a chance to stuff the hat in my jacket.

Sutter yanked off the towel; his shirt and pants were soaked clear through. "To think some people come here for a vacation."

"We should go." I gave a little salute, Donna picked up the box and we scurried toward the door.

Sutter's big hand landed heavy on my shoulder. "What did you find here?"

"Zo's a slob and the geranium shampoo is incredible?"

The hand got heavier. "When you find Fiona, tell her to be at my office at noon. And she better get to me before I get to her, and if you're hiding something, that makes you an accessory."

And it makes me pretty darn clever, I added to myself, but thought it best not to poke the soaking wet bear. The door closed behind us, and Irish Donna and I trotted down the hall. "Bless the saints, Fiona was there in that very room. Ye think she found that phone you been talking about? What has the girl gotten herself into?"

We stopped at the top of the grand red-carpeted staircase; hotel guests milled around below. "We've got to find Fiona and let her know the local cop's hot on her trail." I pulled out Sheldon and held him up in one direction, then another, trying for reception. "No bars. How can we have no bars in the middle of the Grand?"

" 'Tis a hotel on an island, me dear, not Verizon." Donna handed me the white box. "Ye best be settling the wedding dress situation first, then have a go at Fiona. My guess is that Rudy is opening up the bike shop for you, but I need to be getting to the Blarney Scone for the morning rush. Shamus is most likely making more passes than a quarterback if I'm not there giving him the evil eye, not that it be doing much good."

"There she is," a guy in a purple T-shirt called, pointing to me from the bottom of the staircase. Four other purple-shirted people gathered around him, all of them looking right at me. "It's that girl who was with the dead guy last night. I bet she has some clues for us."

They galloped up the steps, and Donna

71

took a step back. "Great day in the morning, they all be daft in the head, they are."

"You're leaving me?"

"In a New York minute, me dear. They got a wild look in their eyes, they do." Donna scurried off toward the back stairs that led to where we'd left Paddy. The Murder Marauders — or so their T-shirts proclaimed — surrounded me, pencils and notepads poised for action.

"How did you know this Peep person?" a gray-haired guy with a goatee asked. "Did you live with him in L.A.?"

"I've never been to L.A."

Everyone scribbled in the notepads, and a lady with bottle-blonde hair asked, "Were you jealous he was with another woman? Is that why you pushed him over the porch, then whacked him over the head with the bottle?"

"I'm not a suspect! I just discovered the body."

"Likely story." The blonde gave me a surly look. "You found the body, you're a suspect and I think you look guilty. Your left eye twitches."

"You know," I added in a serious tone, "that cop, Nate Sutter, knows more than anyone what this is all about."

"Heck yeah, the police." Goatee guy nod-

72

ded, and the rest joined in. "Great idea. Thanks for the tip."

"Don't tell him I sent you," I called after the Marauders. I doubted if they heard me, and Sutter was going to blow his top, but the way I figured it, if I sent other groups his way it would keep the guy busy and let me look for Fiona and the killer.

The Marauders reached the bottom of the grand staircase just as Penelope started up. She looked worse than before, with her auburn hair falling out of its neat bun and her blouse untucked. She took my arm, pulled me to the side and leaned against the stair railing for support. "Please tell me you found the killer, that this nightmare is over, that those two lunatic women are not coming back here ever again to drive me nuts and make a scene. The Grand Hotel does not do scenes; we do peace and quiet and elegance and overcharge guests for the experience. This is not tinsel-town Hollywood." She stifled a sob.

I patted Penelope's back. "It's going to take more than one trip to a room to figure this all out; you gotta get a grip."

"I can't afford a grip; I need action now. We'll all be in the unemployment line by the end of the week and have our condos repossessed and have to return the new

73

Coach bag we just bought in four easy installments on QVC. Last year my cousin worked here at the Grand and the Clintons stopped by and Bill played the sax. I work here and get the L.A. loonies playing murder and mayhem."

"Do you know where I can find Idle Summers?"

"And there's another nut bar, but she's nice and she's a darn good performer. She sure packs 'em in at the Cupola Bar, I can tell you that. It's tough to get name entertainment out here, but she enjoys the place, especially today for some reason. Why, she was singing show tunes at the grand piano in the lobby just a few minutes ago. Now she's got her yoga mat and doing downward dog on the front porch, her skinny butt pointing due east, and the male population around here is having heart palpitations."

Penelope held my hand tight, her eyes pleading. "You are going to fix this, right? You're going to make this all go away and get my life back to normal, right? I can't lose my job. I have bills to pay and we need customers coming to the Grand Hotel, not packing up and leaving."

5

Penelope tramped off and I headed across the lobby. It was crowded with guests perched on green brocade couches drinking tea in lovely china cups and eating little pastries as sunlight streamed in through the clerestory windows. I stepped out onto the porch; nearly every seat was taken. Waiters bustled about serving coffee and the best Bloody Marys on earth . . . so I'd been told. At the far end, which was mostly empty, I spotted a human triangle.

"Miss Summers," I said, as I got closer. I bent down to talk to her face and not her hindquarters. "I think you have a dress that belongs to —"

"Not now, you're ruining my chi. Go away."

"I need the wedding dress that you have that you got by mistake, and I've got your yellow rhinestone dress here in this box that I got by mistake, and —"

Idle's face jerked around to face me. She wobbled and the triangle toppled over, trapping me under it, both of us on the floor. "You got my dress? This day just keeps getting better and better."

I tapped the box wedged under my arm. "Right here."

Idle Summers was probably midforties and had enough lifts and tucks to look ten years younger to an audience. She had big boobs and curly blonde hair cut with hedge trimmers. That she could do downward dog wasn't a surprise. That she could overcome gravity and right her voluptuousness from the upside-down position was nothing short of a miracle.

Idle scooted to one side and I took the other. She sat on the porch floor Indian style and tore into the box, then held up the yellow dress. "Isn't it fantastic? Perfect for my 'Ain't No Sunshine When She's Gone' number. I had no idea where to buy some fancy outfits, and then I talked to this nice lady at a fudge shop in town and she put me on to Brides and Bliss, where she bought a lovely wedding dress. Maybe that's how the orders got mixed up." Idle looked a little closer at the dress. "It's got a spot here on the bottom."

"It tangled with a lilac bush."

"Oh, I just love lilacs, don't you? I swear they smell like heaven. My granny had them in her garden in Ohio: pink, purple, white, all kinds. I plan on getting to as many of those lilac tours as I can; they have an amazing schedule of events. I can just have the dress spot-cleaned, so it's not a problem." Idle smiled, or came as close to it as Botox and injected whatever would allow. "The box you're after is in my room. I haven't even opened it. Yesterday was such a stressful day and everything was going wrong, but then my problem just sort of . . . well, it just died away and today is so much better. Isn't that the best news ever?"

I followed Idle into the lobby and she stopped at the grand piano. She tucked her yoga mat under her arm, tossed her curls, squared her shoulders and belted out that song about the sun coming out tomorrow. In seconds she had the whole lobby, kids to grandparents, joining in. Penelope was right in that Idle Summers was a terrific performer and sure knew how to work a crowd.

"That was fantastic." Idle and I took the staircase to the second floor and headed to one of the expensive rooms facing the front of the hotel and the lake.

"I just love to sing," she gushed. "Always have. You know, I was up for a Tony a few

77

years back . . . when things were really getting good for me and then suddenly things got . . . complicated." She fished around in her lush cleavage, which was straining under the electric-pink workout top, and plucked out the key card. Any male with a heartbeat would kill to be that key card. She jabbed it into the slot on the door and pushed it open.

"Home sweet home. They let me stay here as part of my singing gig. Isn't it amazing?"

And it was amazing, with yellow floral wallpaper, coordinating bedspread and curtains, a hooked area rug and a little alcove for reading. I could only imagine what this room went for a night.

"Look at this adorable antique writing desk." Idle nodded across the room. "I just love it. I'm going to try to buy it and take it back to L.A. with me when I go. It'll be a little memento of things gone right."

"You're going back to L.A. soon?"

A smile split her face. "I intended to stay here all summer and just hang low, but things have changed . . . for the better, the much better, who would have thought. I wasn't sure I'd ever perform again, and now . . . I'm going to be singing 'Happy Days Are Here Again' tonight and lots of nights to come." She handed me the white Brides and Bliss box. "Here you go."

I sat the box on the antique desk and whipped off the top to see a blue dress with sequined flowers. But what grabbed my attention most wasn't the fact that Idle Summers did not have Irma's wedding dress and who knew where it was, but that Idle did have a yellow flyer on the desk. It was the schedule for the lilac tours. The only person she could have gotten that schedule from was Fiona.

Okay, what was going on? What was the connection between Fiona and Idle? They had obviously met up for some reason last night. They knew each other in L.A., and now the Peepster was dead here on Mackinac Island of all places. Where in the heck was Fiona, and what were she and Idle Summers up to?

"Well, hot diggity dog. You got the dress," Rudy said to me as I came into Rudy's Rides with the white box tucked under my arm. Rudy was perched on a stool at the workbench and had on his Mark Twain uniform: a wrinkled white shirt, gray vest hanging open and bow tie skewed to one side. His hair looked as if he'd stuck his finger in a socket, and his blue eyes were sparkling and kind as always.

Rudy was Twain on this island of God,

mother and apple pie that relied on tourism to stay afloat, at least financially. The island regulars of about five hundred assumed multiple roles in parades, pageants and exhibits. Rudy always dressed the Twain part. He said it made it easy to figure out what to put on every day and it gave him license to swill whiskey, smoke cigars and spout such things as *Go to heaven for the climate and hell for the company.*

Irma was Martha Washington in celebrated events, and she had the character down pat. I was the new Betsy Ross since old Betsy retired to Lauderdale and bequeathed me the costume, the flag and the sewing basket. I wasn't great on the sewing angle, but the basket made a great place to stash KitKats to toss to the kids along the parade route.

I went over to the workbench and plopped the Brides and Bliss box between a bike seat waiting to get attached and Bambino and Cleveland, who were named after original Twain cats.

"Whoa," Rudy said as I slipped off the top of the box. He put his hands over his face, covering his eyes. "Isn't there something about seeing the wedding dress before the wedding being bad luck?"

"True enough, *if* this were Irma's wedding dress."

Rudy parted his fingers, looking out at me. "I don't much like the sound of *if.* Usually my little fudge morsel is calm and serene and the picture of rational behavior and tranquillity and beloved by one and all. Then this wedding dress business started up and she's been . . ."

"Distracted?"

"Completely off her nut." Rudy was a mechanic in his other life; he'd decided he'd had enough of looking under hoods at carburetors and fuel pumps and retired to Mackinac, where there were no cars and lots of bikes and euchre tournaments. Rudy kicked some major euchre butt down at the Mustang Lounge, called the Stang. The trophies on the shelf over the workbench were proof of the kicking-butt part.

"You know," Rudy said. He held up the blue sequined dress and tilted his head, a smile tipping his mustache. "I like this dress. I like the sparkle. Always been a sucker for sequins. Not exactly a traditional wedding dress, I'll give you that, but like Twain says, *Life's short, break the rules.*"

I sat down on the second stool beside Rudy's where we spent many hours together working on bikes, Rudy fixing them and me painting. "I don't know if Irma would agree, but getting rid of the sequins and bringing back your bride's dress of her dreams is my problem, not yours."

"Dear girl." Rudy put his arm around me. "When Irma sees this dress, pots will be thrown, cans kicked, colorful words will fill the air around us and customers will dive for cover. I'm the one who lives with the disconcerted bride. Trust me, it's my problem."

"If it's any help, I called Brides and Bliss to see what was going on. Seems a clerk had a little too much bliss, came in drunk as a skunk and screwed up the orders. A bunch of brides are on the warpath and the clerk is now living in Peru under an assumed name. Your old recliner is still in the back room if you need a hideout till this gets fixed, and since we're on the subject of hiding, have you seen Fiona?"

Rudy picked up a wrench and added the new seat to the Sesame Street bike that I'd painted with Oscar the Grouch, Cookie Monster, Big Bird and the gang. "You don't really think Fiona had anything to do with this Peep guy being dead?"

"Do you?"

I pulled the purple sequined hat from my jacket and dropped it next to the white box. "I found this in that Peep guy's room. This means Fiona was there, and my guess is she was looking for his cell phone. There's something on that phone she wants kept quiet. Do you have any idea what happened while she was out in L.A.?"

Rudy picked up a socket wrench. "None of us knows, and she never talks about it. Her daddy went to see her a few times when she was on the coast and always came back in a bad mood. Maybe giving her the *Crier* was Walt's way of getting her out of that place. She refused at first, and then suddenly she gave in. All I know is that Walt is mighty protective of her and she's the same, always wanting to please him. That's half the reason she went to L.A. in the first place, to be a big-time reporter and make her daddy proud. I think Walt feels responsible for her being out there."

"OMG, it is you!" came an earsplitting squeal from the doorway. It was the lady from last night, flanked by four others, all wearing yellow T-shirts. "You were the one standing over the body last night." She held out her hand as she came my way. "I'm Gabi and we're the Corpse Crusaders." She pointed to her shirt, stenciled in blue. "It's so much fun to meet one of the actors. Love that they just worked you all right into the town as if you belonged here for real."

"Yeah, it's freaking amazing," I added.

"So," asked one of the men, whose blond hair was cut short, "how did you know the dead man?" As if on cue they all pulled out matching yellow notebooks and pens, poised for action.

Rudy gave me a *the spaceship has landed and the aliens have disembarked* look as I said, "I'm not exactly an actor, but —"

"Were you having an affair with that Peep guy?" an elderly man asked. "Did he come to the island to see you? Are you going to do in his mistress next and then his wife?"

The blond guy let out a long-suffering sigh. "If you are going to knock off someone else, please, for the love of all that's holy, let it be that Zo girl. If I hear one more *like* come out of her mouth, I'll do her in myself."

"For the record," I rushed in, "I didn't kill anyone."

"But you were standing over the body, so that makes you a suspect." Gabi scribbled in her notebook. "And what about that girl in the purple hat who was in the bushes? We saw her hiding there, and look, you've got her hat on the workbench. Is she the killer? Who is she and why was she there? Are you trying to frame her for the murder?

That's a great plot twist you got going on. I love it!"

"No framing," I said as the Crusaders scribbled madly. "I don't know why Fiona was there in the bushes or in the dead guy's room."

"Fiona?" Gabi squealed, proving once again that I totally sucked when under pressure. "Now we've got a name. This is fantastic. And she was in that Peep guy's room!" They all scribbled again.

Rudy did the *keep your mouth shut* gesture of slicing his hand across his throat, and he was so right. "You know," I offered, "the guy who has the skinny on all this is that police officer you saw last night."

"He's so handsome." Gabi batted her lashes, sighed and looked a little faint as the blond guy added, "We tried talking to him and he's really crabby. He threatened to throw us in jail if we harassed him."

"See, that's all just part of the game." I flashed my best reassuring smile. "He's supposed to be that way, and the jail part was added for color. What you need to do is go see him again and be persistent, just keep going back. He knows what's going on, and he had Zo and that wife, Madonna, down at the station, questioning them. Now he knows even more than before. But whatever

85

you do, don't say anything about seeing the girl in the purple hat. Keep that to yourself and find out what he knows first. You all were really clever to have noticed the purple hat, and you don't want that important clue to get around to the other groups."

"You're right." Gabi nodded, and the rest joined in. "We have to keep our information quiet if we intend to win the free weekend at the Grand Hotel. The hotel is giving the prize to the whole team that solves the case; isn't that fantastic? Thanks for your help, and we'll be sure and tell the police officer you sent us over so he cooperates this time around."

Before I could tell her *Oh, please don't do that,* Gabi and her followers trotted out the door. Rudy leaned against the workbench, his mustache curved in an even bigger smile than before. "Nate Sutter will make you the next victim after sending these people over to him; you know that, don't you?"

"I was desperate to get rid of them, and they will keep Nate busy for a while till I can find out where in the world Fiona is." I did a little innocent shrug. "And I sort of already sent another group his way. If Sutter's going to make me a victim, I might as well really deserve it."

Rudy laughed. It was one of those big

laughs that filled the room, but it sent little tremors down my spine. Nate Sutter was all cop and I was one big pain in his butt.

"You couldn't be content with just Irma wanting to string you up by your toenails. Now you've got Nate on your back?" Rudy said. "You really think that shamrock around your neck is enough to keep you safe after all this?"

"Not a snowball's chance in hell, but Fiona's my friend. I can't sit back and do nothing."

Rudy sobered. "Yeah, she's my friend too, and this is serious." Rudy checked his watch and handed me the socket. "Can you finish up? My latest batch of Mojito Madness fudge is ready and I need to get it sliced up and in the display case for the afternoon rush of fudgies." He pointed to a screw and nut under the seat. "Just tighten this. Remember, *righty tighty, lefty loosey.* We want the tighty part, not the loosey. Can't have the seat fall off when the kids are riding. Bad for business."

Rudy gave Cleveland and Bambino some of the treats he kept in his pocket. They purred and cuddled up to him like sweet little darling kitties from some YouTube video.

I rented out the Star Wars bike for a week,

the Grand Hotel bike and all three of the Downton Abbeys. I started in on my newest paint job, the doggie bike. My plan was to get a little cart that hitched onto the back — a pooch caboose — where the dog could ride along. Earlier this spring I tried a cat carrier and took Cleveland and Bambino for a test run. *Bad idea* took on a whole new meaning.

I got out the tube of raw sienna for a golden retriever for the puppy bike and ivory black for the black lab, and spotted a woman putting papers in the *Town Crier* newspaper stand across the street in front of Doud's Market. Donna said Fiona's dad did the deliveries this week, and her mom was here on the island too. My guess was this was Mom, and maybe she knew where Fiona was. With it being ten minutes till twelve, Fiona needed to get to the police station before Sutter imploded.

"Hi," I said, coming up to the newspaper stand. "I'm a friend of Fiona's and I'm wondering where she is. I haven't seen her since yesterday."

The lady was tall and thin like Fiona, her graying hair pulled back in a loose bun with a pencil jabbed through it. My guess was that the pencil part came from running the *Crier* for twenty-five years.

"She lost some tote bag that she really likes," the woman said while stacking the papers. "I don't know what's so special about a tote bag, but it's got her in a state."

The bag! If Fiona left it somewhere, anyone could have taken the olive oil bottle, smacked the Peep over the head and framed Fiona for the deed. "I'm Evie Bloomfield; I operate the bike shop across the street. Fiona and I are friends. In fact, I gave her that tote. It has *I ♡ the Town Crier* on it and —"

The woman stopped stacking papers and stared at me, the thin lines at the corners of her mouth pulling tight, her eyes chilly. "You're the one who ran into the dead guy on the path. You need to mind your own business, missy. You've caused enough trouble."

"Trust me, getting involved in the Peep Show wasn't a planned event."

"Leave Fiona alone. Her father would be heartsick if he knew all . . ." Mamma shook her finger at me. "Look, the guy was slime and he deserved what he got." Her eyes narrowed. "I have everything under control now, so let it be. No one hurts my family, you understand me, no one. We don't need your help. We'll fix this." The woman tramped off and called over her shoulder,

"That's what parents do, they take care of their kids no matter what."

Well, dang. Rudy said Walt was really protective of Fiona, and it carried right over to Mamma Bear. Whatever Peep had on Fiona, the parents knew what it was, or at the very least they had their suspicions.

I started back across the street to the bike shop and spotted Irma coming out the front door of the Good Stuff. Sutter on horseback trotted down Main with his pissed-cop face firmly in place. Both of them headed straight for me, and was that Fiona peeking out the window at Rudy's Rides? How'd I get so popular? It was at times like this that living on an island had definite disadvantages. There was no escape!

6

"Thank heavens you're both here," Irma wailed as I met up with her on the porch of Rudy's Rides. Sutter climbed off his horse and tied the reins to the railing as Fiona ducked back down inside the shop.

"The wedding's falling apart." Irma's apron was splattered with white icing, a smear of chocolate streaked her cheek and she smelled like crème de menthe. Irma looked good enough to eat.

"Mom," Sutter grumbled in a low voice. "We've got a serious problem over at the medical center, and the instigator of that problem is running around here and I have to find him and find Fiona, and your wedding needs to take a backseat to . . ."

Irma glared up at her son, and his words trailed off. Was that smoke curling from her ears and was her hair actually on fire? Irma took a pink The Good Stuff order pad from her apron and smacked Sutter on the arm.

"Backseat?"

"Or," Sutter added, "maybe not."

"There's still time to find your dress," I rushed in. "I've made some calls."

"It's not just that. It's worse." Irma fished around in her apron pocket again and this time pulled out a little white bride figure made of foam and started squeezing it. "This is a stress ball . . . actually it's called the stressed-out bride. Brides and Bliss sent it to me; they thought I might need it. A case of gin would have been a better idea, but this is what I got."

"Look," Sutter said in his *I know everything* cop voice. "It's just a dress. You can find another dress; they're everywhere."

That got him three more whacks with the pink order pad along with, "Who raised you, Nathaniel Sutter! You don't just replace a wedding dress! It took months to find that dress, and it's not just the dress that's got me going. Now I need to find another place besides the Butterfly Conservatory to have my wedding. How do these things keep happening?" Irma gave the bride more squeezes.

"The butterflies escaped?" I asked.

"Infestation." Irma squashed the little bride faster. "It's an aphid outbreak. No one's allowed in or out until the ladybug shipment arrives to eat the aphids. Margaret

Ingram had to strip buck naked and leave all her clothes inside. Word has it she's got a great butt and now has two marriage proposals. She said if she knew men were that easy, she'd have stripped a long time ago."

Irma fished in her apron and pulled out a squishy figure in a black tux with white tie. Eyes bulging and staring at her son, she compressed the bride in her right hand and the groom in her left. "Fix this now!"

"Me?" Sutter took a step back.

Irma's nostrils flared. "I don't remember being in labor for twenty-three hours with anyone else on this island. You know weddings, and you solve crimes. Solve this!"

Sutter put his hands on Irma's shoulders. "Mom, I got a murder going on and —"

"And there's going to be another murder real soon," she grumbled deep in her throat. She pointed at me. "Or maybe even more. I want to get married and you two are going to make it happen, and I don't give a hoot who's belly-up in that meat keeper over there at the medical center. Do something!"

Irma stomped off, and Sutter and I stared after her. "She's your mother," I said.

"And she's bonkers. I've never seen her this way. Even when I painted the cat green for Saint Patrick's Day and ran the snowmobile into the lake. And why is she harping on me when you're the one who lost the dress?"

"Brides and Bliss lost the blasted dress, and I had nothing to do with the aphid plague, and you're the one responsible for the twenty-three-hour thing so you win the prize."

"I should have stayed in Detroit," Sutter mumbled as he climbed up on his horse. He held out his hand to me. "I'll drop you at the conservatory and you can check out when those ladybugs are coming in and how fast they gulp down aphids. I've got to get up to the Grand. Zo said she saw Fiona talking to that singer lady, Idle Summers. They're both from L.A. Maybe there's something going on with those two and Idle knows where Fiona is."

The sun caught in Sutter's hair and for a second — just a second — I forgot about dresses and dead bodies. His silhouette was tall and lean and he looked as if he belonged in the cast from *Young Guns.* I think this all happened because it had been a while — a long while — since I had anything to do with any kind of guns.

"Hey, are you listening to me?" Sutter grumped. "Fiona? Where is she? Earth to Bloomfield, we got a situation here, remember?"

"Why would you think I know where Fiona is? Was it my time to watch her? Does she have a bell around her neck? We are not joined at the hip and — and — why don't you check on the aphids and I'll talk to Idle?"

"Because I'm the freaking police and do the questioning around here, not that anyone cares!" He pointed to the patch on his jacket.

"Fine, I'll walk up to the Butterfly Conservatory." Mostly because putting my arms around sun-in-his-hair Sutter right now was not a great idea with my brain and other body parts already in mush mode.

Sutter trotted off and I refused to consider any more hunky cowboy references coming to mind. What was wrong with me? Sutter was over the hill, forty-three years old. He took life too serious, ate healthy, and most important of all had called me a total of five times — just five, I tell you — all winter, proving beyond any doubt that he wasn't interested. At least he wasn't interested in me. He was back and forth to Detroit, but that's no excuse. They have phones in Detroit!

I stomped inside the bike shop as Fiona poked her head out the door that led to the kitchen. "Is he gone?" She had two ice

95

cream cones, one in each hand, and a split lip and a red knot on her forehead.

"For the moment he's gone," I said, coming into the shop. "He's hunting everywhere for you, the guests at the Grand think Peep's murder is a mystery game and you're tops on their suspect list, so that means they're all looking for you too, and what the heck happened this time? You're all banged up."

"I got pushed down the steps at the Grand Hotel while sneaking around and I thought the ice cream might help my lip. I could have used ice, but Nutty Buddy tastes better and you always have a stash. Want one?"

I took a bite. "Why would someone push you down the steps?" The first bite of a Nutty Buddy was always the best when the frozen chocolate covered with nuts cracked and then melted in your mouth and all the problems of the world melted away too, at least for thirty seconds.

"I've been asking a lot of questions." Fiona took a nibble of chocolate. "I'm thinking it's a warning to back off, which if you think about it is a good thing. I'm getting close to the killer and making him nervous."

"I'm not sure about a nervous killer being a good thing."

"It means I'm on the right trail, but what

I don't get is how in the world did I wind up a suspect in the Peep Show? I was careful, I hid in the bushes, no one saw me."

"And you've got a purple hat." I took two licks to stop the ice cream from dripping, then pulled the hat off the workbench and handed it over. "This thing is like a neon sign. People at the Grand saw it last night when you were hiding out, and then I found it in Zo's room, which was also Peep's room. I know you didn't kill Peep, but Idle Summers was nearly doing cartwheels across the Grand Hotel lobby this morning, and I'm pretty sure it has to do with Peepster being on a rolling rack in the refrigerator and not Raisin Bran. Got anything to add to this?"

"I must have left the hat when I went looking for Peep's cell phone in Zo's room. One of the maids let me in and did lookout. I helped her pass high school algebra, so she owed me. Idle and I knew each other in L.A. Peep had stuff on her and was threatening to go public with it now that she's doing really well on the club circuit. I told her to come here to Mackinac to get away from him, and we'd figure out what to do together."

"As in knock him off?"

"It was on the list."

I bit my lip instead of the Nutty Buddy. "Ouch!"

"Hey, it was just a suggestion." She expertly caught an escaped chunk of chocolate at the corner of her mouth. "The Grand's always looking for name talent, and Idle has a dynamite voice. We got together last night before I met with Peep. Our plan was to talk to him, just talk and convince him to go away. I got nowhere. Peep wanted money and he wanted me to come back to L.A. and work for him on the *Scoop* or else . . ." Fiona let out a sigh and stopped eating her ice cream. "Or else he'd tell my parents about some of the more questionable ways I got info back in L.A. and blab about Idle's checkered past. Neither was an option for either of us. I was so rattled when I left Peep the first time that I lost the yellow bag you gave me somewhere. I have no idea what I did with it, but someone sure found it and the olive oil and used it on Peep and now I'm duck soup."

"You agreed to pay Peep?"

"What if your parents found out you were a stripper, married and had kids?"

Three customers chose that exact moment to come into the shop. Really? Now? With *kids* and *stripper* hanging in the balance? Why couldn't they come in when Sutter was

98

questioning me about something I didn't want to tell him, or when Irma wanted to know about the wedding dress?

I handed Fiona my cone and she hustled off for the kitchen. In a sweat over the last bit of Fiona's news, I somehow managed to rent the pink, purple and white lilac bikes for the week, then took a call for the New York Yankees bike to be delivered up to the Grand by three.

Fiona stuck her head out. "Is it okay?"

"Are you kidding?" I jabbed my hands on my hips. "No, it's not okay. You're married and have kids and never told me!"

Licking her Nutty Buddy, then mine to keep it from dripping, Fiona looked a lot calmer than I felt. She reclaimed her stool, crossed her legs and tossed her hair. "Of course I'm not married with kids."

"You just said that to take ten years off my life?"

"We got interrupted." She handed me my cone. "I didn't get a chance to finish what I was saying, but you get my point, right?" She sobered, looking completely serious. "My parents had — have — high expectations for me, and some things they do not need to know. Peep texted me to meet him again in front of the Grand to get the money, and when I showed up there he was saturated in olive oil. That's all I know about Peep dead, but I don't believe that Idle and I are the reasons he came here. He could have blackmailed us from anywhere. Why Mackinac Island? That piece of crud had something else up his sleeve, but I have no idea what."

"He just needed a vacation?"

Fiona took another bite of ice cream, leaving a white mustache over her top lip. "Vacation for Peepster was Vegas, the craps tables and a bottle of Johnnie Walker." Fiona licked the mustache. "But he did look bad last night, with sunken eyes and pasty skin. And he was jumpy, and he's never jumpy. Peep gets off on making everyone else jumpy."

Fiona stopped dead, her eyes slowly widening as she turned to me, ice cream dripping over her hand. "Jeez Louise, Peep was on the run. That's got to be it. He was hiding out here. Nothing else makes sense as to why the guy shows up on my doorstep in the middle of nowhere. Someone's after the rat for a change instead of the rat chasing the cheese. He knew that Idle and I were both here, and he could hit us up for money and not use his credit cards so whoever's after him couldn't track him that way."

"Any idea who's chasing the rat?"

"Half of Hollywood."

"You need to tell all this to Sutter. Give him someone else to focus on besides you. Right now you've got top billing, my friend."

Fiona shook her head. "Well, I'm not giving up Idle."

"And I hope she comes to visit you in the slammer, 'cause that's where you're headed." I handed Fiona a paper towel from the workbench. "You can't hide forever on this chunk of rock, and if you leave the island and run away, it will look worse."

Fiona reached for her hat, and I took her hand and held it tight. "Idle's your friend, I get that, but she's desperate and not lily pure; you said she has a checkered past. Did you consider that she might have done in Peep on her own?"

"She wouldn't let me take the blame like this. She might go after Zo or Madonna and let them hang, but not me. I'm going to keep a low profile and nose around a little."

"Tall, blonde hair, green eyes, loved by one and all — the low profile isn't happening. Hold down the bike shop and let me see what I can find out."

Fiona spread her arms wide. "Like people won't recognize me in here?"

"Patience, grasshopper." I batted my eyes and looked smug. "I've got a plan, a really good one that will help you out and me too." And fifteen minutes later I was pedaling the New York Yankees bike toward the Butterfly Conservatory with Fiona tucked away safe at the bike shop dressed in my Betsy Ross outfit. Hey, if it can work for Rudy to be Twain, it can work for Fiona to be Betsy, and with a pillow under her apron, a gray wig and white bonnet that covered a lot of her face, no one would know her. She fit right in with the island inhabitants: a real blacksmith who always looked like a blacksmith; the soldiers up at the fort in uniform, their cannon blasting off every day at ten and six; and horses and buggies everywhere. Betsy Ross was in her natural habitat.

Huffing and puffing, my lungs on fire and sweating, I headed up Cadotte. Instead of turning off toward the Grand Hotel to the left with most of the two-wheeled and four-legged traffic, I went straight toward Surrey Hill. The neat white clapboard framed by an array of blooming lilacs was just ahead with the glass conservatory to the back and the adorable green ceramic turtle painted up in white daisies out front. A big *Quarantine* sign in black forbidding letters was posted for all to see, and a British Redcoat soldier circa 1800s — did I know my Mackinac Island history or what — complete with musket on shoulder kept watch. If George Washington suddenly rounded the bend galloping on his horse, smote the ground and brought forth the Declaration of Independence, I wouldn't have been one bit surprised.

But George didn't materialize and neither did anyone else. Fact is, the soldier and I were the only two, and usually the place was buzzing with tourists this time of year. "Hey, Cal, what are you doing here?" I called out as I slid off the bike. "The fort's over that way." I pointed in the other direction.

Cal Sandman was early thirties and an islander. He'd lived here all his life and had no desire to live anywhere else. Last year he won the Great Chili Cook-off trophy from one of the old guys, and he built a special case in his house to show it off. He was captain of the spudding team, an island sport consisting of brave derring-do snowmobilers who ventured out onto the lake when it froze to check the depth of the ice for us sissies sitting on the shore. He and the others like Sutter marked the safe path to the mainland with the Christmas trees we all stockpiled just for this occasion. The fact that Cal used a wheelchair didn't slow him down one bit.

"Mayor Doud called out the soldiers," Cal

told me. "Around here it's us reenactment soldiers from Mackinac Fort. I'm guarding the butterflies till the ladybugs get here."

Anywhere else on the planet, a crack like that would have you on a psychiatrist's couch.

"Good to see you, Evie," he went on. "All I've dealt with today is cranky tourists who are none too happy when I won't let them in to see the butterflies. There was even a group from the Grand in orange T-shirts called the Body Baggers trying to solve some kind of mystery game and find a killer. They just knew the Butterfly Conservatory being closed had to be involved. Took me a half hour to convince them aphids do not kill people, and sometimes butterflies are just butterflies. One gal with red hair tried to call the governor and complain, and when her cell phone wouldn't work she actually sat and cried. Said she didn't know how to live without her phone."

"Did she use *like* every other word?"

Cal gave me a toothy grin. "That's the one. Hey, if you need part-time help at the bike shop, let me know. I could sure use the cash, and now that you got that ramp for getting bikes in and out, I can roll right in. I got my eye on a Newfoundland."

"Dog? Vacation?"

"1812 musket with bayonet. It's a hum-dinger."

Friend or foe, anyone who talked fire-power with bayonets and held the fort against Zo and the Body Baggers probably wasn't into breaking the rules for Irma's wedding. I told Cal I'd keep him in mind for working at the shop and climbed back on Yankee. The Grand was a ten-minute bike ride away that would probably take me twenty minutes at best in my present physical state. I needed to drop off the rental and maybe find a place for Irma's wedding while there. She had her heart set on butterflies fluttering as the string quartet played Pachelbel, but the front porch of the Grand Hotel would work. Enough champagne and all of us would forget someone had just taken a header into the bushes and gotten whacked by olive oil, and that Fiona was the prime suspect.

Midday traffic at the Grand was heavy, and in an hour when the dinner crowd arrived it would be horse-to-horse around here. I parked Yankee in front of the yellow awning over the ice cream parlor named after Sadie the dog, gone but not forgotten. I reminded myself I'd already had ice cream once today and that two times and the ba-zillion calories that went with it was not an option, no matter how cute the shop was, or I'd never be able to pedal these hills.

I asked one of the employees directing traffic to keep an eye on Yankee till the renter picked it up. Deep in thought over the wedding, losing the blasted dress, letting Irma down and the Fiona mess, I started up the crowded sidewalk toward the hotel. How was I going to fix any of this, I wondered as I headed for the main stairway. I stepped around a herd of tourists on a lilac walk, avoided two kids with drippy chocolate cones and was jostled right off the sidewalk and smack into the path of four fast-trotting horses pulling a wagon taxi rounding the corner and coming right at me.

Freaking hell! I jumped back; the driver veered right, saving my bacon, and yelled, "Watch where you're going, lady!"

He was right! I needed to pay attention! Except I thought I was paying attention. Hey, I missed the drippy cones, didn't I? I was on the sidewalk, and then somehow I wasn't on the sidewalk. How did that happen? I was out of shape but I could still walk in a straight line.

Still shaking from my near-death-by-horse experience, I spotted Sutter up ahead. He stood in the middle of the crime scene, which was still surrounded by yellow tape. Gabi and the Corpse Crusaders looked on, scribbling furiously in their notebooks.

A part of me wanted to go over to Sutter and tell him my great plan of getting Irma and Rudy married at the Grand. Truth be told, I wanted to go over to Sutter to feel safe for a moment. Sutter and I had our moments, but when push came to shove — like right now — Sutter was the guy to have around. He knew stuff like how to survive, get the bad guys and keep cool. I was an emotional billboard, I knew how to paint bikes and survival was sometimes hit-or-miss, but I knew how to make kick-ass spaghetti sauce. The secret was a double dose of oregano and a half bottle of Chianti. After that much alcohol, no one cared what the sauce tasted like.

But right now I had other things to take care of besides my jangled nerves. While I was here, I needed to talk with Idle Summers, or maybe I could even poke around in her room if I could sweet-talk Penelope again. Fiona had complete confidence that Idle would not set her up to take the fall for doing in the Peepster, but I wasn't so sure. Idle was a performer, an actor; she had baggage and she had something to hide.

How could Peep do this, I wondered.

What kind of a life was it when you made money off the trials of others? I'd met some slimy people in my time — my ex being top of the list — but the Peepster even had him beat.

Slouching down to keep out of sight, I ducked behind one of the big Grand Hotel carriages. I walked along beside it as it moved, then kept to the far side of the wide stairway and darted up to the big porch. I scurried across, losing myself in the gaggle of milling guests, and sidled up to the long mahogany front desk with massive vases of lilacs scenting the air. Using the vintage house phone straight out of *The Great Gatsby,* I called the guest who'd rented the Yankee bike to let them know where I'd parked it.

Penelope was on duty and chatted with a family of four as she arranged pink and purple lilacs in a vase. She handed them a Lilac Festival flyer from the stack on the counter, sitting on top of the yellow *I ♡ the Town Crier* bag. Holy cow, someone had found the missing bag! Who? Where? Maybe the killer? Someone had taken the olive oil bottle out and whacked Peepster.

Penelope looked more kempt this time with her hair in a perfect bun, understated neat makeup and a pressed blazer, but she still had a deer-in-the-headlights look about her. Madonna and Zo had that effect on everyone.

"No way can I help you again," she whispered to me after the family left. She took out a white lilac sprig and added it to the purple ones already in the vase. "I can't let you in another guest's room." She pointed over her shoulder to a short forty-something guy with sandy hair, brown eyes and *Hotel Manager* scripted on his name badge. "My boss said no way could the room thing happen again, and he doesn't care what the excuse. That policeman guy had a holy fit when he found out. All of us here at the Grand want to get this over with as much as you do, probably more, but we can't lose our jobs. We need the money."

I tapped the yellow stack of flyers. "Where'd these come from?"

"The gardener was cutting these for bouquets." She nodded to the flowers heaped in front of her. "He found the yellow bag this morning right by where the crime scene tape is. I was so happy I kissed him right there in front of everyone. Now I can give the guests the information and they won't be driving me nuts with all their questions of what time are the tours, where do they go, how long does the tour last, can I take my toddler, can I pack drinks, can I take my dog and my personal favorite, what's a lilac!"

Penelope added a pink sprig to the vase, making it beyond obvious that she should stick to running a hotel and not be a florist. "So, how about I call Miss Zo for you," Penelope continued. "That's what she wants to be called, Miss Zo, do you believe it? She just went up to her room with one of the maids to let her in because she forgot her key. I think she's really excited about her Betsy Ross outfit, and —"

"Betsy Ross?"

Penelope leaned over the counter and whispered, "She just bought the costume today. Seems she wants to march in the Lilac Parade on Saturday, and she's wearing the outfit to get in the mood and think of happy things. She said she needed to do something fun 'cause she was so down in the dumps with her guy being toes-up over there at the medical center. I can understand that, can't you? I mean, losing someone you care about like that would just be terrible, and —"

"What costume?"

"All red, white and blue with a gray curly wig, bonnet and padding, and she's even carrying around a flag and sewing basket to fit the part. She looks real authentic, not like herself at all. I didn't even recognize her. I'll make the call and get her down here and —"

I yanked the phone from Penelope's hand and dropped it back in the brass cradle. "Let's not bother Miss Zo, and I know who this yellow bag belongs to, so I can take it to her, what do you say?" I reached for the yellow bag, and a big hand reached for mine and held it tight.

"I say not so fast," came Sutter's voice from behind me.

7

"So we now have the bag that held the murder weapon?" Sutter said as he snagged the bag in one hand and my arm in the other. "You wouldn't be trying to take it, would you?"

"Hey, I'm just dropping off a rental bike and thought maybe I could fix our wedding problem while I was here. And when I got to the desk, lo and behold, do you believe it, there was Fiona's bag."

"Lo and behold?"

"You caught me off guard." My heart settled back into my chest after Sutter surprised the bejeebers out of me. My guess was that Fiona was right upstairs over our heads posing as Miss Zo and searching for an incriminating cell phone while I was here with our resident cop in the lobby.

"But . . . but think about this," I offered, trying to keep Sutter's attention on me and not the stairs if Fiona/Betsy Ross chose this particular moment to appear. "Fiona says she lost this bag. Anyone could have swiped the olive oil out of it to do in Peep and frame her. Sounds pretty good, huh?"

"Sounds like Fiona's lying through her teeth and hid the bag to back up her story."

I swiped a pink lilac sprig out of Penelope's hand and smacked Sutter on the arm. "How did you get to be such a skeptic?"

"Comes with the badge."

"Fine, but now that you're here I'll tell you my great idea."

Sutter let out a long-suffering sigh, and I lilac-smacked him again. "What about having the wedding on the front porch of the Grand? We can use the round area at the far end that overlooks Lake Michigan and the gardens. It'll be adorable, just look at this place."

I swept my hand over the lobby, all posh and beautiful and serving up high tea. I turned to Penelope. "Aren't weddings at the Grand fantastic?"

Penelope fumbled the two lilacs she tried to stuff in the vase. She bit her bottom lip and started wringing her hands. For some reason Penelope didn't like having Sutter around any more than I did.

"Wedding? Right. Yeah, they're amazing. Let me see what I can do." Penelope pulled out a big long black book with *Events* stenciled in gold across the front. "Now what month are you two considering for your wedding?"

I froze. "You . . . two?" Was that high squeaky voice really mine? "No, no, no, you got this all wrong," I said, holding up my hands as if warding off a charging bull. Sutter's mouth opened and closed a few times, but nothing came out. I jabbed him in the chest with my pointy finger. "It's his mother's wedding, and it's in three days. We're the best man and maid of honor, and we're here to set things up and that is all."

Penelope closed the book and perched her hand on her hip. "Let me get this straight. You want to have a wedding here, at the Grand Hotel, in three days?"

She blinked a few times as if hit with a bucket of cold water, then burst into laughter. It wasn't just a polite tee-hee laugh but the kind that draws attention because someone's crazy as a loon.

"You're kidding, right?" She swiped a tear from her cheek and tried to stifle one last chuckle. "This is the Lilac Festival." She waved her hand over the heap of lilacs on the desk. "We are booked solid and everyone's working around the clock to keep up. We have three weddings scheduled every

114

single day and have since a year ago. How about booking a date for next year's Lilac Festival?" Penelope handed me her business card.

I shoved the card in my jeans pocket. "We'll figure out something." I grabbed Sutter's arm and hustled him toward the porch.

"Good luck with that figuring," Penelope called. "Every place is as jammed as we are."

And that was a shame, but it wasn't all bad. At present Sutter was in *where to have the wedding* mode and not *where is Fiona.* I just had to get him out of there before he switched modes.

"We'll find someplace to have the wedding," I said to Sutter, guiding him toward the steps, keeping him distracted with wedding plans, trying to keep the angst out of my voice. "There's got to be a room or an annex or —"

"Betsy Ross?" Sutter stopped dead by the little stand of *Town Crier* newspapers; two people collided into him, but he didn't budge one bit. He glared down at me. "Betsy Ross is *your* costume."

"Don't be silly." My eye started to twitch. "There's more than one Betsy Ross costume in existence."

"Here on the island?"

"That Betsy girl really gets around?"

Sutter hauled me back into the hotel. He stopped at the desk, yanked the pink lilacs from the vase in front of Penelope, added two purples and three whites and fluffed the tall spikes to the middle; the bouquet was done to perfection in thirty seconds flat, and then he headed up the main stairway.

"How'd you do that?"

"Practice." We stopped at the second floor and turned down the hall to the cheap rooms, and Sutter banged on Zo's door. "Fiona, I know you're in there."

"Like, what's going on?" came Zo's voice behind us. "This is my room."

Sutter turned around, dragging me with him to face Zo in green biker shorts, pink helmet and skinned knees. I could relate to the skinned-knees part.

"Betsy Ross, I assume?" Sutter said to Zo.

"Like, what is a Betsy Ross?" Zo fluffed her helmet hair, smiled hugely and assumed a sexy pose. "Hey, like, you know, like, I like it. Great name."

I figured Zo just set some kind of world record for the number of times *like* was used in a sentence.

"Betsy Ross has like a really nice ring to it," Zo went on. "Do you think it should like be my new stage name?" Her lower lip wobbled as a tear slid down her cheek, then

116

another and another. "Peep would have loved that as my stage name. He always said I need something fresh to make it big in the newspaper world. He said *Zo* was so nineties."

Zo opened her arms wide and looked to the heavens. "Oh, Peepy, my honey bunny, how could you leave me at a time like this when I needed you most?"

Sutter snagged the key card out of Zo's hand and jammed it into the lock. He turned the handle and the three of us stepped inside Zo's room. Betsy Ross, aka Fiona, was on top of the dresser unscrewing the air vent. She jerked her head around, her frontal padding throwing her off balance.

"Help!" Eyes wide and arms flailing, Fiona fell backward. She landed on the green-and-pink bedspread looking like Miss Fourth of July in a garden with Zo screeching, "Like, what are you doing in my room?"

"Cleaning?" Fiona forced a smile. "Would you believe this is the new maid's uniform?" Fiona held up the corner of her white apron, rolling her eyes at Sutter as she sat up. "And you know what, that explanation would probably work if *you* weren't here."

Sutter yanked off Betsy's bonnet and wig. "Mind telling me what's going on?"

"Fiona?" Zo gasped. "Like, is that really you? Why are you dressed up? Is it an island thing? Very Hollywood. Makes me home-sick."

She folded her arms and studied the toppled chair. "But why are you on a chair?" Zo's eyes thinned to slits. "You're here for that cell phone, aren't you? That's what you're looking for and that's why you killed my darling Peepster. He knew all about that affair you had and thought you should come clean about it and —"

"There was no affair." Fiona stood, jabbed her hands on her padded hips and faced Zo. "I didn't do anything, and Xavier didn't do anything. Peep just made it look that way and was blackmailing me. But I didn't kill him, though Lord knows he had it coming."

"Fiona!" I hissed, shaking my head in *shut up* fashion.

"Well, it's the truth. Peep was a cretin." Fiona aimed her finger at Zo. "You're the one who killed him when you realized he was just using you for a fun roll in the hay all these years and had no intention of divorcing Madonna. Her family had money and we all know Peep was about the money."

"Are you out of your mind?" Zo screeched. "I would, like, never hurt my

Peep, and I was out riding a bike when he was . . . you know . . . done in." Zo pointed at me. "Ask her about the bike riding. We passed each other. She's the only person on this island who rides a bike worse than I do. Besides, how could I have pushed Peep . . . my darling Peepy . . . off the porch without being noticed, tell me that, huh?"

She held out her arms. "I had on a red biking outfit that I, like, bought in the hotel shop 'cause red is . . . was . . . Peep's favorite color? Red does not blend in with the evening dinner crowd in the hotel lobby around here. Like, someone would have remembered me, don't you think? Instead, they remember seeing that stupid purple hat Fiona wears all the time! She's just a terrible person. I told Peep not to hire her and that she was nothing but, like, big trouble."

Zo yanked a ruffled pink pillow off the bed and swung it at Fiona, hitting her smack in the face. "How could you, like, do this to Peep? To me?"

"I didn't, like, do anything." Fiona's eyes shot wide open. "Did I just say *like*?" She smacked Zo with a green pillow. "You're contaminating us all."

"Don't you like make fun of the way I talk, you . . . you hillbilly."

"This is the Midwest, you geographically challenged Valley girl."

Zo clobbered Fiona over the head, and feathers flew everywhere into the room. "I'm the only one who loved Peep. You, like, hated him, and his rotten wife only wanted his money. That's all she ever thought about; she never had enough. He was my little Peepy and there will never be another one like him."

"God willing and a little bit of luck." Fiona pillow-punched Zo in the gut.

"That's it!" Sutter stepped between Fiona and Zo and a flurry of pillow feathers littering the floor. "Fiona, you need to come down to the police station."

"Me? What about the avocado queen here? I don't care what the evidence is, she's in this up to her eyeballs."

"Avocado queen? Like, you're nothing but a two-bit pencil pusher."

Sutter yanked away the pillows and tossed them on the bed. "There is no way Zo could have been dressed for dinner, pushed Peep off the porch, run around and clobbered him with the olive oil, then changed and pedaled off for Evie to see her on the way to the hotel. The timeline just doesn't work. I was at the Grand and would have remembered seeing a red sweatsuit in the throng of evening wear."

Sutter took out his handcuffs and faced Fiona. "I need answers right now from you, and you keep running off. It's not going to happen again, and how'd you get the split lip and bump on your forehead?"

Fiona took a step back. "Nate, we . . . we've known each other forever, I sold you Girl Scout Cookies, and saved all the Thin Mints just for you. You owe me!"

"And I got you through geometry. We're even."

"You can't put Betsy Ross in handcuffs," I added. "What will the kiddies in the lobby think of Betsy Ross, seamstress of the first American flag, in handcuffs, huh? They will all be in therapy for years over that one, their Fourth of Julys ruined forever, and they'll cry when they salute the flag. And . . . and the mystery groups will assume Fiona's the killer and that the game is no longer afoot."

"Afoot?" Sutter arched on eyebrow.

"You have to admit that you aren't one hundred percent certain Fiona is guilty. What about Madonna?"

"She's on the list." Sutter reached for Fiona.

"See? Not one hundred percent," I shot back. "And it will crush Fiona's parents,

121

who are here for your very own mother's wedding. What will they think of their darling daughter hauled out of the Grand Hotel, the soul of grace and decorum, in handcuffs of all things by the best man and someone they've known since he was in diapers?"

Sutter pulled the yellow bag from his jacket. "Fiona put the olive oil bottle in this, and it was found at the scene of the crime, and people saw the purple hat last night at the crime scene, and she has motive." He gave me a hard look. "I bet you saw Fiona on that path last night, didn't you? I should lock you up too."

"And if you're not guilty," Zo said to Fiona, "why are you running all over the place and not talking to the police like I did?" She jutted her 36-Bs and added a superior smirk. "You're just like making excuses." Zo shook her finger at Fiona. "You did it, I know you did."

Sutter looked mutinous, but he did put away the handcuffs — thank you, Lord — and said to Fiona, "We as in you and me will walk casually and together out of this hotel and all the way down to the police station." He turned to me. "You get Shakespeare."

"Sometimes I get Shakespeare, sometimes

he mystifies the heck out of me," I said, having no idea how *Macbeth* played into this, but I needed time to figure a way to help Fiona.

"My horse. He's around back, and Fiona and I will meet you in the front by Sadie's. Don't try anything cute," he said to me. "I'm not in the mood."

Sutter took hold of Fiona's arm, tossed the flag over her arm and then hauled her out the door as Zo called, "Justice is served."

I grabbed a pillow and swatted Zo upside the head, adding more feathers to the occasion, then headed for the back stairway. As much as I was hell-bent on helping Fiona, she was the one with all the info. She knew what was on that phone, who was tickled to their toes that Peepster was out of the way, and she knew the island and the people here way better than I did. Fiona was loved, trusted and accepted, and people would tell her what was going on. I was still a come-here, and the trusted part was up in the air.

Sutter hadn't locked Fiona up yet, but I knew he had enough circumstantial evidence to do the deed. Being from a family of Chicago lawyers, I'd been exposed to more than my share of legal chitchat over breakfast, lunch, dinners, any and all family gatherings. From time to time the brain-numbing information actually came in handy.

In my own personal preferences of island transportation, horses were one step behind bikes. The only time I'd ridden a horse was on a horse's rump behind Sutter with my arms around his rock-solid chest and bouncing up and down. Truth be told, I'd had dreams of Sutter, his chest and the bouncing-up-and-down part, but it did not involve being on a horse.

"Here you go," I said, handing the reins off to Sutter as we stood in front of the ice cream parlor with carriages and walkers and bikes maneuvering around us. "And once again in case you forgot, you've got the wrong person in custody."

Sutter let out a deep sigh and cut his eyes to Fiona. "I don't like this any better than you, and maybe you had every right to knock off this Peep guy. That should count for something in court."

"Like twenty years behind bars instead of thirty?" Fiona wailed to Sutter, and then she said to me, "You'd better get to the bike shop. I put a *Be back in thirty* sign on the shop, but that was hours ago. You've got a business to run." She grabbed my hand. "Thanks for believing in me."

I stuck my tongue out at Sutter as the

group of three headed down Cadotte, fading into the crowd of tourists enjoying the evening. Okay, the tongue thing was childish, I'll give you that, but I was ticked off and it was the only thing I could think of to do or . . . or was it? The Yankee bike I'd dropped off earlier was still parked where I'd left it in front of the hotel. This was a sign from the gods of the wrongly accused to use my biking ability — or lack thereof — to make things right.

I kicked up the stand, climbed on Yankee and coasted down Cadotte. I didn't need a lot of speed; I just wanted to startle, not maim. I aimed for Sutter's derrière . . . I'd seen worse targets in my life, I can tell you that. I got closer and closer, gaining a little more momentum till my front tire made contact with Sutter's most excellent tush, propelling him forward.

"What the heck!" Sutter let go of Fiona and Shakespeare, using his hands to break his fall. I hit the brakes, then accidentally-on-purpose toppled over on top of him; the bike landed off to the side in the grass. And here again was another dream I'd had of me on top and Sutter underneath, but *not* in front of the Grand Hotel.

"Gallop!" I yelled at Fiona, her mouth gaping, eyes bulging as she looked on, nothing registering. She couldn't ride Yankee as her skirts would tangle in the spokes, so gallop was the escape of choice. Sutter struggled to get up, but my one hundred twenty-five pounds kept him pinned to the road. Okay, a hundred thirty but not a pound more, I swear.

"Shakespeare!" I yelled at Fiona and nodded at the horse. "Go! Now!"

Fiona grabbed for the saddle, flung herself up onto the horse and took the reins. "Thanks!" she yelled down to me. Then Betsy Ross in full red, white and blue regalia with a flag draped across her shoulder thundered off into the sunset.

I rolled off Sutter and stared at the sky as a throng of tourists gathered around. "Are you okay?" A young blonde woman hunkered down next to Sutter, her foot in my ribs. She swept Sutter's hair off his forehead. "You poor thing."

"This crazy woman here ran you down. I saw it all," another woman added.

"Want me to call the doctor?" a brunette asked, her behind perched on my chest. Terrific. The female contingent of the Nate Sutter fan club was now in session. "You should arrest her, she's a menace."

"That's the plan." Sutter reached around the woman and grabbed my arm.

"What?" I protested as I sat up. "You can't arrest me for having a biking accident. Everyone has biking accidents around here. We are probably the biking accident capital of the USA."

Sutter stood and hauled me to my feet, his face inches from mine. "I want to know what's going on now, no more excuses. There's a dead guy and I need to find the killer, got it?"

"This is part of the mystery weekend, isn't it?" Gabi asked, all excited, as she ran up with her iPhone taking pictures. "This woman ran into that dead body last night," she explained to the crowd. "It stands to reason she's a suspect, and now the policeman just confirmed it."

Gabi rubbed her hands together, a crazed look in her eye. "I'm going to win that free weekend at the Grand Hotel if it kills me." She winked. "A little mystery humor thrown in free of charge."

"See," Sutter smirked. "Now I *have* to lock you up on suspicion of murder. It's all part of the game. After all, it's murder and mayhem week at the Grand Hotel, so put on your deerstalker hat and get used to it, Chicago."

The walk to the police station took about five minutes instead of the usual ten. I tried to think of something clever and disarming to say but came up empty. Instead of going right in, Sutter detoured to the side of the building to park the bike. Shakespeare was already there at the watering trough with a feed bag of oats and chomping merrily away.

"Yeah," I said to Sutter, "that Fiona girl is a master killer all right. A real menace to society."

Sutter led me into the newly painted white clapboard building that was multifunctional with the courthouse above and police station below. It was the island's one-stop-shopping version of justice; you could get arrested and sentenced without having to go outside.

"Hey there, Evie." Molly greeted me from behind her desk as we walked into the station. "Are you okay? Poor Fiona. This is such a mess. What are we going to do?"

Sutter stopped dead and glared at his sergeant. Molly blanched white. "Uh . . . I just heard that Fiona might be in a bit of trouble, is all."

"If I find out you're harboring Fiona in any way, you won't be a sergeant for long. Got it?"

"But why is Evie here with you? I don't get it." Then Molly's jaw dropped and she jumped up and wedged herself between

Sutter and me, spreading her arms wide in protective police mode. "This is crazy. You can't put Evie in jail!"

"Wanna bet?" Sutter hauled me around Molly and continued down the hall past his office door with his name stenciled on the frosted glass. I looked back to Molly, who was rolling her eyes and shaking her head.

"You know," I said to Sutter. "This is not Detroit, this is Mackinac Island. Everyone here, all five hundred full-timers, every man, woman and child, loves Fiona to pieces. She was the Lilac Queen three years in a row, Miss Fudge for two years, keeps folks' dirty laundry out of the *Crier* and prints every anniversary, birthday and wedding. They will all lie for Fiona and hide her under desks, in pantries and in attics and you —"

"The mean old Sheriff of Nottingham?"

"If the jacket fits. You will not find Fiona until she wants to be found."

"Think about this: She has a busted lip, so not everyone loves her." Sutter pulled up in front of the jail cell and opened the door. I knew this moment was coming no matter how fast I talked, but gazing into an actual jail cell was downright terrifying. The closest I'd come to being behind bars was when I was a kid and Mother gave me a time-out on the steps and I gazed at the TV through

129

white wood railings. Life was tough back in Chicago.

Holy freaking crap, this was the real deal! "You can't put me in jail, and I can't tell you anything about Fiona 'cause whatever I say will make her seem even guiltier."

"Ever stop to think maybe she is?"

"Heck no!" I swallowed. "You're really going to lock me up? I have a business to run, cats to feed, I'm the maid of honor for your very own mother's wedding!"

"And I'm the best man, remember. Rudy will feed the cats and lock up the shop." Sutter put his face in mine. He smelled of something woodsy and spicy and really-ticked-off cop. "You've lied to me, hidden evidence and led me down the garden path."

"It *is* the Lilac Festival."

His eyes bulged, little capillaries threatening to pop, his face red as the stripes in Betsy's flag. You can only push a Detroit cop so far.

"Now!"

I stepped across the threshold and Sutter slammed the iron door shut, the metal-against-metal clang jarring clear through to my fillings. "I'm in jail! I'll get you for this."

"You're threatening a cop?"

"I'm threatening *you.*" I grabbed the bars. "You locked me up."

Sutter ran his hand around the back of his neck. "As you just said, this is Mackinac Island. There are cotton sheets on the bed, which happens to have a pillow top; the chair is from the new Pottery Barn catalog and there're hardwood floors; and the Yankee Rebel serves the meals. It was written up in *Midwest Living*. This isn't the Black Hole of Calcutta."

"You'll be sorry," I growled, acting all brave and self-assured and feeling kind of sick inside. But hey, if Martha Stewart could handle prison, so could I, right? Sutter turned and walked down the hall. "You're leaving me all alone?" I tried really hard not to whine.

"Dinner's in twenty minutes. It's roast beef, mashed potatoes and Caesar salad. I think you'll make it."

I sat on the teal upholstered chair with cream-colored accent pillow and took a deep steadying breath. Sutter was right in that the place was nice and the expected food delish and way better than the Cheerios I'd probably have had for dinner back at the bike shop. But jail was jail.

So, what did anyone else do in this situation? Sleep? Cry? Sing "Jailhouse Rock"? Tunnel with a spoon? My singing ability was nonexistent and I didn't have a spoon, so I

pulled out Sheldon and hit speed dial.
"Mother!"

8

"Rise and shine, jailbird, it's morning!"

Dazed and confused, I bolted upright and jumped out of bed to see Mother standing at the foot of my bed. "Did . . . did I miss the bus?"

"And that's been the topic of conversation in our family for years, dear, but such is the life of an artist." Ann Louise Bloomfield, aka Carman, unlocked the cell door and handed me a mug of coffee. I blinked a few times to make sure I wasn't dreaming. "Mother? Is it noon already, and how'd you get the key?"

"I remembered that Molly's a pushover for strawberry smoothies, and I paid a college kid a hundred bucks so I could have his seat on an earlier flight. I caught the first ferry. It's not every day my daughter winds up in the slammer."

Mother took a sip of coffee and sat in the teal chair, and I plopped down on the edge of the bed. The caffeine ignited my brain cells and I remembered where I was and why. As for Ann Louise, she was still in her Chicago lawyer mode of perfectly pressed black skirt and white blouse. Her brunette hair seemed longer since I last saw her at Christmas back in Chicago, and today it was pulled into a silver clip with the natural curls combed into submission. She wore a light touch of Chanel makeup, matte lipstick, barely-there perfume and sensible black shoes.

This was the flawless mother I had known for all thirty-four years of my life, until Ann Louise came to Mackinac last year and morphed into Carman. Then she went shopping for a red dress, black lace and a man . . . a once-upon-a-time gangster-type man. And parents wondered why their kids wound up in therapy.

Mother settled back into the chair. She pulled protein bars from her purse and handed over the blueberry crunch. "So why are you incarcerated in this hellhole?"

I peeled off the wrapper and took a bite. "Fiona's accused of murder," I said around a mouthful of crumbs, with more dropping onto my wrinkled black shirt. "I waylaid Sutter so she could get away and find the real killer, and I wound up in here 'cause

Sutter didn't agree with my waylay tactics. Fiona knows the island better than I do, so she has a better shot at finding the killer. Everyone loves her and they'll hide her till she figures this out. She should be okay and Sutter won't find her, you can bet on that."

"Really." It wasn't a question, it was a fact. A smile tipped the corner of Mother's mouth. "So a graphic designer outsmarted a Detroit cop."

"Yep, I did." I noticed the twinkle in Mother's eyes and suddenly didn't feel quite so cocky. "Maybe I outsmarted him?" I stopped eating the bar. "Okay, what did I do?"

Mother took a bite of her bar, not one crumb daring to mar her silk blouse. She waved her hand around the cell with the door standing wide open and us sitting and chatting. "Evie, this is not the way a normal jail is run. There are usually locks, big ones and guards, mean ones. There's no morning coffee with Mother. You were set up, dear. A certain policeman — who we all know and love, though some of us are amazingly slow at figuring that part out — considered there was a good chance you'd call me once you got in here. He knew I'd be living with you till my office is done, and even then I'll be a whopping ten feet from your back door. I'm not exactly the Terminator, but more of an extra set of eyes, and Fiona has the rest of the island looking out for her."

"You're babysitting me?"

"Nate Sutter is aware of the fact that those who kill once have no trouble repeating the deed to keep from getting caught." Mother sipped her coffee and gazed at me from over the rim of her mug. "Anything happen to you or Fiona to give the man the impression you might be in harm's way?"

"Someone did kind of push Fiona down the steps." I sat up straight and stiffened my spine. "That rat! Sutter knew I wouldn't let Fiona go to jail and that you'd come." I wagged my blueberry bar at Mother. "Instead of going through all this drama, he could have just said, 'Evie, you smart intelligent girl, you've got to be real careful.'"

"And of course that would do the trick, just like the last time you went hunting for a killer. Picking locks? Breaking and entering? Nearly winding up as flotsam in Lake Huron? Any of this sound familiar?"

"He could have tried."

"And he could have banged his head against a brick wall and gotten the same response."

Molly hustled down the hall, a pink smoothie mustache decorating her top lip.

"I've got to leave. There's a disturbance down at the Seabiscuit Café. Zo and Madonna are at it again over that Peep guy, and this time there's a food fight. At least the tourists think all of this is part of the mystery weekend, and the pictures winding up on Facebook aren't giving the island a bad name. The whole thing looks more like a tourist attraction. Go figure." Molly smiled at Mother. "Nice to see you here again, Carman. I made a fresh pot of coffee, and Irish Donna should be delivering scones any time. Key to the cell is on the hook in the office, and I'm locking up the place. You two can just enjoy your visit this morning. If you need me, my cell phone number is on my desk *if* you can get any bars on your phone."

Molly hurried off, and Mother arched her left eyebrow.

"All right, all right," I conceded. "This isn't jail. This is the Holiday Inn with iron bars and better food."

"Zo? Madonna? Peep? What in the world?"

"It's the Hollywood invasion, and since Molly left the cell door open we should follow her. Zo's the mistress/secretary, Madonna's the ticked-off wife and Peep's the dead guy those two are fighting over alive and dead, though God in heaven only knows why. Maybe we'll find something out at the food fight; my guess is Madonna and Zo know more than they're letting on. Fiona can't show her face in public, but we can."

Mother finished her coffee, then ran her fingers through her hair, setting the shiny curls free. She undid two blouse buttons, then rolled up her skirt, shorting it above her knees. She redid her lipstick in cherry red. "Ta-da!" She held her arms wide. "Carman lives."

"And I look a mess." I brushed the crumbs from my shirt and tried to smooth out the wrinkles.

"Everyone knows you've been in jail and that you're trying to help Fiona. You look . . . heroic."

"A year ago you would have insisted I change before we go out in public."

"A year ago I was married, a snob with a new boob job, and did everything by the book. Look where that got me: a rotten divorce, my ex now married to Miss Ooh La La Skinny-Pants and suing me for alimony."

Mother closed the jail door and I hung the cell key on the wall hook next to the other one. I looked at the cell, then reclaimed the key.

"A little souvenir of your life in the big house?" Mother laughed.

"The way things are going, and they aren't going all that well, I might wind up in here again. The next time it might not be so pleasant with doors open and local scone deliveries." I walked over to the Pottery Barn chair and stuffed the key between the seat and the back. "Insurance."

"That's my girl." Mother patted me on the back and I locked the police station behind us, and we started down Market Street. The temp hovered in the high sixties as we headed for the Seabiscuit. I filled Mother in on the Hollywood hellions and how it involved Fiona. "You really got the fudgies buying into the fact that there's a murder mystery weekend going on?" Mother asked me. "How'd you get Nate Sutter to fall for that one?"

"It was either go along with it or he'd have to tell everyone there was a murder at the Grand and this island would be a ghost town for the rest of the summer. I figure the killer is still on the island because he or she needs the missing phone. Whoever it is has done a bang-up job of framing Fiona."

"Meaning they know Fiona. This isn't a chance murder, Evie; it's a setup, a smart person who knows Fiona had motive and opportunity. They polish off Peep and Fiona takes the fall. Or," Mother added, a thoughtful look in her eye, "maybe they didn't know Fiona at all, but having her around when they knocked off Peep was a happy accident. Fiona might be nothing more than a convenient patsy."

"You're not making this any easier, you know."

"Murder never is, dear."

Most of the little shops along Main were still closed at eight AM, but a few restaurants were open for breakfast. A crowd including Gabi and the Corpse Crusaders had their noses plastered to the plate-glass window of the Seabiscuit while yelling and screaming spilled out the open door, polluting the island peace and quiet. I elbowed my way past picture-snapping tourists outside and inside to Madonna and Zo squared off in the middle of the horse-themed restaurant. Molly stood between them, arms outstretched to keep them apart, and she was decorated with breakfast shrapnel. Was that part of a Western omelet on her shoulder?

"You're crazy, you know that," Madonna bellowed. "I'm burying him in the family plot back in Iowa, and that's all there is to it." Madonna hurled a sticky bun at Zo, and it landed on top of Molly's head. If it hadn't been sticky it might have passed for a fashion statement.

"Iowa?" Zo roared, her eyes bulging. She flung a half-eaten jelly doughnut at Madonna, hitting Molly on the shoulder. "The Peep, my wonderful Peepster, should be buried in the Hollywood Forever Cemetery, where, like, so many of those he wrote about are buried!"

"Wrote about? Give me a break!" Madonna scoffed. "Try dished dirt and fabricated lies. Peep made their lives a living hell. If you bury him there they'll all turn into zombies, dig him up and toss his bony alcohol-infused carcass onto Santa Monica Boulevard and hope the buzzards eat his liver."

"He, like, made their lives interesting!" Zo added. "Yeah, yeah, yeah, they all griped and complained, but he, like, kept their names in the limelight. Deep down inside they all loved him, and that's more than I can say for you."

"Enough," Molly said, as a sausage link smacked her across the nose. "I'll toss you both in jail for disturbing the peace if you keep this up."

"And jail's where she belongs." Madonna glared at Zo. "*She* killed Peep, I know she did. He wouldn't marry her and she popped him one on the head."

"That's a lie. Like, I was out biking. I even have an alibi!" Zo pointed to me. "She saw me riding around, so I was nowhere on that porch to push my poor Peep off." Zo swiped away a tear. "We all know you're the one who killed him." Zo jutted one hip. "You just couldn't take it that he liked me better than you."

Madonna flipped her hair from her face, leaving a smear of jelly. "You were nothing but an easy roll in the hay, and there's no way *I* could have knocked off Peep 'cause I was having dinner. If I'd hit him with the olive oil bottle, I would have the oil all over my white suit, and I love that suit. Besides, I was arguing with Officer Sutter when they found Peep in the bushes." Madonna pointed to Sutter hustling through the door. "The hotel clerk called the police when you and I were arguing, remember? So, you little tramp, that makes the police my alibi. Beat that one."

"Everybody shut up!" Sutter bellowed, and joined Molly center stage. "Here's what's going to happen," he said, grabbing the sleeve of Madonna's gold jacket in one hand and the back of Zo's pink fleece with the other. "You two are leaving this place right now with me, and the next time there's

142

Peep combat I'm locking you both up in the same cell and not opening it till Christmas. Got it?"

"Oh, this is fantastic," Gabi squealed, and she scribbled in her notebook with all the onlookers nodding in agreement. "Best mystery week ever. The whole island's involved, it doesn't get better than that." She held up her iPhone. "I've been retweeted fifty times and got seventy likes on my Facebook page. I'm viral!"

"This isn't a game!" Madonna stamped her foot. "Don't you get it, this is for real."

Gabi grinned. "You all are amazing actors. I think you should win awards. We'll have a big dinner when this is over and get trophies and ribbons and maybe roll out a red carpet like they do at the Oscars," she added, as the crowd nodded in agreement.

"Red carpet," Sutter mumbled, his eyes starting to cross. "The show's over, folks." He ushered Hollywood one and two toward the door and turned to a waitress with *Mable* on her nametag. She looked startled and totally flustered. Actually she sort of looked like . . . Holy cow!

"Is that Fiona?" Mother whispered to me as Sutter said to the waitress in question, "You need to get a mop and broom. Do it now. People are watching."

143

Fiona/Mable bent down and started scooping up breakfast carnage, and I scooted down beside her and picked up two wilted sausage links.

"What are you doing?" I whispered as Sutter and company disappeared out the door.

"Getting information like you are," Fiona whispered. "How'd you get out of jail? And go away, you're ruining my cover."

"Molly left the door open. I hid the spare key in case I wind up in there again, and you have plastic red braids left over from Irma's Raggedy Ann Halloween costume. The blown ship has sailed."

"I spent the night at Irma's and it was either Raggedy Ann or an orange pumpkin."

"You should have gone with the pumpkin."

Mother yanked me to my feet. "We need to go. People are staring."

"Do you think Sutter knew it was Fiona?" I asked as I followed Mother outside and the two of us headed toward the bike shop.

"My guess is Detroit's looking pretty good to him right now, and is that Rudy waving to us from the front porch of the Good Stuff? He looks sort of frazzled. It's a morning of frazzled. And to think some people come here for a vacation."

Mother and I waved back, and Rudy's

wave got a little more frantic. His wild gray hair stuck out as if he'd been hit by lightning, and his eyes were about the same.

"It's Irma." Rudy wiped his hands on his red apron with *The Good Stuff* scripted in white across the front. "She's been at the brandy cordial fudge since six."

Rudy led us inside to an old CD player blaring "I'm Gettin' Married in the Morning" from *My Fair Lady* and Irma twirling around the adorable yellow-and-white shop that had the marble tables used for making fudge on one side and soda-shop-style tables and chairs on the other side.

"She got this way from fudge?" Mother asked, giving Irma a worried look.

"That brandy bottle in her hand might have spurred things along." Rudy hooked his arm around Irma as she swept by to try to slow her down, except Irma snagged Rudy and pulled him along into the dance.

"I love this song," she belted out in time with the music. "But it's never going to happen. Nope, there's no church or anything else for me and my man Rudy here. We're doomed."

She took a swig from the bottle and burped. "My dress is out there in the great unknown, probably shipped off to somebody else somewhere, and I'll never get it back on time; the Butterfly Conservatory has the plague, and now Reverend Lovejoy has no more love or joy and has been hospitalized for an overdose of Viagra. Seems his twenty-something wife wanted more than just a senior moment."

Mother looked at me. "Irma doesn't have a wedding dress or venue or preacher?"

"It's a sign," Irma singsonged. "A big fat flashing sign that I'm not supposed to get married. I've been done in by a drunk clerk, aphids and a little blue pill." Irma took another swig, her eyes glazing over.

Rudy pulled the bottle out of Irma's hand and passed it off to me as she swung by on another dance twirl. "Nonsense," he cooed to Irma. "We're getting married, we'll figure this out."

On the next go-round I grabbed one of Irma's arms and Mother snagged the other. "You're ruining my fun," Irma protested. "And right now there's not much of it, I can tell you that."

"And there's going to be even less when the hangover sets in," I added. With one of Irma's arms draped around each of our shoulders, Mother led the way to the back kitchen. Rudy opened the door to rows of white cabinets, crisp floral sunflower curtains at the window and two big vats of fudge bubbling on the ginormous gas stove. Little curls of steam escaped over the edge of the pots, and the scent of rich chocolate wafted through the kitchen. Rudy pulled out a chair at the wood table set for breakfast and we plopped Irma down, with Rudy holding her upright.

"I'll get coffee." I grabbed the carafe from the maker as Mother said, "I don't think there's enough caffeine on the whole island to sober her up."

"Sober?" Irma hiccupped. "Who wants to be sober at a time like this?" She whacked a spoon on the table. "I want a dress, I want to dance, I want to get married!" Suddenly she lurched forward, landing face first in the plate of waffles.

"Holy moly! Is she okay?" I asked Rudy as he bent over her.

"Sleeping is all. Soon she'll be snoring like a grizzly and if we wake her she'll have an attitude to match. She's been up all night since she got the Viagra phone call. I think it's the stress that's got her in a state."

Mother held up the brandy bottle. "That and half a bottle of cherry cordial."

Rudy took off his apron and draped it around Irma's shoulders. He turned her face to one side and wiped a drip of syrup from her nose. "You know, I wanted to elope, but we both have so many friends on the island it didn't seem right to just run off like that. I hate to drag you two into this since you're so busy trying to help Fiona out of her mess."

"Fiona said she spent the night here." I grabbed a waffle from the stack in the middle. "Did she tell you anything about who might have done in Peep? Does she have any leads at all? 'Cause I'm running close to empty in that department."

Rudy opened two of the white wood cupboard doors to reveal pictures taped to the inside. The Peepster was on one door with Madonna and Idle Summers taped under him; dishes and cups and saucers sat on shelves in the back. The other door had a picture of Zo. Rudy looked from one to the other. "Last night we tried to figure out what's going on, and to keep things straight we came up with the fudge shop version of a murder board. It's sort of a murder cupboard. Dead guy and suspects on one side, and as we eliminate people we put them on the other side. Fiona said Zo had an alibi. She might be a pain in the backside and *liking* us all to death around here, but she's out as a suspect. That Madonna person had to be plenty ticked that her husband's shacked up with Zo, so we think

148

she's a suspect big-time."

Mother poured herself coffee and sat on the edge of the table. "Okay, I get that Peep's the guy on the right with the bleached hair and gold chains and women were fighting over him. But why? That's hard to believe, but since my husband left me for big boobs and a feathered behind, what do I know. I recognize Madonna and Zo from the Seabiscuit fiasco, but who's the gal in sequins with the microphone in her hand?"

"That's Idle Summers." Rudy took a chair and snagged a strip of bacon. "She and Fiona knew each other out there in L.A. Fiona says Peep had something on her, and he could have ruined her singing career that had just started to take off. She's performing up at the Grand. That gives her motive and opportunity for knocking off this Peep guy."

"But we know it's not Madonna," I chimed in. "She was talking to Sutter when Peep bit the big one, so she's out." I unstuck Madonna from the suspect side and taped her under Zo on the non-suspect side.

"That just leaves Idle Summers, so I guess she did it?" Rudy checked on Irma, then poured himself a cup of coffee. "Fiona said that Peep kept all his damning information on a cell phone and she's looked all over for it. I wonder what Peep has on Idle? If we find that phone, we've got Idle Summers dead to rights, or," Rudy added in a quiet voice, "we find out something that adds to Fiona's guilt. What if that happens? So far everything we uncover makes Fiona look guiltier."

"That's because we don't have the whole picture." Mother studied the board. "And whatever is on that cell phone is backed up on a computer somewhere, and my guess is it's not here on the island. Finding that phone will give us an idea who else he had on the ropes, and we can add them to the suspect list."

Mother took a pen from her purse and made a question mark on a paper towel. She taped it under Peep's picture. "We don't have the phone, so we need to put the pieces together that we do have. Fiona and Idle are blackmail victims. If Peep was on the run, no one would look for him on a tiny island in a fly-over state, so that could be the reason he came here. What was he like on the ferry dock?" Mother asked me.

"Drunk, obnoxious . . . and nervous. Yeah, he was really nervous. He told Fiona to call him Perry and not Peep because you never know who's around. And he told Zo to lower her voice. He said he had on his down-low look." I shrugged. "I can only imagine his out-on-the-town look."

We all turned back to Irma, who was mumbling, "Wedding dress. I do. Damn the pill."

"Oh boy. Come on, sweet pea." Rudy helped Irma to stand and put his arm around her middle. "Let's get you upstairs to sleep it off."

Rudy and Irma shuffled toward the back hallway, and Mother said to me, "Did anyone look suspicious when you and Fiona were on that dock?"

"Peep and Zo had top billing in the suspicious department, and I was busy picking up Irma's wedding dress that turned out to be the wrong dress. I did go back to meet the next ferry to see if the dress was there, and I bumped into Sutter. Madonna came in on that second ferry, so Sutter knew what was going on with the wife/secretary scenario. Do you think maybe Sutter has information that we don't, something important about Peep? Something he's not telling us? The rat."

Mother gave me her *is the Pope Catholic?* look. "One of the joys of being a cop is that they're connected to other cops and they all know stuff that they don't share with the

151

rest of mankind."

"At least not voluntarily they don't share. Maybe I could have a go at the involuntary part. We need to find out what Sutter knows, and you can't get involved or it's bye-bye attorney license. Lucky for me, there's no such thing as a painting-a-bike license."

Mother put her hands on my shoulder and looked me dead in the eye. "Evie, dear, going head to head with Nate Sutter may not be a great idea. You already spent one night in the slammer, and it's my guess there is another jail cell that's for the drunks and troublemakers on the island and it does not have cotton sheets and fresh scone delivery. You're fast approaching troublemaker status, and how do you know the killer didn't find the phone and is already gone?"

I could tell Mother about me getting shoved into oncoming traffic, but then she'd worry. The good part of being pushed and shoved meant that someone was starting to sweat, someone besides myself, that is.

I kissed Mother on the cheek. "Just a guess on my part, is all."

Mother folded her arms and gave me her *Mother knows all* look. "And I don't believe that for a second."

9

"Where do you want these?" a porter asked me as he lugged three suitcases and a garment bag into the bike shop. It was noon and I hadn't seen Mother for three hours. What was she doing back there in her half-finished office? Finishing the place off herself?

"How about I give you ten bucks to haul all this stuff upstairs and into the bedroom?"

"How about I give you twenty bucks and I drop them here and leave?"

Just what I needed in my life, a sarcastic porter, and I didn't even get the twenty bucks. I wheeled the Nancy Drew bike I was working on to the side to let the paint dry and put a bicycle bell on the workbench with a note that said *Ring for Service* beside it. "Hey," I said to Bambino and Cleveland as they gave me a disapproving stare that said *this is no way to run a railroad.* "Most people around here are honest and won't steal my bikes, and even if they do take one out for a spin I'll get it back. What are they going to do with the thing, pack it in their suitcase?"

I crossed the sun-bleached deck that had a terrific view overlooking the harbor and passed through the back door of the bike shop to the front door of Mother's office/apartment. There was also a paved walkway that led to the office from Main Street.

Soft swells lapped at the rocks some ten feet below, and a seagull swooped down perching on the railing. Winters here sucked, no doubt about it, but summers were spectacular.

"So, how's it going?" I asked Mother as I opened the glass-paned door that still needed a second coat of paint.

Mother shoved her hair out of her face and brushed dust from her skirt. "What do you think?" She spread her arms wide, taking in a piece of plywood across two sawhorses, boxes of nails stacked up for chairs and two trouble lights hanging down from the exposed rafters. "I'm calling the place Law Office 101. 101 is my official address on Main Street — if we ever decide to use addresses around here — and it sounds simple. People get tired of legal mumbo jumbo, and they get frustrated and don't trust anyone. I'm changing that. I know our beloved city council deems no construction between May and October when the fudgies are peak season, and they take it serious. In fact, the town council fined the company that painted the courthouse for not getting the scaffold down, but at least I ordered furniture. I went with cream-colored bookshelves and desk, celery upholstery, cantaloupe accents and a wet bar in the corner. *Therefores* and *whereases* are a lot easier to take with a Bloody Mary in your hand or a kick-ass cappuccino. Nothing's getting delivered till the end of the week, so I have to improvise for a few days. Besides . . ." Mother gazed around. "I kind of like this look, and the place smells fresh and clean."

"With a hint of sawdust."

"There is that."

A *bing, bing, bing* came from inside the bike shop. "Sounds like you have a customer," Mother said to me. "I'll go with you. I need to change and take a walk around town to reacquaint myself with the place and let people know I'm open for business."

"And that business includes a certain Italian stallion?"

Mother batted her eyes Carman style, fluffed her hair and twitched her hips as she followed me to the shop. We cut through the kitchen with cats one and two perched on the windowsill, Cleveland arching his eye and sporting his *I want tuna now* expression.

"Are you here to rent a bike?" I said to the man in khakis and blue polo with a notebook in his hand. "Or are you part of the Grand Hotel murder mystery group looking for the killer? For the record, I didn't do it."

The guy was sixty-something, with intense green eyes, a friendly smile and monk-style hair, balding in the middle. He held out his business card to Mother and regarded me as a glob of wallpaper paste. "I'm Walt McBride with the *Town Crier.* I'm not here about that Peep guy, and I'd like to do an interview about the new law office that you're opening up."

"You're Fiona's dad?" Mother asked, shaking Walt's hand and taking the card.

"We're trying to help Fiona," I added. "Have you seen anyone on the island that you met when you were out in L.A.? Maybe someone followed Peep here and did him in. I'm Fiona's friend and —"

"You and the rest of this island need to butt out," Walt said in a low growl, all signs of friendly gone. "Fiona was done with that guy. He came here and crossed the wrong person, end of story. He was rotten to the core, and I'll take care of Fiona; she's my daughter and . . ." Walt's voice trailed off as two customers strolled in. "Just mind your own darn business."

Mother hooked her arm through his and added a lovely smile. "I'd just love to chat with you. Let's take this interview over to my office for some pictures. The main entrance is out the front door and we take the path alongside. I'm having a sign made; it should be here soon, and aren't the lilacs just lovely this time of year?"

Mother could disarm a nuclear bomb with that smile. More than once that silky voice had swayed a jury, calmed a store clerk or saved me from getting expelled for cheating on an algebra test. Art history I aced, but show me *x* and *y* and ask me what train gets to the station first and I'm doomed.

Walt and Mother sauntered out the door, and I gave the customers a tour of bikes available for rental. Inventory was low, but the Spy Kids bike and the Hardy Boys returned earlier were now clean, checked and back on the road. That was the key, I realized. Keep the bikes rented.

"Hey, Evie the place is bare as Mother Hubbard's cupboard," Angelo said, coming into the shop as a customer left with the new Nancy Drew bike. Angelo had on a black polo and black pants, the color of choice of retired Detroit mob guys. Angelo and his sister moved to the island last year when their Detroit family sort of commandeered SeeFar, a cottage up on the East Bluff. Angelo considered Mother a dish, treated her like a queen and was just what Mother aka Carman needed after the Paris encounter of a feather kind.

"Angelo!" I gave him a hug. "When did you get back on the island?"

"Hey, kid. How's tricks?" Angelo flashed me his million-dollar smile. "Rosetta and I got here a week ago and you know how it is, settlin' in always takes longer than ya think. And now my nephew Luka's come to visit. He couldn't take another Detroit summer with all the smog and traffic, if you know what I mean." Angelo cut his eyes from back to front of the shop.

"Mother's not here. She's out on the town to promote her new law office, which is code for she's out looking for you." I checked for customers, then stepped closer. "If you have a minute, I could use your expert advice and counsel."

"Meaning you got a situation?"

Angelo was my situation go-to guy. He

knew all about situations and helped me out from time to time because I'd saved his beloved Meatball of the canine variety and not the spaghetti variety from the hooves of oncoming horses. Last year Angelo taught Fiona and me how to pick a lock that desperately needed picking, how to avoid security cameras and how to make a great cup of hot cocoa and sneak in extra marshmallows. "I need to break into jail."

Angelo rocked back on his heels, his dark eyes dancing. "I gotta tell ya, kid, that's a new one on me. Where I come from they're trying to stay out of the joint, if you know what I mean."

"I'm not exactly breaking into jail but into Sutter's office that's across from the jail. I can do the lock on his office door, but I first have to get inside the station. I think Sutter knows something about this Peep guy getting murdered here on the island, and at the moment Fiona's headed for the most wanted poster over at the post office. She didn't do it, but the evidence is stacked against her, and sometimes there's more going on than evidence."

Angelo stroked his chin. "Meaning you know something Sutter doesn't?"

If I told Angelo about me and Fiona getting pushed into harm's way, he'd shut

159

down and tell me to get lost. Putting me in harm's way was not going to happen. "You know Fiona, she's a terrific reporter and one of the good guys," I continued. "She's innocent and she's kept you and Rosetta and the family out of the *Crier.* There were no stories of *Detroit Family Invades Island* or *Detroit Family Takes Over SeeFar,* right?"

"You're doing the guilt trip routine on me? That's playing hardball, kid, and I'm betting it's something you learned right from your mother."

"Maybe a little."

Angelo tried to hide a grin as he ran his hand around the back of his neck. "Yeah, yeah, I like Fiona, and I could tell something was bothering her; she had a look about her and didn't finish her beer at the Stang the other night. Fiona always finishes her beer. I can't see her pulling the plug on some guy no matter how big a jackass he is."

Angelo grabbed a pen and my Hello Kitty notepad and drew a box. "The courthouse has cameras here and here." He drew two circles. "So going in the front door's not gonna work. Getting in through windows is harder than getting in through doors 'cause you can't pick them. Personally, if I didn't have arthritis in my left knee, I'd climb the scaffold around back." He made some *X* marks on the other side. "The place got painted a month ago and you can get in through the upstairs windows. No one ever locks second-story windows and there are some big pine trees for cover. Take that old elevator that's in the courtroom down to the police station on the first floor and badda-bing badda-boom, you avoid the cameras and you're in."

Dumbfounded, I stared at Angelo.

"Hey, it's all right there in the *Crier.* I got myself one of the online subscription things for when I'm wintering in sunny Detroit so I can keep abreast. Always got to keep abreast, kid. The town council went and fined that painting company for not getting the scaffold down in a timely manner on account of that maintenance ordnance they got in place. Every day it's up they're fined, and the money they collect gets the elevator up to code. Ya see, some of the fudgies can't be doing the steps when they visit our historic buildings, so they use the elevator. Sutter's office might have a deadbolt, so it'll take time to crack once you get in."

Angelo cut his eyes back and forth, slid a thin black wallet from his pocket and pushed it across the workbench.

"You carry it with you?"

"Old habits die hard, and if your mamma

161

finds out about this conversation she'll string me up by my you-know-what, so you gotta be careful. If no one's in the clink overnight, the office is unattended between midnight and five, and all 911 calls go to Sutter or that cute little sergeant who likes strawberry smoothies."

"That was in the *Crier* too?"

"Not the smoothie part. I kind of got my eye on her for Luka. He's one of those engineer types and not good with the ladies, if you know what I mean."

I had no idea what an engineer for *the family* did, but some things were best left alone. I pocketed the wallet and Angelo patted me on the head as a customer strolled in. "We're done here, doll face." He winked and headed for the door.

A grandmother wanted a basketball-themed bike for her grandson visiting next week and a chemistry bike for the granddaughter. I'd nearly flunked chemistry in high school, but between Sheldon and Google I'd figure it out.

Two ladies came in saying Penelope from up at the Grand told them about the pink and purple lilac bikes I had ready to rent. I wrote up the rental agreement, made a mental note to thank Penelope for the business and then grabbed the ringing phone as felines one and two ambled in from the kitchen. They jumped up on the pool table and I spotted something under Cleveland's collar. Was he playing with the dryer sheets again? It was a piece of Hello Kitty notepaper from my Post-its in the kitchen. Fiona? Who else would send me a *message by cat*? This was what happened on an island of spotty cell phone reception and a BFF on the lam.

I hung up the phone and started for Cleveland to get the note as Sutter came in the door. "So, where is Fiona? I need to talk to her now."

Sutter took up a pool cue, chalked the end and sailed the five ball to the corner pocket, neatly avoiding the perched kitties. From where I stood I could see the note but Sutter not so much. But if meow one moved . . .

"It's not my turn to watch Fiona." I had to say something to keep his attention on me or the pool table, and not the cats. "I've been busy," I added as he sank the nine ball in the side pocket. "I rent bikes, remember? Lots and lots of bikes, and aren't you busy too? I bet someone's trying to break into a house as we speak, or a kid's shoplifting gum over at Doud's Market. Maybe you should check things out there."

"You're trying to get rid of me, Chicago?"

Sutter circled the table to the right. If he went for the ten ball he'd see Hello Kitty clear as day. If I suspected the note was from Fiona, so would he, and who knew what was in it. Something like *I'm guilty and running off to Brazil* would not be good.

"Six ball, corner pocket," I blurted. "I'll bet you a beer at the Stang you can't make it." A beer and a dare . . . no man could pass that up, right?

"What do you know about Idle Summers?" Sutter asked while leaning over the table, stretching the soft worn denim of his jeans nicely over his backside. Oh boy. I hadn't counted on this being part of making the six-ball shot. Feeling a little dizzy, I tried to swallow, failed, then plopped down in Rudy's old wicker chair and swiped the drool from the corner of my mouth. Well, dang. The guy might be over forty but he had the best butt on the island, no doubt about it. The regular female contingent at the Stang had voted on his and other local butts of the male species one cold February night when we needed something to warm our bones. Nate Sutter won best ass by a landslide.

I took another peek just to make sure. Yep, Sutter's backside was definitely not something to be ignored at this angle, or any other for that matter.

"So what's your opinion?"

I jumped up. "Opinion?"

"You got an opinion on everything, so let's hear it."

"Well . . . there's a certain appeal, sort of, least some think so, not everyone, of course. And then there's Cal Sandman, he was in the running too. He's young and . . ."

Sutter peered at me over his shot. "What does Cal have to do with this?"

"He works out and he's cute and we all agreed he has first-class abs and pecs so you had some competition, but you did win by a landslide, and do we really have to talk about this, it was just girls having fun."

Sutter slowly put down the cue stick and straightened. He gave me a curious look with a smile tripping across his face. "First-class abs? Thought we were talking about Idle Summers?"

Holy freaking mother of pearl! "Right! Sure! Of course! Idle Summers!" I could feel a red-hot blush inching up my neck. *Oh dear earth, part now and swallow me up whole.* The only good thing out of all this was that Sutter was so enjoying the conversation he didn't see the blasted note.

"Idle and Fiona knew each other back in L.A.," I rushed on. "And Fiona thinks Peep had something on Idle to blackmail her, and Fiona thinks Idle would never do in Peep and frame her for it 'cause they're friends, but I'm not so sure, and I think Idle has a past and not of the goody-two-shoes variety, and that's all I know, I swear." I made a cross over my heart and held up two fingers Girl Scout Promise style.

"How did you vote?"

"Vote?"

"At the Stang." He knew! How did he know about the vote? This was an eight-mile island; of course he knew and I'd just confirmed the whole thing.

"I . . . I abstained."

The grin broadened. "Abstinence is no way to go through life, Chicago." Sutter reclaimed his cue, made the shot and put the cue back in the rack. "You owe me a beer."

Sutter headed for the door and I sank down on the stool by the workbench again, my twenty-four-hour deodorant all used up in less than five minutes. After discussing Sutter's butt right there in front of him, I'd never be able to face the guy again. And now I owed him a beer. He'd never let me forget the beer. If the gods of humiliation and embarrassment took pity, maybe he'd forget the vote at the Stang? Yeah, right.

Cleveland let out an irritated *pay attention to me now* meow, snapping me back to the thing that had started all this, the blasted note I was trying to keep from Sutter. Bambino waited a beat for a treat, yawned, then headed for the side pocket for a nap. Her tail was the only thing fitting in there these days, but cats were creatures of habit. I scooped up Cleveland in one arm, ignored the hissing and snarling and untied Hello Kitty.

Courthouse at midnight. 911 Nutty Buddy alert. It was from Fiona, all right. My guess was she'd helped herself to the last Nutty Buddy and while scarfing it down overheard me talking to Angelo about getting into Sutter's office. As much as the note nearly gave me a heart attack, it was good to have Fiona along. She knew more what to look for in the way of important clues connected to Peep, and I needed someone to hold the flashlight when I picked the deadbolt on Sutter's office door.

I rented out two more bikes for the weekend and took an order for a brand-new bike to be painted with a conductor motif for a dear husband's birthday. Good thing wifey added the music conductor part to the order or she'd be getting a bike painted with railroad tracks, steam engines, and a big red caboose.

"Blessed be Saint Patrick that you still be alive and kickin' like you are," Irish Donna said to me as she came inside the shop during a sudden lull in the bike rental action. She dropped a pink Blarney Scone bag on the workbench. "I figure you be in need of some nourishment considering the circumstance." Donna claimed the other stool, her curly red hair framing her soft face and sparkling green eyes. She opened the bag, plucked out two scones and handed me one.

I was never one to question a free scone, until now. "Need as in I look hungry?"

"Need as in the orange pekoe has spoken to me loud and clear, it did, and more trouble's a-brewing. I had a cup of me favorite tea this morning, and there it was plain as day swilling around in the bottom. Seems that black cloud of yours is bigger than ever. Gave me the shivers, it did."

"How do you know the leaves are talking about my cloud?" I tore paper towels from the roll on the workbench, kept one and handed the other to Donna. I took a bite of scone, totally amazed at what butter, sugar and a handful of blueberries can do to flour. "I bet those leaves didn't spell out *Evie Bloomfield beware, the world's coming to an end for you.* The cloud could be anyone's

and I refuse to take ownership, and in fact"
— I tipped my chin in defiance — "I'm
thinking your soothsaying gift is broken or
just plain gone. Look what happened to
Fiona. You told her holy oil and garlic kept
evil away, and Peep not only got off the boat
but things went right to hell for Fiona in
less than a day."

"Ah, but the man up and died, he did,
and that's about as away as it gets in my
book." Donna bit into the scone. "The way
I see it, I'm sharp as a tack and there's no
arguing with the tea leaves. Whatever you
got planned, me dear girl, you best be
forgetting it. You need to be hiding out and
barricading the door. Bad times they are
a-coming."

"If I don't help Fiona, that's exactly what
will happen. What kind of friend would I be
if I left her to fend for herself?"

"An alive friend. The whole town is
a-watching out for Fiona, so you can take a
break and hide under your bed for a few
days, is what I'm saying. Even Walt and
Mamma Geraldine are filling in up there at
the *Crier* to keep it going. I'm thinking the
two of them are feeling a mite responsible
for Fiona staying in California, with Walt's
bragging and Geraldine all snooty over their
high-flying daughter. Fiona had to be feel-

ing poorly about that and not want to be proving them wrong by hightailing it home. She stayed there in California all miserable for who knows how long until . . . Now that's the tricky part, it is. I can't quite figure why she came back here when she did."

I stopped midchew and stared at Donna. "I thought her parents gave her the newspaper?"

"That they did, love. They tried for months and then all of a sudden and out of the blue Fiona shows up on the ferry dock with one measly bag and fire in her eyes. None of us could even mention California without getting our heads chewed off. We all figured something pushed her over the edge out there, and now that we got a glimpse of this Peep person, that something must have been a whopper."

"And maybe Walt and Mamma Geraldine decided to make Peep pay for the way he treated their daughter?" I said, thinking out loud. "Neither one of them wanted my help in finding who did in Peep and told me to back off." I swallowed my last bite of scone; the delish morsel now tasted like wallpaper paste. "It could be that they were worried I'd find them out as the killers?"

"Or you'd be finding out that whopper

thing Peep did." Donna leaned closer and whispered, "And they be worried you would be a-finding Fiona as the killer? Something happened in California to get the girl riled, and then Peep shows up here on her doorstep upsetting her something fierce."

Donna tossed her paper towel into the trash can by the workbench and started for the door. "I need to be getting back to the shop before Shamus scares off the paying customers with his endless flirting. Shameful he is, the old coot. One of these days someone's going to bop him one right in the snoot. Lord knows the man's got it coming."

"Someone like you?" I added with a laugh, glad for the distraction.

"Worse things have been known to happen around these parts, but it's not gonna be his snoot I'd be aiming for but six inches below his belt. Bless the saints above, men got themselves a one-track mind no matter how old they be."

"Yeah, well, I'll take your word for that."

Donna gave me a pathetic look. "Been a dry spell, has it? 'Tis all 'bout the cloud, me dear, and you need to be doing something about it before you go and shrivel up like a giant prune."

Donna tramped across the back deck and

I stared off into the blue abyss of sea and sky feeling very wrinkly. Under normal circumstances I would refuse to believe that sludge swirling around in the bottom of a cup heralded bad news. But nothing was normal these days, and I had Walt and Geraldine to add to the Peepster who-done-it list of suspects. On the surface, adding to the list should be good news, but Walt and Geraldine were Fiona's parents. If I found evidence against them, Fiona would be off the hook but her parents would be on the hook, and I'd lose her friendship forever.

Walt and Geraldine were up to their eyeballs in motive, and the fact that they delivered the *Crier* to the Grand gave them opportunity. If Fiona left her yellow bag in the Grand Hotel lobby and either of them had found it and the olive oil bottle and got seriously pissed at Peep, hitting him over the head was a natural reaction. Heck, I wanted to hit him and I'd only known him ten minutes.

Idle Summers was still tops on the suspect list, I reassured myself. With a little luck — which seemed to be in really short supply lately — I'd find information in Sutter's office tonight to implicate someone else. Even if Sutter did drive me nuts in more ways

172

than one, and deep down inside I personally held him responsible for my onset of pruneness, he was a good cop and knew stuff. This was one time I hoped to heck the guy knew a lot more than I did.

10

"You're late," Fiona grumbled to me as she stuck her head out between two pink lilac bushes behind the courthouse.

"It's dark back here," I said, rubbing my leg. "I can't see a blasted thing and I was afraid to use my flashlight just yet, and I hit my shins on the scaffold and we haven't even started to climb yet. I bet you're feeling like bushes are your second home."

"Beats wearing a plastic wig and cleaning food off the floor. Zo and Madonna are drama on steroids; it's a miracle they haven't killed each other."

Fiona crawled into the open, flipped on her flashlight now that we were behind the courthouse and together we gazed at the tangle of pipes crisscrossing their way upward. "You know," Fiona said to me as I zipped my fleece and settled into the cozy warmth. "We could be at the Stang right now catching up on gossip. Do you ever wonder how we get into these messes?"

"Tonight we *are* the gossip, and we got here 'cause you worked for a Mr. Jerkass and I have a pox upon me. We're both screwed, so start climbing, monkey girl."

The lake breeze caught in the pines behind us, swishing branches across a crescent moon. All was quiet except for an owl hooting in the distance and horses clip-clopping on Market Street. Fiona flipped off the flashlight and stuffed it in her jacket so she could use both hands, grabbed the first railing and swung her leg over. She pulled herself up, then grabbed the next bar and then the next with me right behind her.

"The rungs are really far apart on this thing," Fiona panted. "How tall were these workers anyway?"

Huffing, I hooked my foot onto the next pole. "My guess is there was a ladder here that they took down when they finished the paint job."

"Not very considerate," Fiona groaned. "I'm writing a letter." She grabbed the next bar and flung herself across it. If she had an apple in her mouth her silhouette would be a skinny pig on a spit.

"What was that?" I stopped dead.

"My heart exploding," Fiona wheezed. "I think I'm going to die up here and . . .

and . . . Evie!" Fiona gazed down at me, her eyes huge against the dark. "This whole thing is moving. Why is it moving?"

"Because it's not bolted together anymore! They're taking it apart because the town council is fining them for every day it's up here, and I didn't think about that till now. Can you reach the window?"

Fiona stood as the scaffold swayed more and shoved at the window. "It won't budge. It's painted shut. What kind of cheap painters did the town council get?"

"The usual kind. Push!"

Fiona angled her hands against the glass and shoved hard, opening the window and propelling the scaffold away from the building. "Oh crap! This thing is going to make a lot of noise when it falls."

"So am I! Do something!"

Fiona hooked one leg over the windowsill and grabbed one of the metal bars. "It's too heavy, I can't hold it!"

I snagged Fiona around the waist as the scaffold slid away under my feet, leaving me dangling in mid-air. The pipes teetered backward for a second, then toppled the rest of the way into the pines. Fiona grabbed the waistband of my jeans and yanked hard, giving me the wedgie of all wedgies. The momentum sent us through the window and we landed together with a solid *whoop* on something hard.

"We made it," Fiona panted, as faint moonlight cast shadows across the room. "Though I don't know how we're going to get out of here. I think the judge's desk broke our fall. That pox of yours isn't as bad as you think."

I rolled to the side into nothingness and landed on the floor, my head banging against the wood with a solid *whumph.* I sat up, with little stars — yeah, they really were stars — dancing in front of my eyes, Fiona staring down at me, her eyes huge in the dark. "Then again, maybe the pox is that bad. Are you okay?"

"Peachy." Stumbling, I stood, wobbled and grabbed my butt. "Fiona! It's gone!"

Fiona looked back at me. "Eat ice cream, girlfriend, it's instant fanny food. You'll grow another one in no time. We gotta get going."

"Sheldon's gone. I was going to use the flashlight app and he's not there. He must have slid out of my jeans pocket when you wedged me, and now Sutter's going to know for sure we were here and he's going to blow his top . . . again."

"Trust me, Sutter doesn't need your lost iPhone to tell him what's going on." Fiona flipped on her flashlight and we maneuvered around the court benches, heading for the green exit sign glowing in the corner. "Around here a scaffold in the trees is an Evie/Fiona calling card, and tell me this contraption in front of us isn't an elevator."

"Circa Cary Grant and Doris Day. I recognize the brass grating from watching the oldies with my grandpa Frank at Sleepy Meadows Retirement Center. Not that there's much sleeping there, but the movies are a great cover for sipping afternoon tea with good friends Jack Daniel and Jim Beam."

"I could do with a visit from Jack and Jim right now. This thing is a coffin with bars."

"Think vintage. Think charm. Think of it as our way down to valuable information that will set you free." I slid the brass grating shut behind us with a clang. A dim light blinked a few times, and then, miracle of miracles, it stayed on. I turned the ancient handle to the number 1 and our coffin chugged, lurched a few times, then inched downward. Fiona grabbed my hand. "How old do you think this thing really is? And . . . and we just went past the doors marked one. That was our stop. Why isn't this thing stopping?" Fiona buried her head in her hands. "We're all going to die and I can't

die tonight, I have on really crappy under-
wear."

The coffin shuddered, then jerked to a
halt. I pulled back the grating that could
really do with a spray of WD-40 to loosen it
up and gazed to the ceiling. "Okay, the first-
floor doors are right there." I pointed. "I'll
pry them open, you boost me out and then
I'll pull you up. How hard can it be?"

Standing on tiptoes, I wedged my fingers
between the doors and forced them apart;
little shafts of light from exit signs and probably the front desk area shone down into
the elevator. Fiona braided her fingers
together to make a boost; I stepped in and
gave a hop and she propelled me up. I
banged my head on the ceiling, hooked my
fingers over the edge, then kicked and belly-
scooted the rest of the way and resisted the
urge to kiss the solid floor. "I'm in."

"And so are we," came a woman's voice
over me. "Hey, Evie, is that really you?" I
blinked into a blinding flashlight beam. "It's
me, Gabi, and the Corpse Crusaders, and
what in the world are you doing in that
elevator this time of night?"

Gabi gasped and lowered the flashlight,
her eyes big as softballs in the dim light. "I
know what this is, it's the Clue in the Old
Elevator like one of those Nancy Drew

books. It's to go along with the mystery weekend. Whoever thought this all up is so darn clever, but why is the elevator between floors?"

Thank the Lord for overactive imaginations. "An *old* elevator, right? Got to be authentic, and how did you get in here?"

"Front door." Gabi pointed to the three others behind her. "Lloyd, Sylvester, Trixie and I came here to ask that girl who's usually at the front desk a few questions. We heard that she liked strawberry smoothies." Lloyd held up a to-go cup from Millie's on Main to prove the point. "And when we got here, the front door was unlocked. We figured there must be clues in here somewhere if it was open, and here you are. So, what is it?"

"What's what?" I stood and dusted myself off.

"The clue, silly." Gabi laughed. Lloyd, Sylvester and the other girl whose name I forgot joined in.

"Uh . . ." *Think, Evie, think.* I jammed my hands into my jeans pockets to look like I was searching for something like a clue. I pulled out a gum wrapper, a receipt for beer and fried green beans at the Stang and Penelope's business card that she had given to me when she thought Sutter and I were getting hitched.

"Here we go." I passed Gabi the card and she focused her flashlight and read, "Penelope Woodward, associate manager, the Grand Hotel?"

"Let me tell you," I stated in a serious voice. "Penelope knows what's going on up there at the Grand, and that's where the murder was, so she'll have something to tell you for sure."

"You know, we suspected her all along." Gabi's voice had a serious edge. "She gets real antsy when we bring up Peep and talk about that cell phone that's missing and everyone's interested in finding. Peep must have had the goods on her too, and now you give us her card. That means she's got something to hide and could have knocked off the Peep to keep him quiet."

Gabi threw her arms around me and hugged tight, making it hard to breathe. "You are the best, you know that. The Corpse Crusaders are going to win." She hooked her arm through the tall guy's arm and the other girl snuggled up to the shorter guy. "We sort of found each other in all the fun. Isn't that fantastic? Murder, mystery and a little romance to add to it all. What could be more fun than that?" Gabi hugged me again, and the little band trooped to the door and left.

"Penelope's going to kill us for doing that." Fiona's voice echoed up to me from below.

"Yeah, well, she'll have to take a number, there's getting to be a list."

I reached down, took both of Fiona's hands and helped her wiggle out of the elevator. Just for kicks I hit the elevator button and the piece of crap sprang to life, inched its way up to the first floor and stopped where it should. I followed Fiona down the hall to the frosted-glass door with *Nathaniel Sutter, Chief of Police* stenciled in black.

"Nathaniel. Looks very official," Fiona quipped.

"I think it's the gun and badge that are the official part." I hunkered down, Fiona beside me.

I pulled out Angelo's wallet and Fiona held the flashlight over it. "We should get our own lock-picking tools so we don't have to keep mooching Angelo's."

"That would be like inviting trouble, and I'm done with trouble. We're going to save you from the slammer, and then it's nothing but keys and I never want to see these pick things again."

I slid the L-shaped tension wrench into

the lock to hold the cylinder in place. "Did you hear what Gabi said about Penelope and Peep? Do you really think he had something on her, and what could it be? She's a desk clerk, not working for the CIA." I added the hook pick to push the lock pins out of the way.

"I think Zo and Madonna are just making Penelope and the whole place jumpy. No one's acting right, and can you hurry it up a little?" Fiona squirmed and made a face.

"Do I look like 007? I'm going as fast as I can here."

"I have to pee."

"Seriously? Now? And you couldn't take care of this before?"

"A lot's happened since before."

"It's down the hall and around the corner." That I knew where the bathroom was in a police station said a lot about my life lately. I clamped the flashlight between my teeth and Fiona scurried off; the exit sign glaring from the front offered enough light to move around. I fiddled with the lock again and it finally gave way.

I opened the door to Mr. Neatnik Does Mackinac. All papers were in folders stacked on the desk, pens in holders, desk chair facing front and center and not one Snickers wrapper or scribbled Hello Kitty Post-it in sight. I'd heard that a person's desk reflected the state of their mind, and in this case it was true. Sutter was orderly, methodical, precise, and efficient. I considered my workbench back at the bike shop. My brain was a recycle bin.

I sat in Sutter's chair and flipped open the top folder to police reports. Well, dang, there really was shoplifting at Doud's Market, and someone had stolen a whole ham from the Village Inn. How do you get away with that? Stick it under your shirt and look pregnant? There was an official-looking fax from the Detroit PD about Luka Vellardo followed by a question mark. What did that mean? And there was a picture of a guy I wouldn't want to meet up with in a dark alley. He had a diamond stud earring, dishwater-blond ponytail and bad teeth. Can we say whitening strips? There were also three attractive forty-something women in nice suits who —

"What are you doing here?" Sutter asked from the doorway.

I nearly bit the end off the flashlight and flipped the folder in the air, with paper drifting down around me like oversized confetti. *"Da ca crsadrs dud e."*

"What?"

I took the flashlight out of my mouth.

"The Corpse Crusaders did it."

When caught red-handed, blame someone else. A little something I learned from having two siblings. Not that Mother ever bought it, because my siblings were perfect and me not so much. "They came in through the front door, and I followed them 'cause I'm a good citizen and I knew they didn't belong in here."

Was that Fiona standing in the doorway?

"They tried to get in, though, by the scaffold," I added to keep Sutter busy, something I was doing a lot of lately. "It collapsed, and who would be stupid enough to try to climb scaffolding in the back of a building in the first place, and if you don't believe me you can check your camera. The yellow shirts they wear are hard to miss."

Of course if Sutter did check the camera footage, he'd see that I didn't follow them in, but in the grand scheme of whopper lies out there right now, that was a minor detail.

Sutter's eyes narrowed and he stomped his way to the desk. "You're going through my stuff?"

"Checking on what the Crusaders were up to. I wanted to see if it was important."

When Sutter didn't offer some sarcastic comeback to my really lame explanation, I cut my eyes his way. He was staring at the

185

pictures of those three women and the scary guy and absently rubbing his leg. For a split second concern crossed his face. Anyone else would have missed it, but for better or worse I knew Sutter. Something was up and it wasn't just me breaking into his office.

"Who are they?" I tapped the paper.

"Nobody," Sutter answered in a cold, flat cop voice, giving nothing away. He snagged my arm and hauled me out of his chair, propelling it across the office.

"You're lying."

"So are you, I'm just a lot better at it."

"Hey, the Crusaders were here, they came in through the front door. What do you know about Luka?" I tapped the name on the fax.

"Word has it he makes a mean lasagna." Sutter led me to the police reception desk where Molly usually sat, then through the police station door, past the steps that led upstairs to the courthouse, then to the main door. He opened it, took my hand and slapped Sheldon into my palm. "I got seven 911 alerts about the scaffold falling and you left this. Molly had a hot date tonight and probably forgot to lock the front door when she left here."

Curls of fog drifted over the street and twined around our feet and ankles. Halos of mist glowed from streetlights and porches. "You're not going to arrest me?"

A smile tugged at the corners of Sutter's mouth. It wasn't a *you're so cute* kind of smile but more one that said *gotcha.* He leaned against the doorjamb and folded his arms, with little droplets of moisture clinging to his too-long dark hair, and a hint of stubble darkening his jawline. "With you wreaking havoc around here and entertaining the troops with deeds of breaking and entering, Betsy Ross on the run, food fights —"

"I didn't do the food fight."

"And instigating murder week at the Grand Hotel, that lets me fly under the radar and find the killer."

"I'm . . . I'm a distraction?"

Sutter stilled, the laughter in his eyes fading to serious, then mysterious as the night around us. He stood, hesitated for a second, then took a step closer. He tucked a strand of hair behind my left ear; the brush of his fingers against my neck sent chills down my spine. "Chicago, you are always a distraction," he said in a voice smooth as warm brandy on a cold night.

"Is that a good thing or a bad thing?" I could barely breathe, my voice just a whisper, his gaze meeting mine.

He wove his fingers into my hair, his hand steady, protective, possessive. He kissed me . . . slow . . . then hot, then sizzling. "I have no idea." His lips formed the words against mine.

Then he closed the door, leaving me dizzy and alone and an inch away from being a melted blob in the middle of Market Street.

"They cancelled my flowers!"

I pried one eye open as Irma flopped back across my bed and tossed a pillow over her face. "Suffocation's not the answer. There won't be any flowers for the funeral, it'll be a bust."

I felt around on the top of my nightstand for Sheldon. "It's six in the morning. Don't you have a man in your house who needs tending to at this hour?"

The foghorn out in the harbor let out its mournful warning as I pushed myself up; Cleveland and Bambino, sleeping on my chest, did not appreciate the disruption one bit. The eerie thirty-second blasts always gave me a creepy feeling of not knowing what would happen next, and considering the present situation of *killer on the loose,* the creepy was worse than ever.

I clicked on the light and peeked under the pillow to Irma. Her eyes were glazed and her honey-blonde hair was in big O's all over her head, like she'd just taken out the rollers for that nice springy-hair look. "Now the flowers have bugs?"

"The flowers are gone, as in ta-ta, *sayonara, arrivederci* baby." Wiping her nose on the sleeve of her blouse, Irma stared at the ceiling. "I told Francine over there at Francine's Flowers I'd take whatever she had left in the way of anything blooming, and she has nothing except one artificial Christmas tree, an Easter basket and a half-eaten heart left over from Valentine's Day. It's the Lilac Festival and weddings are everywhere and every flower down to the last rose, lily of the valley, baby's breath and daisy within a hundred miles is spoken for and my flowers are missing. That I ordered them six months ago doesn't matter diddly to that old battle-axe."

Irma rolled over and faced me, her eyes blazing. "I'll tell you what I think happened. I just bet there was a last-minute wedding and that money-grubbing Francine sold my lovely flowers of pink peonies and white roses for triple the price." Irma crinkled her nose and snorted. "That little harlot has always had her eye on Rudy, and it just frosts her lilies that I got him and she didn't. Na-na-na-na boo-boo."

189

Irma grinned in triumph, then flopped back. "I found out last night about the demise of my flowers, and I tried to hold it all in and be stoic, but not having flowers is a big deal — at least to me it is — and I can't tell Rudy."

"He'll beat up Francine? She's seventy but feisty. You have to watch that one."

"Rudy will say we should just elope, and I don't want to elope. I want to get married on Mackinac. I've been hoarding tulle and lace for months to decorate the Butterfly Conservatory. I bought those yummy little almonds, bottles of bubbles shaped like wedding cakes and I even bought *I married my best friend today* champagne flutes. Nate's here, you're here, so is Irish Donna and that no-good Shamus and the Douds and the gang at the Village Inn and the euchre club at the Stang. Walt and Geraldine even came back from Arizona to be with me. All my friends are here and I want them to be at my wedding. I've been on this island for forty years; I want to get married here where it means something, not in front of some judge I don't even know. I just won't feel married if it's not here on Mackinac. I want Fiona to put my wedding in the *Crier.* That paper is like our island scrapbook of what happens, and I want Rudy and me to happen here."

"Fiona!" I bolted upright. "I forgot she was in jail!" My brain flashed back to Sutter, the courthouse and the kiss. "I was distracted."

"Must have been one heck of a distraction to make you forget Fiona in jail."

"You have no idea." I scrambled out of bed and couldn't find my last pair of clean jeans I had here somewhere. I grabbed my dirty jeans from last night off the floor, then stuck Sheldon in my pocket next to Angelo's wallet.

Irma's eyes started to sparkle, a grin pulling at her lips. "You know, this is perfect," she said, sounding a little breathy with excitement.

"Fiona probably wouldn't agree with the perfect part." I shrugged on a sweatshirt I got from the Chicago Natural History Museum with *If history repeats itself, I'm getting a dinosaur* scripted on the front.

"We'll do a jailbreak," Irma gushed. "Something drastic is just what I need to get my mind off things. Time's a-wastin'. Grab a crowbar, Chicago, let's get a move on; we'll pry Fiona out of jail if we have to. We all know she's innocent."

Crowbar? I flung myself in front of the door, spreading my arms and legs spidey style to stop Irma. "Nate is your son, he's the police chief, remember? And Fiona isn't exactly *in* jail but hiding in the police station bathroom since our great plan of escape by scaffold sort of bit the dust . . . or in this case the trees . . . and don't give me that *you've got to be kidding* look; no way can I make this stuff up."

"Scaffold? So you're the one."

"And an elevator. You and Rudy try to hunt up some flowers and a venue and a preacher."

"And a dress."

"Oh, yeah, the dress. If I'm not back by ten, ask Rudy to open the bike shop for me," I called over my shoulder as I started down the hall. "Getting Fiona out of the bathroom may take some doing. I'll commandeer Mother to help."

"You're going to need help in the shop when Rudy and I are on our honeymoon, dear, and your mother's not in her room," Irma yelled after me. "I have no idea where she is. Maybe you should rethink the crowbar."

11

I wasn't absolutely sure where Mother was, but I had a pretty good idea. I had no intention of visiting SeeFar at this hour to check if I was right, and I probably couldn't find the place with fog covering the island like a big wad of cotton.

Mother was the perfect distraction for my jail rescue in that she knew just the questions to drive Sutter nuts and leave Molly shaking her head, giving Fiona a chance to sneak out. Irish Donna was my second choice as diversion queen. She'd be up baking at this hour, and no one would pay attention to Fiona if they had fresh warm blueberry scones to focus on, and —

"Yikes!"

I jumped a foot to someone tapping me on the shoulder. I jerked around to . . . "Fiona?" I threw my arms around her. "You're out of jail, that's terrific. How'd you get here and . . . and is that my new blue sweater you're wearing?" I looked closer. "It *is* my new sweater!"

"J. Crew, great choice, girlfriend. It was in your room just sitting there on the dresser screaming, *wear me, wear me.* After I took a shower I couldn't very well put on my filthy clothes that I crawled around in all night. And you need to do laundry since I've got on your last pair of clean jeans." Fiona spread her arms wide. "Don't you love this fog? It's perfect hideout weather. I feel invisible."

"You showered at my house and took my clothes?"

"And slept on your couch and ate two Nutty Buddies. I think I'm addicted. Thanks for distracting Nate with that kiss; it was brilliant." She gave me a curious look. "That's all it was, right? A distraction?"

"So I've been told. And you got out of the station by putting your finger alongside your nose and going up a chimney?"

"I snuck out the window. They lock from the inside, so it was a piece of cake. Who's this Luka guy you were talking about with Sutter?" Fiona framed her face with her hands, looking forlorn. "I'm so out of the loop. I used to *be* the loop, and now I have no idea what's going on."

"I think Luka just got here and there's a

194

good chance he's dating Molly. If Sutter finds out his sergeant is spending time with the family engineer he's going to blow a gasket."

"There something with being a family engineer?"

"There something with being a family godfather?"

Fiona's brows arched to her hairline. "*That* family."

"And what if this Luka guy and Peep got here around the same time? The *Inside Scoop* doesn't exactly scoop sugar and fairy tales, and maybe someone had enough and knew who to contact. Luka could get rid of Peep, frame you, date Molly so everyone thinks he's Mr. Law-Abiding Citizen. Does the name Luka mean anything to you?"

"The fog's still hanging in there. I should visit SeeFar and take a look at this guy; maybe I do know him. We can peek in the window and stay out of sight. If we get caught, I take off and you go with returning Angelo's lock picks that are probably in those gross jeans you've got on from last night." Fiona wrinkled her nose. "How can you wear those dirty things?"

"Because someone has on my last pair of clean ones!"

"There is that."

I followed Fiona through the fog. After a lifetime here she could probably navigate the island in her sleep and on one foot. We cut across the wet grass of Marquette Park; the big bronze statue of Father Marquette, who watched over us all, was hidden in fluffs of white. At the back of the art museum we caught the steps — officially called Crow's Nest Trail, but I'd personally dubbed them the steps from hell — that zigzagged straight up the hillside. Wheezing and panting and trying to ward off death by exhaustion, we reached the East Bluff. "Hope we don't peek into the wrong house or fall off the blasted cliff," I panted. "I can't see a blasted thing."

"You need to get to the gym," Fiona said, not breaking a sweat.

"You never go to the gym. Why aren't you ready to pass out?" We headed up Huron Street, with the Mackinac Bridge in the distance and the town below swallowed in clouds, the ghostly foghorn echoing around us.

"It's a proven fact that we islanders are born with great lungs, can smell a snowstorm twelve hours before it hits and know from birth how to drive a snowmobile. What are Chicago babies good at?"

"Putting toppings on pizza."

196

Fiona stepped around the black wrought iron gate that marked the entrance to See-Far and squeaked like something from a Hitchcock movie. It also announced intruders and was most likely why *the family* never oiled the thing. We did a stealthy tiptoe up the walk, flattened ourselves against the side of the house, then clam-crawled around the concrete statue of the Virgin Mary to the kitchen window. A light was on; the window was open a crack and the scent of burned bacon washed over us.

The Seniority was the older contingent of *the family* and last year acquired SeeFar in a real estate settlement. They also got the owner as a live-in cook in retribution for trying to swindle them out of a boatload of money. My guess was that the *live* part of the deal had definite appeal over the obvious alternative. That the window was only open a crack this morning and not flung wide meant former owner Dwight Wainwright the Third's cooking was improving.

Angelo sat at the table drinking something steamy. A younger guy with dark wavy hair, intent black eyes and a backward Detroit Tigers ball cap stood beside him studying something spread out on the table.

"I know him," I whispered to Fiona as I pointed inside.

197

"You mean you *wish* you knew him. Hubba hubba, come to mamma. That is one delish Italian stallion, and I got to tell you he is a fine way to start the day."

"And Luka belongs to Molly," Mother said from behind as she joined in the staring. "Angelo set the two of them up and they seem to be getting along." She held up a pink Blarney Scone bag. "Breakfast?"

I took a blueberry scone, Fiona cranberry, Mother chocolate. Mother was definitely Carman this morning in her fringe jacket, skinny dark denim jeans, hair tumbled and curly, and not one hint of Ann Louise anywhere. "He got off the same ferry as Peep and Zo," I said. "I remember the hat."

"If the hat's what you remember about the guy, you need a shot of that hormone therapy stuff." This time Fiona was the one panting and it had nothing to do with climbing steps. "I'm getting a cardio work-out just looking at the guy."

I took a bite of scone and mumbled, "So, what exactly does the family engineer do?"

"Fixes things like SeeFar's crumbling foundation," Mother chimed it. "He's got the blueprints right out there in front of him. He's so shy I don't think he's ever been out of Detroit till now."

"Or it's a great cover," I added. "It's those

shy quiet types you have to watch out for."

Mother patted me on the back. "Luka isn't like that. He leaves the exciting part to his brother. He got the personality genes, and I think he's a cover model for books or magazines or something."

"In L.A.?" I dropped my scone, then picked it up quick to stay within the no-germs rule of things retrieved off the ground within five seconds. "That's the connection. What if Peep had something on Luka's brother and Luka went after Peep?"

"And," came Angelo's voice out the window as he leaned over the sill. He had a *Kiss Me I'm From Detroit* mug in his hand, dark eyes dancing, hair mussed and sexy. "What if the moon is really blue cheese and those astronaut guys didn't let any of us know so they could corner the market and make a killing? I know you're all trying to find out who plugged that Peep guy, but Luka here's not your man. We're a family here, and just like all families we got our ways of doing things. Wasting good olive oil is not our style; we save it for the lasagna and a nice ziti. And we pick up after ourselves — no messes left behind, if you know what I mean — and Peep croaked was a big mess. Now I'm making my hot chocolate here, so if you girls wanna come on in instead of stomping all over my new red geraniums, that would be fine by me."

Mother stood, kissed Angelo through the window then sauntered off toward the back door. I passed Angelo the wallet with the picks and mouthed *thank you,* and Fiona and I faded into the fog, neither of us up to facing a guy we'd just accused of being a killer.

"Well, that was a little awkward." Fiona popped the last bite of scone into her mouth when we reached the steps leading down to town. "Do you think Angelo's hacked off that we accused Luka of murder? I mean, we've got enough problems around here without adding him and the rest of the family to the list. And I think it's all for nothing. Luka didn't come here to kill Peep. When I was in L.A. I never met him or his brother or heard anything about either one."

"Yeah, but you've been gone for a year. Whatever got Peep dead was something recent that came up. But why come to Mackinac?" I stopped Fiona before we started the steps. "You're the link in all this, the one thing that's in common with the island and Peep. What aren't you telling me?"

Fiona puffed out a deep breath and stared down at the wood platform. She kicked an acorn, sending it flying over the side into the white abyss. "Peep wanted me back. The *Scoop* is doing well and he needs an editor, someone who already knows the paper and the contacts. He said he wanted to start cutting back on work, which makes no sense since Peep is all about work and money, but that's what he said. I hated the *Scoop,* but I was a good reporter until . . . until I got fed up and had to get out of there no matter what."

"Okay, so Peep was using the stuff he had on you to get you back to L.A., I get that. But like we've said before, he could have bullied you over the phone. He didn't have to come to a place he didn't know existed. Everyone loves you on Mackinac. No matter what you did or got involved with, it's over and you've moved on." I took Fiona's hand. "What's so important that Peep thought he could get you back?"

"Threats up close and personal are more effective than three thousand miles away." She pulled in a deep breath. "And if you really must know, I just happen to have Orlando Bloom's phone number. Nothing's more important than Orlando Bloom except maybe that new hottie, Channing Tatum."

"I'm trying to be serious here and save your butt and you're not cooperating, and who the heck is Channing Tatum?"

"Girlfriend, you so need to get out more." Fiona raced down the steps, her footsteps slapping against the wood planks breaking the early-morning quiet as she faded into swirling white puffs.

I did a quick Google on Channing while considering the fact that whatever was on Peep's phone meant a lot to Fiona personally, but I couldn't imagine anything that would have her so upset and —

Holy mother of pearl! I stared at Sheldon, my retinas starting to sizzle. Fiona was right about one thing, I really did need to get out more, especially if that was what was out there. Yowzer!

Weak in the knees, I stumbled down the steps, then followed the sound of the fog-horn out in the harbor, figuring I'd either wind up on Main Street or stumble into the lake.

"Glad you're here, but the ferries aren't running in this pea soup so you didn't have to hurry," Rudy said to me as I came into the shop. He was standing on a teetering stool and lovingly polishing his euchre trophies displayed on the shelf over the workbench. Bambino and Cleveland were sprawled across the pool table enjoying an early-morning snooze that would morph into a noonday snooze that would give way to an afternoon snooze interrupted periodically by meows of *servant, give me tuna now or I pee on your clothes.*

"But once the fog lifts," Rudy continued, "all those fudgies waiting on the other side will descend upon us like a swarm of locusts, and I know that's a good thing but it sure does make for a crazy day." He cut his eyes my way. "And what's wrong with you? You're all flushed and you just knocked over two bikes and didn't even notice."

I picked up Nancy Drew and Babe Ruth. "Well, since you asked, there's this guy, Channing Tatum, that Fiona was talking about and —"

"That new pooper-scooper who follows the horses around and cleans up? I hear he's terrific and doing a great job."

"Not exactly, but you got the terrific part right."

Rudy's shoulders slouched as he climbed back to earth, and he plopped down heavy on the stool where he'd been standing. He picked up a brown wicker basket and a screwdriver. "At least something's going right around here. Like Twain says, *the world owes you nothing, it was here first,* so I'll just have to figure things out on my own."

I took the stool beside Rudy and patted

203

him on the back as he attached the basket to Harry Potter. "I wish there were something I could do."

"Finding a new euchre partner is going to be tough." Rudy nodded at the shelf of trophies. "There's room for two more and I need someone who can help me whip the pants off Trevor Fallon down at the Stang."

I looked from Rudy to the trophies. "I . . . I thought you were having a meltdown over the wedding."

Rudy waved his hand in the air as if shooing a fly off a beer. "Not to worry, things'll work out just fine. I love Irma and she loves me, so what else really matters? We're friends who found each other and now we're inseparable; we're together for better or worse, through thick and thin. The wedding is just window dressing."

I didn't think Irma would agree about the window dressing part; she wanted the celebration, the ceremony, the romance, but I was sure she'd agree that she and Rudy were . . . friends.

"Actually," I said, as little gears in my brain started to turn, "you're best friends."

"Nothing better than that."

"You two would go to the ends of the earth for each other. If one of you showed up dragging a dead body, the other would grab a shovel, lead the way to the garden no questions asked and start digging, and when the cops came you'd hide each other in the attic."

Rudy put down his screwdriver and looked me dead in the eyes. "I got a feeling we're not just talking about me and Irma now, are we."

"I think Fiona has a friend, a really good one, and my guess is that whatever's on that phone that we can't find involves someone Fiona's close to. She's not freaking out about her own well-being but someone else's, and she is not going to give him or her up. I'd say it's why Fiona left L.A. She'd had enough when Peep's peepholing got personal. Maybe she even got fed up enough to knock Peep off when he showed up here with his threats. You know Fiona, I know her, and she's true blue, one of those till-death-do-us-part kind of people."

Rudy's eyes darkened. "That's a big leap, Chicago. And we have other suspects, you know, good ones."

"We do have other suspects," I said, not feeling nearly as confident as I wanted to. I grabbed the screwdriver and handed it to Rudy. "But it's a darn good thing we have an attic in this place, 'cause we just might have to use it."

"Use what?" Cal asked as he rolled through the door.

Rudy gave me a wide-eyed look that said *what do we do now?* Cal was a great guy, a soldier for real some years ago, and it was how he ended up in the chair. He did the reenactment thing now but still took protecting the law seriously, proven by the *protect our butterflies* assignment. And he was a good friend of Sutter's. This was not a man who needed to know about Fiona in the attic.

"Use our connections to find Rudy a euchre partner," I blurted, needing something to fill the void. "I don't know a spade from a club, so I'm out, and my mom's a ringer, so no one will play with her."

Cal shrugged his broad shoulders, pulling his T-shirt that read *Honk if you find men in wheelchairs sexy* tight across his broad chest. "I do a little Texas hold 'em, so I'm not much good either."

He rolled his way to the workbench. "Thought I'd stop by to see if you'd take me on here. I bought the Newfoundland and now I've got to figure out a way to pay for the thing." He grinned. It was the boyish kind of grin that made women swoon. "I was over at the VI and Nate was there getting coffee to go; he was on his way to the

Grand. Seems one of those Hollywood hellions got her bracelet stolen, a gold turtle or something. This Peep Show thing sure keeps old Nate hopping; we'll never get a chance to do some fishing if this keeps up. He said you needed a fill-in for Rudy here when he's on his honeymoon."

Zo's turtle? The one that used to belong to Fiona? Drat! Another nail in Fiona's coffin, and the reason I found out about it was from Cal here in the shop talking to me. So, maybe Cal being Sutter's pal wasn't such a bad thing after all. Maybe it was a good thing in that if he worked here I'd be the one getting information for a change.

"You're hired," I said to Cal. From behind him Rudy shook his head and mouthed, *Have you lost your mind?* Okay, I got that because just as I might find stuff out about Sutter and what was going on, Cal could very well carry tales back to our dear police chief. A lot of chitchat went on at Rudy's Rides, but it was worth the gamble of what got spread around. I needed information.

"And," I added, "Rudy here will teach you how to play euchre."

"I will?" Rudy's eyes bulged.

Another great place for local gossip was the Stang. I put my hand on Cal's shoulder and pointed to the trophies. "Wow, just look at those beauties all big and shiny. One of those babies is what you need to keep that Best Chili Ever trophy you got company. Just picture them side-by-side in your mahogany trophy case with the light shining on them. Great idea, huh?"

Cal's eyes glistened, his jaw slacked and a little drop of drool caught at the corner of his mouth. It was the same reaction I had when looking at a new Coach purse. "Yeah," Cal said, all breathy. "It is a great idea."

"Perfect," I rushed on before Rudy could protest. "You can start now. Rudy will show you around the shop and how it works and where he keeps his lucky euchre deck. I'll get us some fresh scones to celebrate. Yippee."

Both dudes looked at me as if I needed Prozac. I guess the *yippee* was a bit over the top. I grabbed Nancy Drew and raced out of the shop. I hoped it dawned on Rudy what I was up to with getting Cal as an in-house informer. If not, I'd explain things later. Hey, Rudy couldn't be too upset; I found him a euchre partner, didn't I?

I pedaled toward Cadotte and the Grand Hotel instead of heading for the Blarney Scone. I was a quart low on fat and sugar and could really do with another scone, but it would have to wait. What mattered most right now was Fiona. What had she gotten herself into with stealing the bracelet, and how close was Sutter to locking her up for real?

It might also be a good idea to pay attention to what I was doing and not get lost in the fog. I still couldn't see a blasted thing and someone was behind me, I thought. Another bike? I heard them approach and pedaled my little heart out to get to the side and out of the way, till I was rammed hard.

What the — I held on to the handlebars but it didn't help. Again I went flying ass over appetite, not sure which of those body parts would hit the ground first because this time there was no dead body to stop me.

12

"Like, my favorite turtle bracelet is gone, I've looked everywhere for it," Zo screeched from inside the Grand Hotel. I could hear her as I limped up the back steps, nearly running into Idle coming down. She took one look at me and hurried off.

"It was that Fiona person, I tell you," Zo went on as I got to the lobby. I joined the growing crowd of hotel guests, maids and waiters and even a few of the morning gardeners wandering in to see what all the hoopla was about. Hoopla was not a common occurrence at the Grand; the place was more martinis, Manhattans, high tea with piano music . . . usually. Today the yellow-shirted Corpse Crusaders, orange-shirted Body Baggers and purple-shirted Murder Marauders wrote furiously in their notebooks and Sutter had one of those *Lord take me now* expressions on his face.

"Like, she still thinks that bracelet belongs

to her even though she, like, gave it to me years ago," Zo ranted on.

"It *is* hers." Walt elbowed his way through the crowd. Geraldine followed behind him, clutching a refill stack of *Town Criers.* "Her mother and I gave Fiona that bracelet with the turtle when she graduated college to remind her of Mackinac. The island's shaped like a turtle, in case you didn't know."

Zo sneered. "Yeah, right. This place is, like, nothing but a chunk of rock in a lake. Big deal."

Geraldine jabbed her finger at Zo. "You got that bracelet when Fiona was desperate for money out in that L.A. hellhole, and you wouldn't let her buy it back like you promised."

"I didn't promise anything. That turtle is my good-luck charm; I wear it all the time except to sleep. I even had a turtle necklace made to match it." Zo reached in her blouse and slid out a thin gold chain with a turtle suspended at the end. "And now Fiona's broken the set, she's broken my good luck." Zo glared. "She never did like me or Peep."

"What's to like?" Geraldine roared.

Zo gazed toward the ceiling and made the sign of the cross, only she did it backward like someone who didn't do it all that often,

211

probably never, and this time was just for effect.

"Fiona robbed me of my favorite piece of jewelry and my beloved Peepy and my luck," Zo sobbed, a tear trickling down her cheek. "She even stabbed a knife into the pillow on my bed to prove just how much she hates me. She's a full-fledged lunatic. First she got Peep out of her life, and now she's going after me. I think she wanted Peep for herself, that has to be it. When he, like, chose me instead, she left L.A., and now that we're here she's jealous that we were, like, so happy. Oh, the shame of it all."

"You're the lunatic," Walt growled.

"I'm not the one accused of murder and stabbing pillows," Zo blubbered.

"We should take this into my office," Penelope interjected, looking pale and nervous. "This isn't the sort of thing to be talked about in public at the hotel." She hooked her arm through Zo's and faked a sweet smile. "We'll give you some privacy so you can collect yourself and sort this all out and —"

"Like, I don't want privacy." Zo yanked her arm away and jabbed Sutter in the chest with her index finger. "I want justice, like, right now for my Peepy, and I want my luck back. I want everyone to know Fiona for the kind of person she is. You're the law around here; like, arrest her."

"We don't know who's responsible for what," Sutter insisted in his flat cop voice, his face unreadable except for a little vein throbbing at his temple. "But we will look into the matter, and you need to go down to the police station and give us a formal statement about the theft. Maybe you just misplaced it."

Zo's face turned the color of the geraniums in the carpet. "Like, you're going to wait till that woman puts a knife in me before you do anything about all this?"

"One can only hope," Penelope muttered under her breath.

"Like, I heard that," Zo huffed. "You're probably in cahoots with Fiona. You didn't like Peep any better than she did, I could tell. You put us in a crappy room."

Penelope smacked her palm against her forehead. "There are no crappy rooms at the Grand Hotel. You got the room you paid for; if you wanted a better room you had to pay more money. I personally gave him that option when he checked in, so quit your whining."

Sutter held up his hands as Molly made her way through the crowd. "Miss Zo, you go with my sergeant here to the police station and give a statement."

"And you'll find Fiona," Zo insisted as Molly led her out of the lobby with Zo still calling over her shoulder. "She took my bracelet and she took my Peep. She should pay for her sins."

The crowd paused for a beat, then burst into wild applause. "That was the best performance yet," Gabi insisted as *bravo, bravo* erupted from the rest of the onlookers. "I think Zo should get the award for best actor. She's fantastic."

"Our own little Penelope here should get an award too," one of the Body Baggers chimed in, patting Penelope on the back.

"Or you, Mr. Dreamboat," a brunette gushed. She gazed up at Sutter and batted her eyes, both hands perched on his chest. "You're as good as that Hugh Jackman guy any day of the week."

"Are you kidding, he's so much more handsome than that," a blonde panted. "I think we should put up a poster here in the lobby and let people vote on who they think is the best actor and supporting actor and" — she looked to Sutter and sighed — "the most handsome."

"I'm ordering the trophies tonight," Gabi added. She turned to Penelope. "We need to have a banquet for the presentation at the end of the week. We can have it as part of the dinner hour right here in the hotel with an open bar and a red carpet right down the middle of the dining room. We all want the red carpet; it makes it official looking."

The blonde glanced at me and snickered. "You sure won't be walking on any red carpet or winning any awards; you're always a mess. Just look at you now. I think you look this way 'cause you want people to feel sorry for you. Well, honey, it's not working. Get a life and take some acting lessons, and you really need to clean yourself up."

"And with a little luck maybe you'll be the next one on the slab over at the morgue," I offered with a fake smile, every bone in my body hurting. "That would get the award for best live-action scene for sure."

Sutter hauled me toward the hall behind the reception desk with an *Employees Only* door on one side and farther down the hall *Annex 1* and *Annex 2.* "You're not helping to calm things down here."

"Hey, that woman started it, and will you slow down?" I whined. "This isn't exactly my best day ever."

"Maybe you should just hide under your

bed and do us all a favor." Sutter entered the *Employees Only* room as Madonna was coming out. She waved a stack of papers at Sutter. "All this legal stuff about Peep has to be faxed to L.A. I need a death certificate; I need the doctor to sign off on the body. When can I take Peep's sorry cheating butt home and get out of here?"

Sutter hunched his shoulders. "When we catch the killer."

"Fiona *is* the killer." Madonna slammed the door shut behind her, and Sutter tramped across the room. Guess that flat cop voice and bland look was more of a front than I thought. "How'd I ever let you talk me into this murder weekend idea?"

"At the time it beat yelling *killer on the loose, barricade the doors.*"

"And it's good for business," Sutter ground out.

"There is that." I sat at a desk cluttered with printers, fax machines and telephones. Office supplies lined the far wall; a small table with breakfast goodies sat off to the side next to the utility box and a stack of bottled waters. A well-hydrated staff is a happy staff. "I just hired Cal and all the shops are making money. Think of it this way, you're our hero."

"I'd rather just be the police chief, and

216

what the heck happened to you? You look like you fell in a blender."

Lying to Sutter was always a little tricky, but if I told Sutter the truth, that someone had tried to run me down, he'd either toss me in jail again and this time not let me out or stick to me like white on rice. With the possibility of needing to hide Fiona in the attic, I didn't need Sutter hovering.

"An accident." When you're lying, a partial truth works best. Another little something I learned from siblings Trevor and Lindsey and one of the reasons why they were really good attorneys. "Bikes and I aren't a great mix."

"You should put that on a T-shirt." Sutter pulled tissues from a box on the desk and handed them to me. "I'm guessing the reason you showed up here is that Cal mentioned the bracelet being stolen."

"He said you were up here and I knew you'd think Fiona took the bracelet, and that's crazy. Why would she do such a thing? It makes her look guiltier. She's too smart for that." Oh, I so hoped I was right.

"Or after knocking off Peep, Fiona figured stealing a bracelet is no big deal."

"What about Walt and Geraldine?" I swiped at my knees to clean out the scrapes and bit back a string of ouches so as not to

217

look like a wuss in front of Sutter. "Those two are out there in the lobby right now and would steal the bracelet they gave Fiona in a heartbeat. And they hated Peep."

"But they love Fiona. Love trumps revenge. They wouldn't do anything to get her accused of murder or robbery."

"Idle Summers sure would. Maybe she's setting up Fiona. It gets her off the hook. Or maybe Peep and the bracelet gone aren't related, what about that, huh? Madonna could take the bracelet to drive Zo bonkers, and then there's the maid. If I had to clean Zo's room I'd knife her pillow too, and something's going on with that Luka guy. I don't think he's just an engineer."

Sutter wandered over to the breakfast table, no doubt to take the chocolate bagel I had my eye on. Instead he stared out the window and started folding the paper napkins into neat triangles and arranging them into a circle. "Neither do I."

Agreement? Well, dang, that got my attention, and so did the napkin thing. "What does Molly say?"

"Molly's taking Italian classes, and I can't understand a word she says half the time; she's waltzing around the office singing 'That's Amoré' and answers the phones with *ciao baby*. When she signs her name the end of the *y* forms a little heart."

Sutter lined up all the coffee mugs, then turned the handles in the same direction. He started for the door. "I got to get back."

"To set out the dinner plates and ring for the butler?" I nodded at the napkins and mugs. "Are you moonlighting as a waiter or something?"

A blush inched up his neck. Sutter never blushed. Sutter growled and swore and grumbled. "I really have to go. When I left Molly she was on her third double espresso and reorganizing the office. By noon I won't be able to find a blasted thing, and you need to stop off at the medical center and get cleaned up, you're still bleeding."

"Ah, you're worried about me?"

"Heck no, you're upsetting the fudgies and that makes you bad for business."

I hurled a poppy seed bagel at Sutter's big thick head. He snagged it right out of the air, laughed, took a bite, opened the door and left. I started to follow, but there was a chocolate bagel that needed eating, or so my stomach insisted. My hips totally disagreed, and my head had no idea who to listen to as Penelope's voice drifted in through the partially open door.

"Okay," she whispered. "That Peep's history, but I still can't find that dang phone and I've been through her room twice."

I grabbed the bagel and crept closer to the door as Penelope continued with, "What if L.A. girl out there has the phone and starts blackmailing us? It'll wipe out all that we've worked for." There was a reply I couldn't make out, and then Penelope added, "We're shorthanded tonight and I don't get off till after the last show up at the Cupola Bar. Without the big bosses hovering around, it's better for us. We'll talk then."

The door opened more and I darted under the desk as Penelope walked in. Well, dang. Peep really did have something on Penelope? How'd that happen, and what could it be? The guy was one fast operator; he was only here a few hours before he croaked. Maybe Penelope orchestrated the croaking, and who the heck was she talking to in the hall?

Penelope walked around the room, her footfalls heading for the breakfast table. With a little luck she'd get her coffee and leave. Her cute black shoes with little tan bows passed in front of the desk, heading for the door. They looked expensive; in fact, I think Mother had a pair. If I were on my feet as much as Penelope, I'd get good, expensive shoes too. I heard the doorknob turn and held my breath. I was almost home free till the phone rang on the desktop right above my head and Penelope's footsteps hurried back my way.

Okay, don't panic, I reassured myself as she picked up the phone. If Penelope didn't sit down at the desk, I was okay. She'd never know I was here, and I could find out what she was up to and what Peep had on her. And was it enough to do the old boy in. Penelope gave information on reservations and location and spieled off a list of things to do on the island, and for crying out loud, couldn't whoever was on the other end of the phone just Google *Mackinac Island*?

Penelope hung up, started for the door, came back and sat in the desk chair, our knees touching. She bent down, eyes huge, her gaze fusing with mine.

"Hi." I held up the chocolate bagel. "I dropped it and it rolled under the desk. Slippery little devil."

Penelope backed up the chair and I crawled out. My poor knees would never be the same. "So," I said, all smiles and happiness as I stood and dusted myself off, though, considering my ripped blouse and muddy jeans, it was an exercise in futility. "You think it's going to rain today? I see some clouds out there on the horizon."

Penelope cut her eyes to the door, then back to me, her lips forming a sour pout. "Where I come from it's not healthy to stick your nose where you shouldn't. Sometimes it can get shot right off."

"It's all the bagel's fault. Next time I'll try toast; toast doesn't roll." Hobbling, I took the steps down to the congested back parking area, where I'd left Nancy Drew. Banged up like we both were, I didn't think the front door entrance was appropriate. The morning sun had managed to burn off most of the fog, but pockets still swirled around the delivery drays and bike racks for the employees. I started for Nancy and spotted Zo and Idle behind a discarded refrigerator. From the looks on their faces they weren't about to hold hands and skip off to have breakfast together.

Stooping down, I crept behind a red-and-green dray. Peep had something on Idle and Idle hated Peep, I got that, but how did Zo fit in with Idle? I clam-crawled under a gray dray and worked my way over to Trayser's Trading Post's carriage, which was probably dropping off a purchase to one of the guests.

"I got your note and I'm here," Zo hissed. "What do you want?"

"You have that phone," Idle said in a low voice. "I know you do, and you're going to blackmail us all just like Peep did. You were his secretary; you know the business. You're not as stupid as you'd like to have people believe you are."

"Now that you got right, I'm not stupid."

"Well, I'm done paying. I'm through."

"We'll see about that."

The trading post carriage started to move and I jumped back as it took off, leaving me right out there in the open air face to face with Idle and Zo. "Lost my contact lens. It rolled over here. Sure hope that buggy didn't flatten it like a pancake." I hunkered down on the ground and started patting the ground. "Where could it be?"

"One of these days," Idle said, coming over to me, "you're going to hear something you'd be better off not knowing and it's going to bite you right in the butt."

Zo headed for the front of the hotel and Idle folded her arms, her eyes narrow slits as she watched me. "I guess it's gone."

I stood, unwedged Nancy from the bike rack and started for town. Idle was right in that Zo probably did know what was on Peep's phone and she wasn't nearly the airhead she pretended to be.

It took a lot to shove Nancy along. Her front tire was flat, handlebars bent, basket squashed and she needed a new paint job. I wasn't the only one who got wrecked today, and Nancy was one of my favorites. I read her books when I was a kid and used to get so involved in the mystery I did the flashlight-under-the-blanket trick. Nancy was my hero. She was smarter than the guys, braver than the guys and she had a really neat car.

After the fifth person stopped me to ask if I was okay, I turned down Market and made for the medical center. For sure I was getting too close to the truth or this bike thing wouldn't have happened. But what was the truth? I didn't even feel close to having an answer, but someone thought I did. I needed to get patched up and it would also give me a chance to chat with Sparkle. She was the nurse/receptionist and dating Fiona's brother when he wasn't away at a blacksmith convention.

The Stang and the Village Inn were hubs of gossip for sure, but it was the same crowd. On the other hand, everyone went to the medical center and Sparkle knew all. Most of the time she kept to that patient confidentiality thing, but after a handful of Oreos the girl was known to let a few things slip. Maybe she knew why Fiona and Idle were such good friends, and maybe she knew what Penelope was up to.

I had no idea what Sparkle's real name was, but she wore sequins on her jeans and beads on her smock, and on holidays she had tiaras to liven the place up. I loved the Valentine one with the springy red hearts and dancing cupids.

"Hey," I said to Sparkle as I came in the door. "How's it going?"

She helped Mrs. Witherspoon into a side room and called over her shoulder, "Take a number, take a magazine and if you can take two aspirin and call me in the morning that would be great."

"It's morning now."

Sparkle stopped in the doorway and looked at me, her eyes bloodshot, her clothes wrinkled. "Really? What happened tonight?"

"I ask myself that every time the alarm goes off. Are you okay?"

"You're not. What happened? Never mind, I know it's a bike thing, with you it's always a bike thing and I swear if Doc doesn't get back soon I'm going to row across that lake out there and drag his bony behind back here myself."

"Where is he?"

"He won't tell me." Sparkle shrugged and gave me a lopsided grin. "Smart man. He hasn't had a vacation in years, so he's got

225

one coming. I did rent-a-nurse, but she keeps sneaking out for lilac lectures and flirting with one of the dray drivers. You should make us tea."

"Tea?"

"Yeah, trust me, you really want tea."

"Sure, I'll make tea." I headed to the small kitchen area, where Fiona sat at the round wood table munching Oreos. She had on clean clothes that were a little big and the blouse had rhinestones around the collar and down the front. She looked tired, the kind of tired that came from worry with no answers. "Fancy meeting you here."

Fiona held up an Oreo in salute. "One of the advantages of Sparkle dating my brother, and lucky for me she feeds felons."

Fiona gave me a second look. "And lucky for you she has an endless supply of Band-Aids and Neosporin. You got to put training wheels on one of those bikes, girlfriend; the summer's just starting and you're not going to make it to August at this rate. So, what did you find out about my turtle bracelet being stolen? Mrs. Witherspoon told Sparkle all about it when she came in for her vitamin B shot, and I'm guessing you weren't riding around in the fog this morning just for kicks. You were up at the Grand. What's going on?"

I got a mug that had *Classy, Sassy, Macki-nac Smarty-assy* scripted in red from the shelf over the sink. I added water and Earl Grey and hit the two on the nuker. "I have no idea where the bracelet is," I said while watching *Smarty-assy* rotate on the glass tray. "Did you know Sutter's into folding napkins?"

"What's that got to do with anything?"

"I have no idea, but he's scary good at it. Did you know that Peepster had something on Penelope and was blackmailing her? I overheard Penelope talking to somebody in the hall and —"

"You were eavesdropping."

"Tomayto, tomahto. And Penelope's been through Zo's room twice looking for the missing phone, and I'm thinking she could have left your purple sequined hat behind so you'd get the blame for breaking in."

"I did break in and if there's dirt to dig up, Peep had the shovel. I wonder if Penelope was at the hotel the night Peep bought the farm? I could have left my bag anywhere in the hotel; I was so upset I can't remember what I did with it. You said Penelope has an accomplice, so one of them could have given Peep the old heave-ho over the railing and the other whacked him with the olive oil from below. Teamwork. I wonder what

Peep had on them?"

"That is the sixty-four-dollar question. Penelope's working late and I could go hear Idle Summers singing at the Cupola Bar and poke around and see what slithers out." And I could talk to Idle and maybe figure out how she fit into all this mess. Not that I'd tell Fiona that. She thought Idle Summers was a true friend and trusted her to the end of time.

Fiona pried an Oreo apart and licked the filling. "The Cupola? That means heels and a skirt and a lot of makeup for the scratches."

I retrieved my Earl Grey. "I'll manage, but whatever you do, don't you show up at the Grand. The evidence is building and you need to stay out of sight. It's not just Sutter gunning for you, those mystery groups are everywhere and it'll be a chorus of *There she is.* Sutter will lock you up for sure." I dunked the tea bag a few times in the hot water to release the flavor. "I'll take this to Sparkle; I think she needs it more than I do."

Fiona stood and hugged me. "You haven't looked in the mirror, have you?"

I started for the reception area and stopped dead as Madonna followed by the Body Baggers barged through the front door. "Okay," Madonna bellowed, her face red and jaw set. She had on black slacks and black top to match her black attitude. She had her blonde hair pulled back into a ponytail and wore enough mascara to make Maybelline proud. "Where is that piece of scum? I want to see him right now, and I want to get him ready to fly today. This whole thing has taken long enough; we're out of here."

Sparkle poked her head out of examining room 1. "What piece of scum are you looking for?"

"Peephole Perry."

Sparkle looked beyond Madonna to the Baggers. "And you are . . . ?"

"Trying to solve the mystery of who killed the Peepster, of course." An older woman in denim capris held up her orange notebook.

Sparkle blinked a few times. "And just when I think things can't get any crazier around here . . ." She peeled off her exam gloves and came over to Madonna, who was standing in the middle of the waiting room. Sparkle tugged Madonna down into a chair and sat beside her. "Honey, Peeps is dead. Getting him through the security line is gonna be a challenge."

Madonna parked her hands on her hips and scowled. "Not if he's in a coffin. I need

229

to get him back home and drop his lying, thieving carcass in the ground before the lawyers will execute the will. So pack him up and toss in some ice; we're hitting the bricks, baby."

"It's not that easy," Sparkle said in an adult-to-cranky-kid voice. "We have a situation; Mr. Peephole met with an untimely demise."

"And it's the only good thing the jackass ever did in his entire life."

"The medical examiner needs to release the body, and I'm not the medical examiner."

Madonna gazed around the room. "Well, where the heck is he?"

"That's a very good question."

Madonna jumped up. "What kind of town is this?"

"How long you got? It could take a while. Look, Mackinac is a nice island; find something to do for a few days like horseback ride, hike, take a cooking class or maybe something lilac, lilacs are really in right now. This will all get straightened out soon and you can be on your way."

Madonna harrumphed and stomped to the door. "I got a singing career to launch here. I got plans, big ones. I need clothes, new ones, fancy ones, and a lot of my money is tied up in Peep's business." She gave Sparkle a curious look. "Where are Peep's things?"

"It's a murder investigation," a Body Bagger volunteered. "Nothing on the victim can be released."

Madonna seethed. "Peep always carried a lot of cash; I want to make sure you all didn't take it. It wasn't murder by money. I want the money now." She tossed her head and folded her arms. "Or I can just sit here all day and keep you company and chat about Peep. Trust me, I can chat about that man all day long."

Sparkle jumped up, ran to her desk and pulled out three big see-through sealed baggies — forensics Mackinac style — and dropped them on the desktop. "You cannot touch anything, but here it is." She read from the list. "Leather belt with rhinestone buckle, stainless flask half full of vodka, key ring with six keys, shoes with three-inch lifts."

"I don't care about those things."

"And a wallet with various ID and nine hundred fifty-three dollars in cash."

Madonna's eyes glistened as she studied the bags, turning them over. "I want the money now before that grubbing Zo gets her hands on it."

"Thank God you're nothing like that." Sparkle pulled on gloves, opened one of the bags, and slid the wad of cash from Peep's wallet. Madonna took it, then stomped to the door and slammed it shut behind her.

The Body Baggers applauded and the denim lady added, "Isn't she fantastic? I think she's going to win best actress for her performance. This mystery week at the Grand is the best time I've had in years. I've never seen acting like this, and I've been to Broadway plays."

The Baggers scurried out of the clinic and I handed Sparkle the *Smarty-assy* mug. Fiona dropped a handful of Oreos in her palm. "That must be one hell of a will," Sparkle said around a mouthful of chocolate crumbs.

"She probably inherits the *Inside Scoop,*" Fiona said, gazing at the closed door. "Not that she'd have a clue what to do with the thing. Madonna knew how to spend the money, not how to make it. She had some assets tied up in her name in case Peep got sued, which happened all the time, but that's about it. She's probably going to sell the rag, and she wants her money, the sooner the better."

Sparkle popped the last Oreo in her mouth and headed toward the room she'd come out of earlier. She said to me, "I'll just be a minute with Mrs. Witherspoon, and then I'll clean off your knees and elbows. When was the last time you had a tetanus shot?"

"How about yesterday?"

Sparkle grinned. "That's what they all say." A half hour later I left the medical center and shoved Nancy Drew — I was beyond pushing — toward Rudy's Rides. My knees hurt, my elbows hurt and now my butt hurt. It hurt a lot thanks to not getting tetanus, whatever that was. I passed the perfectly restored Biddle House, the oldest building on the island, where Melissa Graves dressed in full colonial garb and told fudgies more about fur trading than they ever wanted to know.

My butt buzzed and for a second I thought it was a side effect of the tetanus thing till I heard a *bing.* I eased Sheldon from my back pocket and checked the screen. It was a text from Abigail. How r wedding plans C U soon.

I didn't really work for Abigail now, just a few freelance gigs in the winter when her ad agency got swamped and I wasn't. No one did ads better than Abigail; no one ran a better agency and got business the way she did, and how she and Rudy could be father and daughter boggled the mind. Getting a text from her still made my insides liquefy and with being the maid of honor, no way was I telling her the wedding was in serious jeopardy.

Can't wait to C U, I lied back.

When I got to the bike shop, a working dray with two behemoth brown horses pulling the wagon sat parked at the curb. Big guys muscled boxes marked *Furniture by Design* off the wagon, as Mother pointed the way up the side walkway to her office. She turned to me, beaming. "My own office." I'd never seen Mother happier. "Law Office 101 is now official. Guess you're never too old to have your dreams come true. Angelo's taking me to dinner at the Grand tonight to celebrate, and you should join us, Evie. I wouldn't be here without you."

I kissed Mother on the cheek and gave her a hug. "And I wouldn't be here without you. Have fun tonight."

I took the ramp into the bike shop, where Cal was rolling back and forth across the floor . . . pacing wheelchair style. "Good, you're back," he said as I parked Nancy next to the workbench. "The ferries are running now and we had a big crowd in here and two little girls would like you to paint a couple of" — he pulled a paper from his jeans pocket — "My Little Pony bikes, one pink, one purple, and if you could find a way to add a swishy tail off the back they'd love you forever. Rudy had to leave to make more fudge and it's almost ten, I got to get out of here."

"You turn into a pumpkin at ten?"

"I have to get up to the fort and fire the cannon, it's one of my duties."

"Right, what would we all do around here without a good cannon blast to scare the crap out of us at ten o'clock every day."

Cal grinned, his sandy hair falling over his forehead. "You're cute when you're sarcastic, but at the moment you kinda look like roadkill."

"Ah, Cal, you're one sweet-talking son of a gun."

"And don't I know it." He swaggered and held up his arm to show off his very fine muscles. "Me and the guns here got serious juice. We'll make it up to the fort in time to scare the crap out of you at ten, you can count on it. See you tomorrow?"

"See you tomorrow."

Cal zoomed off and I plopped down on the stool and sprang right back up like a jack-in-the-box. It hurt to stand, it hurt to sit. The only good thing was that the worst part of the day had to be behind me, literally, right?

"Stick a fork in me, I'm done," Irma blubbered as she barged into the shop. "Now the Happily Ever After quartet can't make my wedding. They're in Canada and can't get out. Got arrested for taking smoked salmon across the border."

"Seems a little extreme for a few fish."

"Try a semi full, and the Happily Ever Afters sure aren't happy and neither am I. It's a sign, the final one in the long list of no dress, no flowers, no minister, no venue, no food."

"The caterer?"

"Max eloped with Eugene that bartender over at the Pink Pony. We all saw it coming and that's good, but it's another sign that I'm not supposed to get married. The wedding's off."

13

"Wait a minute." I put my hands on Irma's shoulders. "There's no such thing as a sign; Rudy told me that a long time ago."

"That's 'cause he's a sweetie and didn't want to upset you. You got the black cloud for sure. Just look at yourself, you're a mess. And now I got the sign too, only mine is a smoked salmon in Canada. You can't buck a sign like that."

Two customers came in, took one look at me and stopped dead. "I got run over in the fog," I explained, needing to say something. I pointed to Nancy Drew. "It was a wreck, all because of the low visibility this morning, but it's nice out there now; you can see for miles. Riding a bike is really safe and a lot of fun."

"Doesn't look safe." The customer in a straw hat started for the door.

"What about these terrific Downton Abbey bikes? I have two left. See, there's the castle there on the bumper."

After more fast-talking I rented the Downtons, demonstrated how to strap on helmets and even threw in kneepads and elbow pads and directions to the medical clinic just in case. I turned back to Irma sitting in Rudy's white wicker rocker with Bambino and Cleveland snuggled in her lap purring their heads off.

"See," she sniffed, "this proves it." She petted one, then the other. "I'm destined to be a crazy cat lady and these two know it. It's over for me. My window of marital opportunity has closed."

"Irma, you were making fudge, you smell like butter and cream. These cats would snuggle with Godzilla if he smelled like that. Go talk to Rudy and I'll think of something to make this wedding happen."

Irma looked up at me with watery eyes. "Here on the island tomorrow? Tomorrow's my wedding day; we've been planning for months."

"Of course, here on Mackinac. Tomorrow." I had no idea how to pull it off in twenty-four hours, but Irma looked so sad I had to say something positive. She and Rudy were the perfect couple and they deserved to be married their way. But by six thirty I had no idea how to pull it off. Irma could get married in any nice dress, but what about food, venue, minister and music? I had no idea how to handle any of those problems.

I locked up, grabbed the box of Cocoa Puffs from the kitchen for dinner and headed for my bedroom upstairs. I wanted to stay open till seven with business being so good, but Idle's show started at nine and my plan was to catch her before and talk so I could follow Penelope after.

I didn't want to talk and I didn't want to follow. I wanted to take a bath, eat peanut butter right out of the jar and watch reruns of *Gilmore Girls* and then go to bed. I wanted this day to be over.

Instead I pulled out my blue silk dress with the flippy skirt that I hadn't worn since my Chicago days, dug my strappy heels out of the back of the closet and trashed my old mascara that had congealed into a clump of goo. I had to go glitzy to blend in with the evening crowd at the Grand. And after one shower and a half bottle of Cover Girl to cover scratches and bruises on my face and arms, followed by wiggling into panty hose to hide the scrapes on my legs, I caught a taxi. I never took taxis; they were expensive and someone else did the driving, not that I was a control freak or anything. Tonight I was just too tired to freak.

"Hey, lady," a voice said, as someone tapped me on the shoulder. "Wake up." I cranked open my eyes, gazing into dark brown ones. "You said you were going to the Grand. Well, rise and shine, this is your stop. You were really zonked."

"Been a tough day."

"That explains the snoring." He offered his hand and I climbed from the wagon into the milling crowd on the sidewalk. The yellow crime scene tape still cordoned off the path at the far end of the hotel, and a cool lake breeze ruffled through the trees. I pulled the lace pashmina over my shoulders — *thank you, Mother* — and took the steps to the porch. Piano music drifted from the big open doors, servers scurried about taking drink orders and I caught sight of Penelope working the front desk. If she saw me after our knee-to-knee confrontation this morning, she'd be suspicious as to why I was here again. I didn't need suspicious. I needed Penelope feeling perfectly safe so I could follow her and find out what the heck was going on.

To stay out of Penelope's sight I ducked behind a feathery palm, then shuffled over to a portly porter. I edged my way past the

Terrace Room with a wedding reception in full swing and made my way to the elevators and rode up. The Cupola Bar was to the right, a long hall to the left. A murmur of voices and clinking glasses came from the bar side, but since the show hadn't started yet I figured Idle would be in her dressing room getting ready. I took the hall to the left. The first door was storage for the bar; the second door had a gold star.

"Wow, I love that dress," I gushed as Idle opened her door, her perfectly penciled brows raised in surprise at seeing me. "You look great in coral, and before you slam the door in my face I'm here to talk about Fiona. What's going on with you two? Whatever you're hiding that Peep knew about, it's making Fiona look guilty. You need to come clean to Sutter for Fiona's sake; it's the right thing to do."

"I'll be the judge of that," Fiona said, coming to the door and standing beside Idle. "And we won't have to wait for Nate to hunt me now because everyone's going to see me if you keep that door open much longer."

Fiona nodded down the hall to Gabi and one of the Corpse Crusaders getting off the elevator, and she grabbed my arm and yanked me inside. My foot caught on the carpet and I stumbled against a side table, knocking a box to the floor. A Hello Kitty sweatshirt, PJs and a fuzzy pink HK purse tumbled out. Idle dropped down and scooped the goodies back in the box and closed the lid, shoving it all under the table.

"It's for my niece," Idle blurted at the same time Fiona said, "It's for her cousin."

"It's my second cousin who I think of as a dear niece." Idle faked a smile.

"In L.A.?" I prodded trying to get to the truth. Idle might be a terrific singer but she sucked at lying.

"Yes, right, L.A." Idle nodded, looking like one of those bobble-head dolls, but the strangest part was that the address on the lid read *Lisa Willis in Wisconsin.* "Look, I really have to get ready," Idle went on. "Fiona was helping me button and zip; you know how hard it can be to button and zip. You should leave."

"This room has a fantastic view," I said, gazing out the back as the last rays of sun caught the treetops of woods below us. "This is really high up. Is that scaffolding right outside your window? I thought construction was a no-no this time of year."

"The hotel is adding rooms and the bad winter kept them from getting it all done. It's the back so no one can see the scaffold, and you should leave now." Fiona backed me toward the door, gave me a little shove out into the hall and closed the door.

Okay, what was that cousin/niece thing all about and that address in L.A. when it was Wisconsin? Why lie about that and who the person was? I could have called them on it, but then they'd know I was on to them. Idle and Fiona were up to something together, but was it a big enough reason to get rid of Peep permanently?

I headed for the Cupola Bar on the other side of the hall, perched on top of the hotel facing the lake. The lounge was dimly lit with intimate round tables occupied by couples, and here I was the conspicuous single. So much for blending in. I took a table off to the side and ordered a glass of Chardonnay. What I really wanted was a burger, fries and a Bud Light.

Big windows all around offered a terrific view of town below and the long sweep of the Mackinac Bridge twinkling in the distance. There was a really cool white bar with floral padded stools, a glass chandelier overhead made in Venice back when gondolas were more than a tourist attraction and a dance floor. On a small stage toward the front, a trio was playing Duke Ellington. The Duke was before my time, but Grandpa

Frank had a collection of thirty-three-and-a-third vinyls. I never got the number thing, but the music was great and —

"Hi there, gorgeous," a man said, standing beside my table. I looked around for the person he was talking to but . . . but . . .

"You're talking to me?"

He laughed and sat down. "Humor, I like that."

Idle came out on stage, introduced herself and opened with "You're Nobody Till Somebody Loves You." The guy signaled for the waiter and ordered champagne. I was a Nutty Buddy connoisseur to be sure; champagne not so much, but it sounded French and expensive and I couldn't place this guy to save my life. He was in his fifties with salt-and-pepper hair, and his suit could probably pay for my bike shop. Maybe I'd run into him over at Doud's or here at the Grand? Why would he buy me champagne?

"My wife's off at some lilac lecture this evening," the man explained. "And here I am all alone."

"So, you came over for the lilac festival. Ah, you're a customer. The island is a great place for a good time and a nice ride." I held out my hand. "Evie."

"I'm . . . Johnson and I'm always up for a good ride." He put his hand on mine and smiled, except it was kind of a weird smile, and he laughed deep in his throat, and why hold my hand? I reclaimed my hand and Idle ended the "Nobody" song and started in on "Georgia on My Mind."

"Hey," Sutter said to me, drawing up to the table as the waiter poured the champagne. "Who's your friend?"

Sutter had on a jacket and it wasn't the black Windbreaker with the *I AM THE PO-LICE* patch. It was a blue blazer and he had on a tie. Sutter owned a tie? "This is Mr. Johnson," I explained. "He's a customer of mine and here on the island for a good time and a nice ride of course, and he bought me champagne, isn't that sweet."

"I was here first, buddy," Johnson said good-naturedly, holding up his glass to Sutter. "Better luck next time. Get lost."

Sutter looked from me to Johnson, a slow grin breaking across his face like he was really enjoying the moment. "Mind if I join you?" Sutter didn't wait for an answer and took a seat. "I'm Nate Sutter, chief of police on the island, and there will be no riding."

Johnson froze with his glass halfway to his mouth, eyes bulging. He choked and sputtered, then jumped up, knocking his chair backward on the floor, and raced for the door.

I looked from Johnson to Sutter. "You know him?"

Sutter's smile broadened. "You really don't get what's going on here?"

"Holy cow! He's on the most wanted list?"

"You'll figure it out." Sutter righted the chair, took the champagne from my hand and set it on the table. "We should dance."

"You . . . dance?"

"On occasion. I think this is one of them."

Sutter led me onto the floor as Idle broke into a swing version of "All of Me." Okay, I'd taken dance lessons as a teen; it was one of the social graces in the Bloomfield household along with what fork to use when and how to select the best 401(k). I could shuffle my way around, but Sutter . . .

"How'd you get so good at this?" I asked as he added some footwork and gave me a twirl. I hadn't twirled in years.

"Practice." Idle flowed into "Old Devil Moon" and Madonna strolled out on the stage with her, the two of them now singing a duet.

"Madonna said she had plans, but I never suspected this." And another thing I hadn't counted on tonight was my hand in Sutter's, his hand at my back and us together . . . close. Chest to chest close. His chin touched my cheek. He'd shaved . . .

close. And he smelled like . . . a man. My leg brushed his. My hip grazed his. My stomach flipped and I couldn't breathe. I went hot all over. *Okay,* I said to myself. *Get over it.* I'd had these feelings before with Sutter and they went nowhere. No follow-up phone calls, no texting, no stopping by for a cup of sugar or anything else that came to mind. Not that the guy ever said he would. It was me; I was reading too much into a few kisses and a dance, a really sexy dance.

"The woman can sing," Sutter said, his warm breath across my cheek. "Who would have thought?"

And that was the problem; I couldn't think about anything but Sutter. "What are you doing here?"

"I want to talk to Idle after the show. What brings you here?"

"The elevator. I need to powder my nose."

I cut across the dance floor, leaving Sutter alone in the middle. I needed to get a grip. And I needed to warn Fiona. If Sutter found her and Idle together it would look like they were up to something. IMO they were, but Sutter didn't need to know that.

I took the steps to the second floor and spotted Penelope at the bottom of the red-carpeted staircase, jacket and purse in hand, walking across the lobby. She was leaving now? No, no, no! What happened to her shift ending when Idle finished the show? Hey, the show wasn't finished! Do I warn Fiona about Sutter or follow Penelope?

I crossed my fingers that Fiona had already left, and I headed down the steps and out the front door. Penelope climbed into a taxi, the one headed to the East Bluff and Mission Point and up to Arch Rock.

Huffing and puffing and stumbling in heels . . . blast heels . . . I power-walked beside the taxi as it circled to the back of the hotel to catch Annex Road. I needed a bike. What I needed was a car! How was I going to keep up with the taxi?

"Evie?"

I spun around to Mother running after me, though with auburn curls flowing out behind her and her lovely red dress swishing at her knees she was definitely more Carman than Mother tonight.

"Where are we going?" she panted. "And we're going somewhere for you to be following that taxi like a hound on the scent."

"This might be one of those questionable situations, and you're a lawyer," I said to Mother. "You uphold the law. This might be more breaking the law. You don't want to get involved in that."

"I'm your mother first, dear; I'm involved

and have been for thirty-four years, and if there's no question, then where's the fun? And as for upholding the law or breaking it, that's always a gray line, take it from a lawyer. Besides, Angelo is inside having drinks with Luka, and I know they want to get rid of me and talk shop. Spill it."

I pointed to the wagon fading into the night. "I'm following another suspect in the Peep Show, but we can't keep up and we're going to lose them in the dark and. . . . Shakespeare! Just what we need."

"If you say so, dear, but I never did get *Othello*. How does Shakespeare figure into this?"

"Horse." I ran over to Shakespeare, tied casually to a post by the back entrance of the hotel 'cause no one would be stupid enough to take the sheriff's horse. I gave Shakespeare a pat, put my foot in the stirrup and shimmied up. I slid my leg over the saddle, very unladylike considering I had on a dress, hiking the thing up to my thighs. Thank heavens for the dark, and I never thought I'd be glad I had on pantyhose.

Mother held out her hand to me.

"Uh, this is horse stealing; no gray lines, just a big black one in law books everywhere."

"They have to catch us first."

"I think that's what Bonnie said to Clyde." I grabbed Mother's hand and she slid up behind me with her dress cascading over her legs. Mother always knew how to dress for the occasion. I flipped the reins. "Giddyup."

Shakespeare didn't budge. He flicked his tail and snorted and tossed his head.

"Giddyup, you handsome gorgeous stud," Mother said in a sweet sexy voice, and Shakespeare trotted off at a fast clip. "Sometimes it's not so much about the facts but how you present them."

Mother held on to me and I held on to the saddle, both of us bobbing along; we weren't exactly a proficient equestrian mother/daughter team. "Who are we tailing?" Mother asked, her voice bouncy with the horse's trot as we passed under a canopy of trees leading into the woods.

"Penelope. She's a desk clerk at the Grand. Peep was blackmailing her and I wanted to find out why. Everything she does at the hotel seems normal, so I thought I'd check out her life away from the place." I pulled on the reins to slow Shakespeare so as not to get too close to the taxi. "We don't want to be conspicuous."

"We're in evening dresses riding the sheriff's stolen horse," Mother said with a laugh. "The conspicuous ship has sailed, dear, probably to Fiji by now, knowing how fast the gossip mill is here on the island. The best we can hope for is that this Penelope person doesn't catch on."

The taxi took the turnoff to Mission Point Condos, where the long stretch of buildings was outlined against the night sky in the distance. I guided Shakespeare into the trees. More likely he went there on his own when he spotted a patch of nice grass. "That's Penelope, in the red jacket getting off," I whispered, as the night quiet closed in around us.

Mother and I slid to the ground, our feet crunching the leaves. Penelope started down the lit brick sidewalk. Mother and I tiptoed after her as Shakespeare trotted off in the other direction, back to the Grand. "I guess I should have put him in park and turned off the engine," I said. "Now what?"

"Now we walk back and hope we find something juicy here to justify ruining really expensive shoes."

Penelope opened the door to a condo that had a view of the woods out the front and the lake out the back. We slunk across the neatly mowed grass, kept to the shadows, climbed up on a decorative urn and held on to a window box. We peeked in at Penelope and the forty-something hotel manager guy from the Grand playing a rousing game of tonsil hockey with a little Twister thrown in just for sport.

"Whoa. So that's what they're up to." I staggered and fell backward into the bushes, knocking over one of the urns when I landed. The porch light flipped on and Mother and I squished down behind the bushes as the door flew open. I froze; Mother was dead still beside me as forty-something grumped, "Blasted deer." He slammed the door.

I started to run for the woods and Mother took hold of my hand. "Running draws attention. If we walk nice and slow we're just two lovely ladies out for an evening stroll."

"Do you think they saw us?" I asked as we strolled. I spit out a leaf and picked bark off my blue dress, which was probably ruined.

"They saw something, and there are deer around here." Mother looked as if she just walked out of a Macy's ad. "You know, these are really expensive condos out here. They have porches and crushed-stone paths, nice views, custom doors and windows, good curb appeal, perfectly maintained. I'd say they go for a half mil and up. In my book that's kind of steep for a desk clerk. Maybe the guy's the one with the money?"

"He's a hotel manager. They do okay but not this okay. Maybe one of them inherited money? But then why work at the Grand?"

"We're on to something, Evie, and I smell a rat." Mother's eyes twinkled. "Make that two rats, and whatever they're doing it's paying off very well indeed. And Peep caught them at it or at least figured out what they were up to. I wonder how he found out so fast? What did Peep do that we haven't done? Something between the time he checked in and taking a swan dive off the porch."

"That's about three hours. He and Zo took the carriage to the hotel, then probably had dinner. It's a long trip from L.A. to the island, so they were probably tired. My guess is they never left the hotel."

"Okay, so whatever Penelope and her honey have going on, it definitely involves the Grand. We got that much, but right now it's the least of our concerns, dear."

"Because deep down you really think Fiona's guilty of knocking Peep off?"

"Because there's a murderer on the loose, and when Shakespeare shows up and we don't, the chief of police and a certain retired Italian tough guy are going to go berserk wondering where we are." Mother nodded up ahead. "And guess who's headed our way right now."

Terrific. My scrapes were worn raw under my panty hose, and my behind situation had not improved thanks to our recent horse bouncing. Sutter would be pissed and I wasn't in the mood. "We should tell those two that we don't need them worrying about us, we don't need being saved and we're doing just fine on our own except for walking in heels."

Mother laughed. "You really think all that advancing testosterone is going to buy that line? And then there's the little fact of stealing a horse to deal with." Mother paused, a grin still on her lovely face. "You know, I had a case once where a woman stole her boyfriend's Mercedes. She didn't get the car, but she didn't go to jail either. I have an idea, dear, just follow my lead. Like I said before, it's all in how you present the facts."

14

"You found Shakespeare!" Mother gushed as Angelo and Sutter drew up beside us. "That's just wonderful. Evie and I were so worried, weren't we, dear? We heard he was missing and we've been searching all over for him, the sweet little darling."

Angelo looked from Mother to me. "And did you hear that two dames in fancy dresses rode off on him heading this way?"

"We did." Mother gasped and hooked her arm through Angelo's. "They took that nice horse for a joyride, of all the nerve."

"Nerve you got in spades, I'll give you that." Angelo shook his head and kissed Mother on the cheek.

"It's late and I'm tired," Sutter grumbled. "And somebody left me standing in the middle of the dance floor. So if all the BS is out of the way, what were you two looking for up here? And it wasn't my horse."

"Of course it was, and it's a nice night for

a stroll." I waved my hand toward the woods speckled in moonlight, the sounds of crickets all around us.

Sutter put his hands on my shoulders. "Do you know what they do to horse thieves in this state?"

"It wasn't a theft, it was a borrow, a short borrow, not even a long one," I sighed. I hated just handing info over to Sutter like this, but it might get him to focus on someone besides Fiona. "Penelope, that clerk at the Grand, and the hotel manager have a condo around here. They're up to something shady at the Grand, making good money at it, and Peep found out about it."

"And like any astute businessman this Peep guy wanted a piece of the action," Angelo chimed in as the five of us started for the Grand. "Then Penelope iced him to shut him up." Angelo held up his hands in surrender. "Not that I would know about such things, you understand; I'm just doing a little speculating here, is all."

"And what about Idle Summers," I added, facing Sutter. "What did you find out talking to her tonight? There's more to her than singing at the Cupola Bar. She and Fiona are friends, but she's the one hiding something, and Peep knew what it was. Like

Angelo said, Peep wanted part of the action."

Looking concerned, Sutter rubbed his chin as we walked along, the gravel crunching under our feet and moonlight playing hide-and-seek in the treetops over our heads. "I didn't talk to Idle about the case; I wanted to see if she'd sing at Mother's wedding. They've gotten to be friends over this dress thing."

Sutter glanced at his watch. "It's after midnight and today's her wedding day. Idle said she'd sing and get some of the guys to play, at least till nine when she has her show at the Grand. So now we have music but that's all we have. There's still no minister, or venue, flowers or a dress or food. Mom's really happy about marrying Rudy, and they'll get married later on, but today was the day she had circled on her calendar. I've let her down; I should have been able to pull this off."

Angelo stopped walking. "Have you looked around this place? Are you seeing what I'm seeing? We got ourselves an island full of pretty little posies. Not that I'm suggesting anything, I'm just speculating, is all. A few flowers from here, a few from there, what's to be missed?"

Mother yawned as we all started walking

257

again. "I got one of those online certificates last year from Mother Earth Ministries. I can do weddings."

We all stopped dead in our tracks. "Hey," she said. "I had six divorces in a row and got tired of tearing lives apart. I married the two janitors in our building right there in the boiler room where they met. The whole maintenance staff came; they served boilermakers and the best pulled pork I ever ate."

"Least they had a place to get married," Sutter continued as we started walking again. "Everywhere on the island is booked, and we can't ask the Stang or the Village Inn to shut down and host the wedding on one of the busiest weeks of the year just because we're all friends."

"And we don't have a cake or food or the dress," I added when we pulled up to the Grand, where the last of the night crowd was lingering on the porch or catching taxis. "There's nothing we can do now except reschedule for later in the summer when things settle down. I'm really sorry," I said to Sutter. "I have no idea how to fix this for Irma and Rudy."

"The Blarney Scone has tablecloths and napkins, and the courthouse has folding chairs for the overflow crowd at the town

258

council meetings," Sutter said, jarring me awake as he hauled bikes into my bedroom, leaning them against the dresser. "This will work, I've done more with less. I mean some people have. Give Martha Stewart scissors, paper and a glue gun and she'd put together the Taj Mahal."

"We don't need no Taj Mahal here," Angelo said right behind Sutter, dropping the Sesame Street bike at the end of my bed, making me jump and Cleveland and Bambino dive under the covers.

Angelo took out his cell phone and did the *I'm looking for bars* stretch. "Luka's got a guy, the booze is covered, I'm checking now, should be on the next ferry. That Luka is something else, I tell ya. Rosetta's making the ziti that'll bring tears to your eyes, mostly 'cause of the garlic, not that I'm ever telling Rosetta 'bout the garlic if I wanna live to see my next birthday, and why are you sitting there in bed?" Angelo said, facing me, as Sutter headed back down the steps. "We got to get going." He gave me a double take. "Scary hair, doll face. You might want to do something with that. You're never going to snag Nate with hair like that."

"What? Who says I want to snag Nate Sutter?"

"Everybody." Angelo's face split with a wide grin. "Fact is we have a pool thing going on. I got Friday night, three-to-one odds, not too shabby. Keep it in mind."

"I'm not snagging anyone." I grabbed Sheldon off the nightstand and Angelo headed out of my room. "It's six AM," I yelled after him. "There are bikes in my bedroom and Sutter referenced Martha Stewart, and not about her prison days. How does he know who Martha Stewart is, and doesn't anyone sleep on this blasted island?"

Mother stumbled in. "We can sleep when we're dead, dear." She dumped a garbage bag on my bed, and pink, white and purple lilacs tumbled out around me. "Right now we have a wedding to get together, and these flowers need water right away. Where are your vases?"

"In the east wing next to the silver candelabra. This is a bike shop. So, you mean the wedding's on, and where'd you get these?" I held up a lovely purple stem, the aroma straight from heaven as Sutter brought in Baby Ruth and Batman.

"The gardeners at the Grand were trimming the bushes and I took the off-falls. Aren't these amazing off-falls!" Mother slid pruning shears in her pocket and winked at

Sutter. He groaned and hustled down the steps, and Mother turned to me. "You've got cake."

"Chocolate? For breakfast?"

"Wedding. You're in charge of getting it here by five. We'll do a small ceremony on the back deck overlooking the lake at sunset, then have an open house reception so everyone can visit after they close their shops and get off work. That gives Rudy and Irma a chance to visit with their friends. Booze goes on the workbench, food in the kitchen, dancing on the deck. This is all Angelo's idea. He got the brainstorm about four this morning when he couldn't sleep, meaning I couldn't sleep, so he made us cocoa. He's a pro at this sort of thing and he's been handing out orders for the last hour."

"Angelo puts together weddings?"

"He says it's like arranging a sit-down but with a better outcome." Mother held up her hands. "I don't know what a sit-down is, but it's working and I say we just go with it. Now about that cake, got any ideas, and you really do need to do something with that hair, dear. Oh, and I have four-to-one odds for tonight. You are the maid of honor and he is the best man. I think I'm going to win."

"Mother!"

"Just a suggestion, dear, just a suggestion."

Ten minutes later I parked a repaired Sherlock by the back kitchen door to the Blarney Scone and knocked. I needed a cake ASAP, and a cake was just a giant scone with icing on top, right? And if Irish Donna said one word about what odds she had on me and Sutter, I'd wring her neck.

"How do you feel about making a wedding cake?" I asked Irish Donna when she opened the door and the amazing aroma of things baking drifted out.

"How you be feeling about riding that bike of yours no-handed with a blindfold on?"

"That scary, huh? What if I tell you it's for Irma?"

Donna's green eyes danced and she clapped her hands together, making a little white cloud of flour puff out around her. "Blessed be Saint Patrick, now you're talkin', me dear. Come on in, we'll give it our best shot. I'll get in some extra help to mind the shop so Shamus and I can get cracking. That husband of mine, old goat that he is, does a buttercream icing guaranteed to put a smile on your face and an inch on your waist."

I helped Donna hunt cake pans stuffed

back in a cupboard as Shamus rooted through recipes in an old Red Wing shoebox. When I measured out a tablespoon of salt instead of a teaspoon, they tossed me out of the Blarney Scone just as Sutter was heading in.

"We got a cake," I told Sutter; the two of us were standing on the back wood stoop as yelling spilled out from the kitchen window. "Well, maybe we have a cake. How's it going on your end?"

"Bikes are stored in your upstairs, over at the fudge shop and in your mom's office. Mother and Angelo are painting Rudy's Rides; hope you like honeysuckle yellow. I'm here to beg table linens from Donna. Last time I checked on Mom, she was hyperventilating and Rudy was fanning her with a copy of the *Crier.*"

"Think we'll make it."

"I've been through worse. You should have seen MarySue Hollingsworth and the Rose Room at the Hilton and the swan ice sculpture that melted into a big dick . . . ens of a mess. Spread the word that the wedding's on and it's potluck like we do for the Christmas bazaar." Sutter headed inside with me staring after him.

I got the potluck part, and spreading the word was a done deal with Irish Donna onboard, but my brain was still back at MarySue and the Rose Room. What happened at the Rose Room? I would have liked to see that ice sculpture, and that Sutter even knew the Hilton had a Rose Room boggled my brain. Was it a shoot-out to end all shoot-outs, and was that what happened to Sutter's leg?

"Buongiorno, Evie," Molly yelped as she ran up to me. "The Grand Hotel just called and they got a guest swilling vodka, dancing on the tables and singing 'Heartbreak Hotel.' I tried to figure out how to say all that in Italian, but I don't have enough time. Anyway, she's giving the place a bad name; it's the *Grand* Hotel, not the Heartbreak, and people don't pay the big bucks up there to hear about getting dumped. Nate's knee-deep in getting that wedding together and I got to mind the office. This gal says she knows you and keeps yelling things to the waiters like *just do it, I'm lovin' it* and *good to the last drop.* That last one she used when polishing off the vodka and demanding more. I got to go, I have four slow cookers brewing up Italian wedding soup for tonight and I got to keep an eye on it. *Arrivederci.* Oh, and just so you know, I have next Monday at five-to-one odds, so you and Nate can take your time getting it on." She kissed me on both cheeks and hurried off.

I couldn't talk. I could barely stand and it wasn't because of the odds thing going on. Only one person I knew would rattle off ad slogans like casual conversation. Abigail? Here now? Except the Abigail I knew never did alcohol; she said it clouded her creativity and impeded her work ethic. I knew I'd have to face Abigail sooner or later, but deep down I'd hoped some urgent work would keep her in Chicago and she'd send an office staff person to the wedding in her place.

I could ignore Abigail, let the Grand fend for themselves, but she'd find me sooner or later, and maybe I could even convince her to go home! I climbed on Sherlock and pedaled for the Grand. It was a lovely day for a wedding. Not too hot and a slight breeze off the lake, and I had to admit that as much as I hated Abigail being here, Rudy would love it. I needed to suck it up and forget that Abigail was the boss from hell. Besides, this was different; she wasn't my boss. She couldn't drive me nuts and maybe she'd just be one of the girls, right?

I'd done the snatch-and-grab version of getting dressed and my hair looked more rat's nest than coiffure, so I made for the back entrance. The big refrigerator had been picked up for recycle, leaving more room to park bikes. I headed up the stairs and stepped around the long reception desk, festooned this morning with vases of pink and purple lilacs. They were nice but not as nice as the ones Mother had brought home. Did the woman know how to pick flowers or what? When I got to the lobby I could hear someone bellowing — no way could this be labeled singing — "My Kind of Town."

"For the love of God, do something," Penelope pleaded as she raced up beside me. She clutched my arm tight and propelled me toward the dining room with its white tablecloths, elegant green and white striped chairs, vases of lilacs everywhere and the crazy lady on top of the center table using a saltshaker as a microphone.

"People are arriving for the wedding on the porch and reception in the Terrace Room, we need to get things ready for the lunch crowd, the busboys are going nuts and this is gearing up to be one of our busiest days of the year. Get rid of her! We're in the hotel business, and that means renting rooms and making money, and who in the heck is this person? She says she knows you from your days in Chicago and that you're besties."

Penelope seemed her usual self this morning; the two of us were bonding against the crazies who invaded the island. There were no incriminating looks my way or suspicious stares. Maybe she'd bought the dropped bagel story I dished out yesterday morning when she found me in the employee room? Maybe she really did think it was a deer in the bushes outside the condo? And maybe pigs fly. Penelope wasn't that stupid, and she had something going on that brought in cash, lots of it. This morning she was playing it cool to try to cover her tracks? Heck, that was what I would do too.

"If you could just shut her up, I'd be eternally grateful." Penelope hurried off as Gabi and the Crusaders hustled into the dining room. "It *is* true," Gabi gasped. "This is a new suspect." Gabi nodded to Abigail, who was starting in on "Heartbreak Hotel," round two, as the rest of the Crusaders crowded around.

"She has to be a suspect," the tall corpse guy chimed in. "She's way too over the top to just be a guest here." He pulled his yellow notebook from his back pocket. "She's singing about a heartbreak, and maybe that's her motivation. I got it, she was having a fling with Peep and he wanted to end it. That's a heartbreak, all right."

The shorter Crusader guy added, "Then

Peep came here to the Grand Hotel and she followed and knocked him off? Or is she just a red herring?" He shook his head. "No, that's not it. I think she's here for a reason."

"Yeah, like to drive me nuts," I said under my breath.

"From the looks of it, she's driving everyone nuts." Gabi wrote in her notebook. "We need to find out more about her." Gabi made a sour face. "The one thing we know is that she's not a singer. With a little luck she'll be the next one to get polished off and put an end to this god-awful racket." The Crusaders trooped off and Abigail's gaze landed on me.

"Evie? Evie Bloomfield, is that really you?" Abigail's eyes focused on me. She flashed a lopsided grin and scrambled down off the table, losing one of her sensible two-inch heels as her navy skirt slid up to her thighs. Her long blonde hair slid out of the bun, and she had raccoon eyes from smudged mascara.

"Abigail," I gushed. Well, I tried to gush, I really and truly did, for Rudy's sake. Abigail and I hadn't had a warm fuzzy relationship back in Chicago, more glacial ice and scratchy wool. "Let's get you to your room." I smiled sweetly and ushered her toward the elevators. "You need to freshen up. Doesn't that sound nice?"

"I'm fresh enough. Let's get us to the bar, and what sounds nice is a lot more vodka." She laughed then, her lips wobbling as a tear slid down her cheek. "Oh, Evie, Evie, what am I going to do? Things are just terrible. I'm so glad you're here."

I pulled Abigail into a chair at a vacant table. "No, no, you got it all wrong. This marriage is a really good thing; your dad's happy, and you'll love Irma. It's going to be great, just give it a chance."

"Irma who?"

"The bride?"

"Whatever." Abigail waved her hand in the air. "Dad's always happy, and it's me we're talking about here. Evie, I'm never getting married."

"I didn't know you wanted to."

"I met this guy . . . tall, rich, connected." She sniffed, more tears trailing down her cheek. "Did I mention that he was rich? He left me, Evie. Roberto ran off with that digital designer person in the art department. Suzie or Sally or something S. Why would he choose her?"

Because Sarah is sweet and cute and fun to be with, I added to myself.

"I own the company," Abigail demanded, pounding on the dining room table, making the tableware and glasses jump and nearly overturning the vase of flowers. "I'm the boss. You understand what I'm going through, not that me getting dumped is anything like you getting left at the altar. Gads, nothing could be more humiliating than that. I don't know how you manage to go out in public after that fiasco. I'd have to dye my hair and move to Alaska, though living here is about the same as Alaska, I suppose, maybe worse. Did you go into therapy? Of course you did, you poor pathetic thing."

Abigail grabbed my hand and looked me in the eyes. "You and I, we're not getting any younger, Evie, and our biological clocks are ticking, can you believe that?"

"You . . . you want children?"

"Children?" Abigail's brows shot up and she added another one of those hand waves to shoo away such an idea. "I'm talking Botox, liposuction, lifts, tucks, implants. Least I can afford it. You? I don't know what you're going to do, and are those crow's feet around your eyes, and do I see freckles? You poor thing! Freckles, what are you going to do about those?"

"Look for a bottle of olive oil; it's been known to put an end to an annoying problem."

"Olive oil? Really?"

"It's a proven fact. Let's go to your room and order room service with lots of coffee; you'll feel better after coffee."

Abigail stood, holding on to the table for support. "I do have a nice room with a lovely view. I had to pay extra for it when I got here, but that nice receptionist switched me from a crummy room to an expensive one."

"That's great. Now you can get some sleep and rest up from traveling." *And being on a bender.* "You'll want to be at your best for the wedding. You know, there'll be a lot of really good-looking men there, think of that. Maybe you'll meet someone new and he'll whisk you away, far, far away."

Abigail brightened. "You do have rugged men, those outdoor types who can build a bridge with a knife and a toothpick. The strong virile hunks." Abigail made a growling sound. "One of the maids here said the police chief is a real hottie. I got to meet him. Nothing's better than a man in uniform." She flipped back her hair and jutted her chin. "You know, I feel better already. A sultry island affair is just what I need to perk myself up."

"It's Michigan, not the Bahamas."

"So we'll have to make our own heat. I'm

getting together with that cop guy and having some fun tonight, you can count on it."

Abigail strutted over to the elevators and got on as Madonna got off. A waitress in a smart black dress with crisp white apron hurried my way and handed me an envelope with *Evie* scrawled across the front. "This was left at the front desk. Penelope said to look for the woman with messy hair, no makeup, denim capris and skinned-up knees and elbows." The maid gave me the critical once-over. "You win, or lose, depending on your point of view."

The maid took off and I tore open the envelope and unfolded a piece of hotel stationery: *If you want to know what's going on around here, Annex 1 in five.*

Five minutes? I raced off for the lobby, then slowed, then stopped. What if this was a setup? I'd already been pushed into a line of horses and off my bike. Walking into this felt like a really bad idea. I needed a sidekick, an extra set of eyes to watch my back. I needed someone with a vested interest in all this, and I needed them now. I had no idea where Fiona was, and Mother was knee-deep in honeysuckle yellow. Molly was keeping Mackinac Island safe and . . .

"Hey," I said to Madonna as she strolled past. Okay, Madonna wasn't exactly an armed guard, but right now another warm body was better than nothing. "Can you help me out? Actually I think we can help each other out."

Madonna did sort of look like Madonna today if you squinted a little and added forty pounds. I pulled Madonna off to the side and showed her the note. "This person might know who the killer is. What do you think?"

"I think that you didn't get the memo. Fiona's the killer."

"There are other suspects, and the police aren't going to release Peep until they are absolutely sure they've got the right person behind bars. Let's see where this takes us. It could help you out."

"I need to find Zo, little harlot that she is. My lawyers are trying to reach her. If she thinks she's getting anything from Peep's estate, she's crazy, though she does get to keep the condo he bought her, the creep."

Madonna started off, and I snagged her arm. "I thought you wanted to solve this murder as fast as possible, get back to L.A., read the will and live happily ever after. I need you because this sounds like one of those movies where the stupid girl goes up the dark stairs looking for the killer and the audience is yelling, *Don't go, dumbass!*"

"It's the Grand Hotel, not *Psycho*. You'll be fine."

"Tell it to the guy cooling his heels at the medical center. I've had enough close calls lately and I know you're looking for Zo and . . . and, you know what, I think this might be Zo." I tapped the note. "I think she might have done in Peep. It fits, it really does. I should have thought of this before; it's perfect. And now I'm getting close to the truth and she wants to do me in too."

"Not so perfect; she has an alibi, remember."

"For not pushing Peep off the porch. She could have paid someone to do that while she waited below and whammed him with the bottle."

"Seems kind of far-fetched, and besides, she loved Peep."

"But he didn't leave you to marry her, did he? She had to be furious, and I think all that uproar about the stolen turtle necklace was to throw more suspicion on Fiona. It was probably her idea to come here; I doubt if it was Peep's. Mackinac Island isn't exactly a Peep kind of place. Her plan all along was to knock him off and pin it on Fiona or Idle or both. She knew they were here."

"Hell hath no fury like a woman scorned?"

"And I think Zo was feeling scorned and used and had enough of Peep. He probably promised her the earth and handed out peanuts."

"I know that feeling."

"And if Peep's out of the way, she does have the dirt on everyone to keep blackmailing. Maybe I'll get one of the staff to go with me. If she thinks I'm getting close to finding her out, it could get ugly." I rubbed my elbows. "I've had enough ugly."

I started off and Madonna grabbed my arm. "All right, all right. I'm not the Marines, but I got a scream that'll strip wallpaper, and you're right: If I don't get some straight answers, I'm never getting off this rock. If we get the hotel staff involved, they'll call the cops and Zo will just run off."

I followed Madonna past the *Employees Only* door and headed farther down the hall into the older part of the hotel, still maintained to absolute perfection. Madonna pointed to Annex 1. "Okay, we're here, now what do we do?"

I knocked.

"This isn't the presidential suite; we probably have to go in on our own." Madonna turned the knob and opened the door. "Are you ready?"

"I'm ready." *Maybe.* "Awfully dark. Where's the light switch?" We stepped inside and the door slammed shut behind us.

"Evie?" Madonna said in a flat voice, her voice echoing in the room. "I think we just reached the dumbass part."

15

"Hello? Anybody here?" I called out, with Madonna yanking on the door handle behind me trying to open it.

I reached in my back pocket, snagged Sheldon and poked the flashlight app. Thank you, Steve Jobs. "There's got to be a light switch somewhere."

"There," Madonna said as the beam zeroed in on the wall by the door. She flipped the switch back and forth, and nothing happened. "Any more brilliant ideas?"

I scanned the room with the light. "I think we're alone. We'd be dead by now if we weren't."

"I feel so much better now."

"It's a storage room of some kind. Dining room storage, judging by the bins on the shelves labeled *cups, saucers, tablecloths, napkins, dishes, candleholders.*"

"Oh good, now we can have a dinner party, and is that an envelope with your name on top of that big box in the middle?" Madonna took my hand and directed the beam. "It is. How much you wanna bet it's not the key to get us out of here." Madonna handed me the envelope, and I slid out eight-by-ten glossies.

"Cats?" Madonna said, looking over my shoulder. "Why cats on a pool table? Is this like cats playing a piano, one of those YouTube things? What is going on?"

"It's Cleveland and Bambino, they're my cats and in the middle of my pool table, well actually it's the town's table but it's in my bike shop for the summer."

I flipped over the pictures and Madonna read, "*Butt out or lights out.* I don't think they're talking about the lights out in this room."

"Neither do I." My blood ran cold. I couldn't breathe; little dots danced in front of my eyes. "What kind of sick bastard would harm cats? My cats? Okay, they're a little testy at times . . . most of the time . . . and ill-tempered and crabby and grumpy and critical and bossy, boy are they bossy."

"If this means what I think it means, you might be in line to get some nicer cats."

Holy freaking hell! My hair stood on end. "I have to get out of here!"

"If you remember correctly, I never

wanted to come in the first place."

"The door's locked, but I can pick a lock. Do you have a hairpin, nail file, even a safety pin? Underwire from a bra will do. My state of noncleavage doesn't warrant a wire. It's all because of that blasted cloud!"

"I sure don't see any clouds." Madonna jutted her boobs. "And I didn't pay ten grand for boobs that need wires. We can bend a fork and use one tine, except I can't see the Grand Hotel using forks that bend, and I'm guessing knives are too big for your little Houdini trick. I say we take turns banging on the door. We'll just have to wait till someone finds us."

"Everyone's busy and I don't have time to wait. No one's going to find us for a long time, and I have to find Bambino and Cleveland."

"Um, why?"

"The door is thick, really thick," I said, trying not to panic. "Like soundproof thick and . . ." I focused the light to the ceiling, with fancy moldings still intact and a mural that needed work. "And the reason it's soundproof," I said as much to myself as Madonna, "is that this was a gambling room back in the day that the hotel served smuggled-in booze. I bet there's another door. There would never be just one way in and out. Think about it; if the cops come in through the door we just came in, the escape exit would be across the room so guests could exit into another area, probably a nightclub or bar, and look as if they were there all along."

"I don't see any door." Madonna sat on the box in the middle of the room and crossed her legs.

"It's a secret door in case the feds went snooping around. We'll have to move these bins off the shelves to find it. Come on, let's get going."

"I think you watch too much TV, and I'm a singer, not a mover. Let me know what you find."

"Really? You're just going to sit there?"

"Of course not, I thought I'd take a nap."

Holding Sheldon in my teeth so I could see what I was doing, I tugged the bin of dishes to the edge of the shelf, then lifted them as best I could onto the floor so they wouldn't break. Didn't seem fair to have the Grand Hotel pay for my mishap. I did the same with the cups and the saucers, and when it came to the tableware I sort of accidentally-on-purpose dropped it to the floor with a thunderous *clank*.

"Hey, a girl's trying to sleep here!"

I got a silver candlestick holder from the

candlestick bin and started tapping the walls.

"What in the world are you doing now? You're giving me a headache."

"I'm listening for a hollow sound that should be the door. The walls are solid plaster, the door filled with Styrofoam or whatever they used to muffle sound back then."

Madonna sighed. "Maybe they boarded it up and plastered it over, ever think of that? We're talking almost a hundred years ago with this gambling room idea."

I gave a few more taps. "This whole place is built on history. My guess is that sooner or later the Grand will rehab this room as the Rum Runner Room, say that Al Capone had a shoot-out here, sell bathtub gin at an exorbitant price and make a killing and . . . Here." I tapped again, listening closely. "I think the door's right here, I really do." I searched the seam for a spring or latch.

"You know," Madonna said with a yawn, "I don't think this is Zo; seems a little elaborate for her pea-brain, but whoever set all this up never considered the extra door idea. You were probably supposed to sit here in the dark and worry so much about your kitty cats that you'd give up on finding this killer person to protect them from future harm."

"That's because the imbecile who did set this up doesn't know that Evie Bloomfield's a Midwest girl and meaner than a junkyard dog when pissed. I passed pissed an hour ago."

I gave one hard shove on the panel and it sprang free, with me tumbling headfirst into a lovely room draped in greens and mauve. There were maybe a hundred guests in tuxes and long dresses all holding champagne flutes, and right now they were all staring at me and not the bride and groom cutting a five-tiered wedding cake.

"Congratulations," Madonna said, offering a big toothy smile as she stepped over my back. "And to the groom, a little piece of advice — always remember those three magic words that keep a marriage strong: *You're right, dear.*"

Madonna headed for the exit with me right behind her.

"Where have you been? We're running out of time," Sutter said as I bolted into the bike shop. He was standing at the workbench expertly arranging lilacs in white wicker bike baskets, the whole thing looking like *Better Homes and Gardens.*

"Where are Bambino and Cleveland? They're not on the pool table; why aren't they on the pool table?"

"Because there's blush tulle bunting spread out on the table so it doesn't wrinkle. It'll go over the white cloth bunting that —"

I grabbed Sutter by the front of his navy T-shirt and yanked him around to face me. "Cats now!" I tugged the crumpled glossies from my pocket and crammed them into Sutter's hands. "I got locked in a room for two hours with Madonna and cat death threats."

"I'm not going to ask which was worse." Sutter smoothed out the glossies and read the back, his jaw tightening, cop face firmly in place. "When the cats aren't on the pool table, where are they?"

"In the kitchen snarling and hissing at me till they get tuna."

"The kitchen's a zoo with cake, chafers, chillers and dinnerware. No cats. Try again."

"They sleep with me, one on each side. They bite my hair to wake me up at three AM for a treat." My voice cracked and I swiped away a tear.

"You sure you want to keep these cats?"

I choked back a sob.

"Right." He grabbed my hand and we tore

up the steps to my bed, which was surrounded four deep in a jumble of bikes, with Cleveland and Bambino in a tangled heap of calico and black asleep in the middle.

Oh, thank you, God! I backtracked out of the room, sank onto the top step and dropped my head into my hands.

"Are you okay?"

"The one good thing about this is that it's proof positive Fiona is not guilty. She'd never threaten to catnap Bambino and Cleveland thinking it would get me to back off finding the killer. That's what this was all about; even Madonna thought so."

"Fiona wouldn't hurt your cats, I'll give you that. And of course she'd never hurt you. But this is a warning, Evie, and next time it might be more. You've got to be careful." He closed his eyes. "I'm serious here. The next threat won't be against your cats."

"I'll stay out of dark alleys. I'll stay out of dark anything." I held up my little finger. "Pinky swear." Sutter's finger circled mine and we shook. "Okay, we got that over with, but right now we've got to get a move on. We really do need to get the bunting up. Who made these napkins into swans? They're adorable."

Sutter picked up a bird. "I got it off You-Tube."

Sutter started to get up, and I pulled him back down. "That's it! Bunting? Swans? Chafing? Tulle? Either you're gayer than a picnic basket, Nate Sutter — though that is such a stereotype and I apologize and if you are that's fine — or the Detroit police department has added events planning to their new and improved public services for the city and you're in charge. What the heck's going on?"

He shrugged, his broad shoulders rubbing against mine. "Nothing's going on, just normal stuff, except for the John up at the bar. That was kind of interesting."

"Johnson. So I guess he was one of those most wanted people."

"The only thing he wanted was you. Not that I blame him. You looked hot."

I stared at Sutter. "Really? You know, I think it was the white shawl and the blue dress and —" I jumped up. "John?"

"John." This time Sutter pulled me down.

"He thought I was a . . ." I laughed, and Sutter joined in. Then he kissed me again, making my insides boil and my toes curl and scrambling my brain. "I get it," I said, all out of breath, my heart racing. "You're not gay."

"You're right." He smiled, his eyes peering deep into mine, his fingers twining into my hair. "And you're going to love your bouquet, and as much as I'd like to prolong this activity, it's two hours to TBE and the flower baskets need lace bows along with everything else that needs to be done around here."

"TBE?"

"The Big Event."

"So, you're saying the Detroit police really do have an events planning department?"

16

"And by the power vested in me by Mother Earth Ministries, I now pronounce you husband and wife." Rudy and Irma held hands and gazed adoringly into each other's eyes as the sun dipped into Lake Michigan, setting the world ablaze in reds, pinks and blues.

Friends and family cheered and blew bubbles because throwing food would invite swarms of seagulls. We all burst into "All You Need Is Love" — like Rudy said — led by Idle Summers and the string quartet from the Grand Hotel.

"We did it! Fantastico!" Angelo swiped away tears, kissed Nate on both cheeks, then picked Mother up and spun her around. Luka popped champagne corks, Irish Donna cried and draped a lovely gold shamrock over Irma's head that set off the yellow rhinestone dress borrowed from Idle and I snuck upstairs to check on the cats.

With a house full of friends, Cleveland and Bambino were safe, but I had to check anyway.

"Will you slow down?" Molly panted behind me. She was not in wedding garb but police shorts and jacket. Someone had to hold down the fort while Sutter did the best-man thing, not to mention tie bows, arrange flowers, stream yards of bunting folded from tablecloths and drape enough blush tulle to make any bride happy.

I held up my hands and stepped back. "Molly, we're friends, good friends, and if you say we got a problem I'll scream." I held out my dress. "I'm in lavender silk here, I have flowers in my hair. I have a bouquet, one that Sutter made for me and I still don't get how that happened but it's lovely, and I'm wearing strappy heels and have on perfume, the expensive stuff. I'm pretty."

"Zo's dead, at least Madonna thinks she is and she's raising holy hell up at the Grand that nothing's being done about it and we're all a bunch of slackers and the killer is getting away."

"She's dead? Is Zo breathing or not breathing? Pulse, no pulse? And why does Madonna care if Zo's kicked the bucket? The way those two get along, Madonna should be doing a jig and gulping martinis.

Heck, the whole staff at the Grand should be drinking and dancing."

"Madonna's afraid she might be next. There's no body, but Madonna's been trying all day to get hold of Zo over some will stuff and couldn't find her anywhere. Madonna convinced the managers that something was wrong, and when they opened Zo's room the place was trashed, not messy trashed but torn up, Johnny-Depp-the-early-years trashed, like someone was looking for something."

"And you don't want to bother Sutter."

"Do you? I'm not exactly Perry Mason and you've been in on this dead-guy stuff since you ran over him. I thought we'd go together. It's not a murder scene or even an official crime scene, but Zo is missing and with all that's gone on . . . If something happens to Madonna she's already on her last nerve and the fur will really hit the fan around here."

"And if you stumble across Zo's body you don't want to be alone."

Molly gritted her teeth and gave a little nod. "There is that. A reporter from Condé Nast showed up this afternoon to cover the mystery weekend as one of the ten best summer getaways. We've got to find the killer fast before the truth comes out that

Peep the dead guy is for real. And you're right, your dress really is pretty."

"You can borrow it sometime when you and Luka go out. Hope it brings you better luck than what I'm having. Meet you at the Grand in fifteen."

Molly didn't budge, and bit her bottom lip. "Evie, what if we do find Zo's body?"

"We'll hold hands, scream like little girls and I'll bring vodka."

"Grazie."

"Prego."

"I'm getting good at this." Molly and I exchanged high fives and she hurried off. Using an excuse of needing more ice because all events need more ice, I scurried out the front door, changed from cute strappy heels to old worn flats, and hoofed it to the Grand. The town was hopping with the festival being in full swing. There was lilac ice cream, lilac fudge, lilac scones and lilac tea at the Blarney Scone; the Island Bookstore had books galore on lilacs; and of course there were lilac bikes. The ones I'd rented out got a day free because we closed the shop for the wedding. Saturday was the parade and Sunday was vintage baseball using gentlemen's rules and no gloves — ouch — and —

I was yanked into the alley next to Little

290

Luxuries. "Fiona?"

"Shh." She pulled me deeper into the shadows. "I missed Rudy and Irma's wedding." A tear slid down her cheek. "Was it beautiful?"

"When this is all over we'll have them get married again just for you."

"And we'll have cake."

"Yes, cake for sure." I took her hand. "You look bad."

"Zo's missing and her room's a wreck. I borrowed a maid's uniform and some of Idle's makeup and a wig, and I've looked all over that hotel for Zo and she is not there. Nothing. She's gone. Someone made it look like I did in Peep, and now with the missing-bracelet mess I think they're going to pin Zo's murder on me too."

"Hey, we don't even know for sure that Zo's dead."

"She'd dead, all right, and don't even mention Idle as a suspect in all this. The only other person who could have killed Peep and Zo is that desk clerk, Penelope. She and one of the hotel managers are awfully chummy, and they've got some kind of operation going on, but I can't figure out what and I think Peep knew about it."

I held Fiona's hand tighter. "Someone locked me and Madonna in one of the back rooms of the Grand and threatened to catnap Bambino and Cleveland. I thought it might be Zo; I actually thought she might be the killer. She has that alibi, but she could have paid someone off to give old Peep the heave-ho over the side. I think being trapped in the room was a threat to get me to stop looking for the killer. We're close, really close. We just need to live long enough to figure it all out. Meet me at the Good Stuff at midnight. You can spend the night in my attic. You'll be safe there." I gave her a hug. "I cleaned."

The Grand was packed. It was always that way, but tonight it was elbow to elbow with guests all decked out to see and be seen.

"Finally," Penelope grumped as she rushed up to me. "That policewoman said you were on your way. This place is going to the dogs. Zo's missing, Madonna is having a meltdown and someone broke into Annex 1 and tore it apart for God only knows what reason."

"No!" I stage-whispered.

"Yes!" Penelope stage-whispered back. "Nothing was taken, far as we know, and someone crashed the Fallers' wedding reception and now they want a full refund."

"Hey, congratulations were offered along with sage advice."

Penelope gave me a wide-eyed look and I quickly added, "So I heard."

"I want this over with. Zo's disappeared and if Madonna would too, then all these L.A. la-la people are out of our lives." She nodded as if agreeing with herself. "We need them gone. Everything was fine until they showed up with their sneaky phone and threats. Why can't they mind their own business? That's what we do around here; this is not Hollywood."

"What threats?"

Penelope jumped up, smoothed back her hair and pointed to the steps. "You should go on up. The mystery groupies are outside looking for Zo now. It won't be long before they want to see her room, and I have to let them so they think it's part of the game. I swear, some people are so gullible you can get them to believe anything."

I took the stairs to the second floor and made for the back of the hotel. Penelope seemed genuinely surprised over Annex 1. If she'd been the one to trap Madonna and me, she probably wouldn't have brought it up. But she did. Unless she brought it up to cover her tracks.

I knocked and Molly answered the door. "Whoa," I said as I walked in to see all the bedding torn off, drawers overturned, the dresser and nightstand and even the bed pulled away from the wall and toppled. "Trashed is an understatement. If the phone was here, whoever did this found it."

"If the phone was here at all. And if it was, I bet they got rid of the phone and Zo as a package deal. All of Zo's stuff is still here and no one's seen her since last night. There was a *do not disturb* sign on the door handle and housekeeping came back twice. When no one answered this evening and Madonna asked about Zo at the desk, managers checked her room and found this. Madonna screamed and fainted dead away."

"I'm sure housekeeping did too; they'll have to clean this up. Okay, so if Zo isn't here, where is she? If there's no body here, where is it?"

"I hate this body stuff; I hate the word." Molly swallowed and made a little whiny sound.

I put my arm around her. "Why did you go into police work? Bodies and —"

Molly made another whiny sound.

"Criminal things are part of this. You had to know that just from watching TV. Why take the job?"

"It's a good job. Nate's really sweet and the chief before him was too. I look hot in the uniform and the pay's not bad. All my friends bring me strawberry smoothies and we chat and this is Mackinac Island, so people behave; rich families hate scandal and the b-o-d-y thing never happened around here . . . until you showed up."

"Sorry about that."

"It's the cloud. You won't tell Luka about the b-o-d-y thing, will you? He thinks I'm badass."

I looked at Molly's sparkling blue eyes, slender build, freckles across the bridge of her nose and unicorn hair clip holding back her blonde hair. "Totally badass."

I opened the door to study the hall and literally ran into Sutter, still in his gray suit, white shirt open at the neck, tie trailing out of his pocket, lilac boutonnière still in place. A man in a good suit . . . was there anything sexier? Except maybe taking that good suit off piece by piece and dropping it on the floor as —

"Any sign of Zo?" Sutter asked, snapping me back to the hotel hallway, and that was a real shame.

"How'd you find out about this?" Molly asked Sutter. "We wanted you to enjoy your mom's wedding."

"Irma and Rudy have a whole town to celebrate with, and there's no place better for gossip than a wedding. Zo missing is top billing."

"There you are, you," Abigail purred, drawing up next to Sutter, hooking her arm through his. "My room's back the other way; why don't you stop in? There's this drink called Sex on the Beach; I do great Sex on the Beach. I do great sex anywhere."

"I'm kind of busy here," Sutter said, looking in Zo's room.

"Of course you are." Abigail paused and blinked a few times. "Evie? I didn't even notice you standing there. Nice dress, so last year but nice. Were you at the wedding?" Abigail did the dismissive hand gesture and turned back to Sutter. "I nearly lost you in that crowd in the lobby, sweet thing. The elevators here are so slow. This afternoon one of the maids coming out of this very room took me down on the back service elevator. She had a laundry cart and it was hard to get through the crowd, and I might have been misbehaving just a teeny bit because I just hate waiting on things, so she suggested I come with her."

"This room?" I asked, feeling a little sick.

Sutter pulled out his iPhone and punched up a picture of Zo.

"No, not her."

Sutter flipped to Fiona.

"That's her," Abigail said. "She was nice,

but her hair needed product and her nails weren't done." Abigail batted her eyes at Sutter. "I'm in the deluxe rooms. I had to pay a holiday surcharge, but it was worth it. Room three fourteen, don't forget." Abigail pressed her voluptuous self up against Sutter and kissed him full on the mouth, adding a little tongue. She strutted down the hall, waving over her shoulder. "Ta now."

"You worked for her?" Molly asked, shaking her head. "No wonder you have a dark cloud."

I looked up at Sutter, with Abigail's lipstick on his mouth. I could strangle her, but we had a surplus of dead bodies at the moment. "There's an explanation for this," I told Sutter. "Fiona didn't do anything to Zo. She was here at the hotel looking for her just like we are."

"Then where is Zo, and where the heck is Fiona? Maybe Fiona found Zo and she wouldn't give up the phone." Sutter strode off toward a waiter in a white coat pushing a room service cart draped in a white tablecloth with dishes, silver serving bowls and a rose centerpiece. The waiter stopped in front of a wide unmarked door as Sutter pulled up behind him. "Guest elevators are around the corner," the waiter said to Sutter.

Sutter flashed his badge. "We're taking this one down with you."

"Hey, you're the boss."

Sutter cut his eyes my way. "Something I don't hear nearly enough around here."

We all crowded into the elevator and chugged our way to the lower level, where the door slid open to a hallway. We could see the kitchen off to the right. "What's down there?" Sutter asked, nodding in the other direction.

"A ramp out to the loading area so we can roll in supplies and take out trash." The waiter pointed in the other direction. "Laundry room's over there to the left. The late crew's back there now. It's been a heck of a week around here for everyone."

"See," I said to Sutter. "The laundry is right here and that's what Fiona was pushing. Probably trying to help out the overworked staff; she knows a lot of the girls."

"And they won't rat her out. My guess is she's been hiding out here with Idle and living off room service." Sutter headed outside, with Molly and me following. The parking area was lit; night crew bikes jammed the racks and Shakespeare was parked off to the side snoozing.

"Hey," Gabi called out, as the Corpse Crusaders rushed up to Sutter. "Look what

298

we found, the gold turtle bracelet. Isn't that great?" Gabi held it up, as the shiny gold caught the fluorescent light. "We heard about Zo missing, so we started looking around for clues, and there it was over by the side of the hotel. This is so exciting, another body, and with this bracelet the clues are pointing to Fiona being the killer all along. This is her bracelet and Zo said she stole it, and I think she was right. My guess is Fiona wanted to shut her up once and for all."

The tall Crusader nodded and added, "I'd say Fiona whacked Zo and stuffed her in a garbage can."

"Or poison," the other girl Crusader added. "Rolled her up in a carpet first and then lugged her down in a laundry cart or maybe a room service cart and put her in the trash. They do it in the movies all the time."

The band of Murder Marauders hurried up; a lady in a Sherlock hat was shaking her head. "You all are the worst detectives ever. You need something bigger than a trash can to hold a body."

Gabi gasped, her eyes rounding. "The refrigerator! What about the refrigerator?!" She jumped up and down. "I saw an old one back here yesterday all taped up so some kid or animal couldn't get in. I never thought of it being a clue; it's like a coffin just sitting out here all along. I'm getting so good at this mystery-solving stuff, I scare myself. We need to see Zo's room and look for more clues to where the body is. Then we find Fiona and we win the free weekend." Gabi waved her hands in the air and did a little happy dance right there in the parking lot.

"You mean *we* win the free weekend," the Sherlock lady insisted, a scowl creeping across her face. "It was our idea about hauling the body off."

Gabi put her hands on her hips and straightened her spine. "But you didn't know about the refrigerator; that was all us, the Crusaders, and it's the most important part of the mystery. The only thing is we still have to consider that Penelope person at the front desk. I just know she's up to something. The other day she had a Louis Vuitton purse. Do you know what those things go for and on a clerk's salary? Like that's going to happen. It's got to be a clue of some kind."

"I bet the purse was a knockoff," one of the Marauders offered. "It's meant to look like she's guilty of something and she's really not. I'm putting her in my red herring column. She's just there to throw us off."

Sutter held up his hands. "All of you go to bed and forget about purses and herrings and about getting into Zo's room. The mystery party is over for tonight."

"You don't make the rules around here," Gabi insisted, glaring up at Sutter.

Sutter snarled, flashed his badge and snapped into scary Detroit cop mode. "Wanna bet?"

"Party pooper," Gabi groused as the groupies trooped off into the night. "Let's go to the Gate House Bar and strategize about what to do next."

Sutter went over to where the refrigerator sat. He studied the ground, uttered some colorful Detroitisms that turned the air a little blue, then kicked the side of the hotel. He turned to me. "Where's Fiona, and I want to know now."

"Oh come on, you don't really think she stuffed Zo in a refrigerator. That's diabolical and totally icky. Fiona wears a purple sequined hat, on her better days, and matching nail polish. She is not the icky type."

"She's the smart type." Sutter looked serious. "Fiona finds the phone and gets rid of it and Zo. Peep's already history, so whatever he was blackmailing her with is gone.

Yeah, there might be a computer back in L.A., but it'll require passwords, have firewalls and who knows what else to break into, and the thing is probably hidden. If someone found it, they wouldn't know what to do with it. Fiona's problems are over." Sutter turned to Molly. "Where's the refrigerator now? How does this recycle thing work around here?"

"Drays haul it out at British Landing to get hauled off the island. The trash scow might have already picked it up. They don't keep eyesores sitting around on the island; it's bad for business. If the fridge is gone, it's halfway across the lake headed to some recycle facility. The Captain runs the landing. If the fridge isn't there, he knows who took it, but I doubt if he'll know where it's going. The island contracts with hauling companies, not the recycle companies."

Sutter and I stared at Molly in wonder.

"Hey, it's all right there in the *Crier;* they print the town council minutes every month."

"And Fiona would know all this," Sutter huffed.

"Ya think?" Molly did the mommy-to-little-boy eye roll.

"Go back to the office in case Zo turns up

on her own." Sutter turned to me. "Find Fiona."

I folded my arms and didn't budge. "I'm not turning in my best friend when we don't even know if there is a body. Do you realize how hard it would be for Fiona to lift a body into a refrigerator?"

"If Idle helped her, it would be a piece of cake."

"Did you save me any?"

"Any what?"

"Cake. I didn't get any wedding cake. Did you save me a piece? You better have saved me a piece."

"And you better have saved *me* a piece," Molly chimed in. "I didn't even get to go to the wedding. I was busy doing your job." She glared at Sutter.

Sutter looked pained and pointed to me, then Molly. "If Miss Marple and Mamma Mia hadn't run off, you two would have your cake. As for needing to find Fiona, I have the olive oil bottle at the scene of the crime, and her in Zo's room once before snooping around and with a laundry cart this time around. We know she and Idle are hiding something. Who knows what the heck that's all about, but it seems to have everyone's attention, and if you think Penelope's a suspect, all I've heard is that she gets people good rooms. That's what hotel clerks do."

"I overheard her talking to someone about Zo and the missing phone and paying Peep off," I offered. "She knows stuff."

"This whole blasted island is talking about nothing else. There's a mystery weekend centered on it, in case you've forgotten."

"Fiona didn't lock me in that storage room; what about that?"

"Idle did. She got tired of you butting in, and on that particular subject we are in complete agreement." Sutter hitched himself up into the saddle and took the reins. "Find Fiona before I do, got it? I mean it, Evie. I need to know where she is."

How could things go from kissing on steps to this? I considered throwing something at Sutter except I'd probably hit Shakespeare, and I liked Shakespeare. "I'm going to wring his neck one of these days. He never listens to me."

"Guess that means whoever had tonight in the Evie-Nate getting-it-on pool lost. Try to patch things up by Monday, will you? I could really do with a vacation to Arizona this winter. Oh, and by the way, we're missing a key to the jail cell; we had two. You don't know where it is, by any chance?"

"When I was a guest at your lovely establishment, I left the key in the police station." And I did, it just happened to be stuffed down in the Pottery Barn chair in case I faced incarceration round two. "My guess is one of the Crusaders took it as a souvenir." I nodded to the group heading down Cadotte. "They were actually in the station poking around. Can you imagine? Of all the nerve."

"Well, thank heavens you're above all that." Molly laughed and climbed on her official black police bike that had flashers but no sirens. I promised her I'd save cake if there was any left, then started off for the bike shop, thankful I'd brought flats. All this in heels would have been killer. I winced at the comment. So who was the killer? Idle? Penelope? I had no idea.

It was after midnight and I wanted to go out to British Landing and see if the refrigerator was there, but I needed to talk to Fiona more. Or maybe I was just plain chicken about the refrigerator thing. What if Zo was there and I opened the door and she fell out! Chills shot up my back. Molly wasn't the only one freaked out about the possibility, and I had a terrific track record of going toe-to-toe with dead people lately. This never happened in Chicago. No toe-to-toe, no dead people in the fridge. Maybe

I did bring some kind of bad juju with me. Was there a way of getting rid of bad juju? A potion or ritual or chant. Maybe I could Google it. Then again, Fiona had tried extra virgin olive oil and garlic and we all saw how great that worked out.

Lights were on in Rudy's Rides, even though Irma and Rudy had left on their honeymoon by now. My guess was friends were cleaning up or drinking up or both, and felines one and two were safely tucked away under the covers.

I cut up the path alongside the bike shop to the back deck, now deserted, quiet, lovely. Moonlight sliced a golden path across the lake, the baskets of pink lilacs that Sutter arranged still lining the edge. A gentle breeze ruffled through the wedding arch Sutter had fashioned from tree branches, tulle and more lilacs; fallen blossoms somersaulted across the wood planks and drifted out to sea.

Most of the food and drink were cleared away, but a slice of half-eaten wedding cake sat on a table off to the side. How anyone could leave even a smidgen of cake was a mystery to me. I was a cake-aholic, no cake left behind ever. I pinched off a section, plopped it in my mouth and licked my fingers, savoring the moment. It was the perfect wedding with family and friends gathered together, just like Irma wanted . . . just like every girl wanted . . . just like I wanted. Heck, considering my last personal encounter of a wedding kind, a groom who showed up would be a big improvement.

I headed for the patch of grass that connected the back of the bike shop to the back of the fudge shop and retrieved the key from under the mat.

"Fiona?" I whispered into the dark as I stepped inside. "It's Evie."

"Over here." Fiona clicked a flashlight on the kitchen table. She was eating a cheeseburger and fried green beans and held up one in salute. "The Stang delivers to felons, and they also gossip with felons. No Zo?"

"And presumed dead." I sat across from Fiona and snagged a bean. "Sutter thinks you and Idle stuffed her in a refrigerator bound for a recycle center and she's halfway to Timbuktu by now."

Fiona chomped a bean and shook her head. "Well, dang! Why didn't I think of that, it's brilliant."

"What if Idle *did* think of it?"

"Idle didn't knock off Peep or Zo." Fiona let out a long, tired sigh and took a bite of burger. "She has people depending on her and she wouldn't risk jail . . . again. And the fewer people who know about the other Idle Summers, the better. She screwed up, Evie, but she turned over a new leaf and she's making a go of it."

"Everyone in Hollywood has screwed up. I think it's a requirement to live there. What's the big deal?"

"There are screwups and then there are screwups. If this one got out, hotels where she performs would have nothing to do with her. The Grand wouldn't have touched her with a ten-foot pole."

"Well, if she killed people she'd still be in jail, so that's not what got her in trouble. She's too healthy to be peddling drugs. Burglary? Burglary would be a big no-no in the hotel business."

"Especially of the feline variety. She was good, really good."

"But not quite good enough," Sutter said as he opened the back door and stepped inside.

17

Sutter held up a key, his silhouette framed in the doorway. Of course he had a key; his mom owned the place. "I thought you were headed out to British Landing? You're a rotten sneak, you know that."

"Right back at ya." Sutter turned on the kitchen lights.

"Idle didn't kill Peep, and neither did I," Fiona said around a mouthful of cheeseburger, too tired to even be panicked. "Idle served her time, and that part of her life is over with."

"Because she changed her name and got a new identity. That worked until somehow Peep found out, and that means Zo found out. You shut them both up, or you and Idle did, and right now the evidence I have with the olive oil bottle and turtle necklace says it was you. Fiona McBride, you're under arrest for the murder of Peephole Perry and Zo . . . when we find the body."

"*If* you find the body." I jumped up. "You can't arrest on an *if*. Didn't the Supreme Court rule on that, and how can you think Fiona would trap me in that room and threaten Bambino and Cleveland?"

"And nothing happened. It was a great way to shift the blame."

"There is no shift because Fiona's innocent. Remember when you arrested Rudy? You were wrong then and this is the same thing all over again and . . . and what about the mystery weekend up at the Grand, huh? You're really going to mess that up big-time, and the Grand will not be happy, and if the guests think this was all a sham they will be really ticked off at all of us. At least wait to see where Zo turns up."

"So you can have Fiona halfway to God knows where. The Crusaders found the bracelet. We'll say that led to Zo's body like they suspected, and Fiona guilty. Fiona in jail proves the point, and they win. That gives them a free weekend at the Grand, and that should make them happy, and finally, thank God, we are done with the mystery weekend."

"Cheater, cheater, pumpkin eater." I had to say something and was so ticked off I couldn't think of anything else . . . except there was something else to say, something important. "At least put Fiona in the good cell where I was. It has the nice chair, a special treat where you can escape your problems."

"Must be some chair." Fiona shoved the burger and beans to my side of the table and stood. She licked the spice from her fingers and wiped them with a napkin. She flashed me a weak smile, then hugged me tight. "You'll find the killer, I know you will, and I'll be okay. I had Doud's put back the last bottle of OPI nail polish, Go with the Lava Flow, for you. Great shade of pink."

I grabbed Fiona by the shoulders and looked her dead in the eyes. "When you're sitting in the chair, think of me, I mean really think of me."

Sutter held on to Fiona's arm and turned my way. "Don't come anywhere near the jail. Do not go out to British Landing."

"Because there's a killer on the loose and it would be dangerous, but this isn't over," I called to Sutter, who was leading Fiona out the door. "I'm going to find the real killer if it's the last thing I do."

Fiona knew how to get out of the police station window, and if she found the cell key I'd stuffed in the Pottery Barn chair, she'd be free as a bird by morning. Not that the Mackinac jail was terrible, but it made

311

getting her off the island a real possibility. If I didn't find the killer, off-island was plan B. Fiona being on the run sucked big-time, but it beat rotting in jail for something she didn't do and being somebody's bitch for the rest of her life.

Desperate for a new take on who knocked off the Peepster, I opened the murder cupboard to see if Irma and Rudy had thoughts on the subject. I picked up a bean and chomped as a knock came from the back door. I jumped, stumbled and banged my shin on Irma's industrial-size Viking stove and hit my head against the string of big copper ladles dangling above. Door knocking didn't usually have this effect on me, but I'd been locked in a room and hunting for a body in a fridge. It was a jumpy kind of night. I couldn't see anyone out the window, not even a shadow of anyone. The handle turned. I grabbed a big ladle from above as the door opened to . . .

"Cal? Oh, thank heavens."

"That's what all the girls say." He flashed his dimpled smile, laughed and rolled into the kitchen. I hung the ladle back with its family.

"I was at the bike shop putting stuff away," he said. "And saw Nate and Fiona leave. When the lights stayed on I figured you were over here."

"Sutter sent you to spy on me, didn't he? I don't need a babysitter."

"Let's go with keeping you out of trouble." Cal rested his hands on his knees, looking way older than thirty whatever and a lot wiser. "God works in mysterious ways, trust me on that, and so does Nate Sutter, you can trust me on that one too. Sometimes you gotta believe in the system or at least that Sutter knows what he's doing. He's a smart man, Evie. He's a really good cop; that's one of the reasons you like him."

"I don't like him. I want to put him in a sack, weight it with a rock and toss him in the lake."

"I don't think Fiona killed that Peep guy, and I'm not sure Nate does either. But he has his reasons for putting her in jail, and for now, like it or not, you'll have to live with it."

"Unless I can make that sack plan work."

Cal pointed to the board. "So, what's this all about?"

I snagged another bean. "Sure, why not. Maybe you'll see something I don't and we can put an end to this." I pointed to one door. "Here in Kelly green marker we have the non-suspect list. There's Madonna the jealous wife, who couldn't have whacked the Peepster with an olive oil bottle because she was wearing Dior silk and having dinner at the time and not a drop of oil on her anywhere. Then there's Zo the mistress/secretary, out bike riding. If she pushed Peep off the porch, the dinner crowd at the Grand would have noticed her decked out in red biker spandex, her outfit of choice for the evening. I thought she might be the killer, but now she's missing, suggesting that the same person who did in Peep did her in as well."

"Walt and Geraldine? Really?" Cal asked. "Then again, I think Walt probably wanted Peep dead more than anyone. He always felt that Peep had something on Fiona and that's why she stayed in L.A."

"Sutter thinks Walt and Geraldine wouldn't do anything to implicate their daughter, and if Peep turned up dead they knew she'd get the blame. For once we agreed on something. Luka and Molly are an item. Luka being a killer while dating a cop seems a little extreme even for *the family.* And there's Idle Summers."

"She did a great job with the music tonight, and isn't she performing up at the Grand?"

"She's big on my who-done-it list, but since she just sang 'I Will Always Love You' at the wedding she's on Rudy and Irma's non-suspects board."

Cal tapped Penelope's name listed under the black marker suspect side. "Who's this?"

"According to Sutter, she's the freaking employee of the year." I stood and closed the cupboard. "I'm going to bed, and you can tell the local rat-fink police chief to take a long walk off a short pier and go straight to the devil." I tossed Cal the key. "Lock up when you leave and slide the key under the mat. I'm going home and putting on my quitters, also known as jammy pants, fuzzy robe, and bunny slippers. I've had enough for one day; I'm done."

I cut across the yard and let myself into the bike shop that at present looked more Martha Stewart than Lance Armstrong. It would take a week to make the transformation back to bike shop, and there wasn't a piece of saved wedding cake anywhere. I found a can of tuna, a plastic spoon and two paper plates with silver wedding bells and went upstairs. Bambino and Cleveland sat in the middle of my bed looking even more pissed than usual since they were surrounded by bikes. Actually it was more their bed, but I liked to pretend it was mine 'cause I changed the sheets once a week and made the thing every day.

"This is not my fault," I said, peeling back the pull tab and scooping out the tuna. "And I want you to listen to me for a change. You're getting death threats, so I need you to be on your worst behavior tonight. Come on, snarl it up, guys, give me some hiss and a big bushy tail, and make with the glowing eyes and sharp claws."

I stood back and watched them scarf tuna. Cats . . . did they ever do what they were told? There was a reason cat obedience school did not exist! My only hope was that if someone did take the fearsome feline duo, a bit of "The Ransom of Red Chief" would kick in and they'd be so horrible that the captors would give them back to me as punishment.

I exchanged my lovely dress for dirty jeans and a black fleece. I took Babe Ruth from my bedroom because it was one of the bikes with a headlight. I locked the bedroom door and put the key in my pocket. If someone really wanted the daring duo inside, they could break down the door, but this was an old house and built to withstand Michigan winters. It would take a lot of breaking to get inside.

I hauled Babe downstairs, banging up my walls and beating up my shins. Bikes down steps was no easy job and made me appreciate how the guys got the bikes up here in the first place. I checked to make sure the lights were out at the Good Stuff, meaning Cal was gone, then started for the back door and —

"Faith and begorrah, what's a woman got to do around here to get a bit of sleep after a hard day's work?"

I spun around to Irish Donna standing in the doorway between the shop and the kitchen rubbing sleep from her eyes. "I didn't know you were here."

"Waiting up for you, I was, and then I wasn't. A bit of the bubbly can do that to a woman. We all figured you were off trying to save Fiona somehow. I fell asleep in Rudy's old wicker rocker out there in front, I did. Right comfortable in a pinch."

She eyed Babe. "If ye be off to where I think ye are, can you be a-waiting till tomorrow at this time? I got four-to-one odds, I do, and having just made up a fine cake for ye on a moment's notice, I figure you can hold off."

"Sutter just arrested Fiona, of all the dumbass things to do, and I'm on my way out to British Landing to see if Zo's body's in a fridge on the dock waiting to be recycled, and if it is, I'm dumping it in the lake."

"Blessed Saint Patrick, you need to run

317

that by me again." She held up her hand, blinked a few times, then reached for a half-finished bottle of champagne and polished it off. "Now I got it." She swiped the back of her hand across her mouth and burped. "All I can tell ye is that the Zo woman wasn't much good the first time around; recycling seems a waste of time and effort, so I see your point with the dumping part."

"This has to do with Fiona charged with Peep's and now Zo's murder. She didn't do either, and at least I can take care of one of the problems."

"Good thinking. Paddy's parked down the street; we best shake a leg." Irish Donna snagged her long green velvet coat that put my fleece to shame and started for the door. I held her arm.

"You don't have to go. Like you said, you already baked a wedding cake today. You've done your part and you have to be tired."

"Me dear girl, the only things I have to be doing in this here world is dying and paying taxes. Getting Fiona out of a fix is sure beating either of those, and I've never been to a body-dumping before. Could be right interesting and get my Facebook page a-buzzing, been kind of dull lately. Now let's get a move on before Nate beats us to that body and goes and spoils our bit of fun. Oh, and

I put aside a slice of wedding cake for ye and Sergeant Molly. I hid it under the workbench. Turned out right nice, it did."

" 'Tis a lovely evening for a body-dumping," Irish Donna said to me as we clip-clopped along Lake Shore Drive, with the Mackinac Bridge off in the distance. There were no houses or businesses out this way, only night birds warbling in the pines, water lapping the shoreline and moonlight slipping in and out of overhanging branches.

"Thanks for the wedding cake." I licked icing from my fingers and zipped my fleece against the chill. "It's great. You should offer it on the menu; people would love it. Who wouldn't stop in for tea and wedding cake?"

"Someone who's just gotten divorced, be my guess." Donna pointed up ahead to the docks dotted with dim fluorescents out in the water. "There be the landing. We should leave old Paddy here to rest up and go the rest of the way on foot. Dillard Prescott's the night watchman and probably sleeping in the warehouse, but we don't need to be caught snooping around all the same. Telling him about Zo in the fridge is sure to get him on the phone to Nate."

"There's a boat at the end of the dock." I

pointed to a dim light at the end of the pier. A low engine rumble drifted our way, as thin curls of gray diesel exhaust faded into the dark.

"Looks like she's a hauler. Could be here to get our fridge, and there's a load waiting for pickup right there on the dock. I think we got ourselves a winner."

Donna started off, but I didn't budge. I pulled in a deep breath. "I . . . I don't know if I can do this. I don't know if I'm ready to face another dead body."

"Are ye ready to be facing Fiona in jail?"

Staying close to the line of parked drays — the horsepower in the barn behind us resting up — we made our way to the pier. The wind kicked up Donna's coat, floating out around her like an Irish Batman. The concrete was worn rough from brutal winters of ice and snow, but tonight moonlight danced across the gentle swells out in the lake.

"What's this refrigerator be looking like?" Donna asked as we hurried along.

"Rectangle, white, GE stamped on the front, big enough to hold a body."

"Nothing here on the dock like that. Must be onboard." Before I could stop her, Donna was halfway up the gangplank. I hurried after her, the drone of the engine vibrating through the boat and into our bones, the scent of fuel heavy around us. Stepping over cables and around big metal things I couldn't see over, we headed to the back.

Donna parked her hands on her hips as the lake breeze tossed her hair in her face. "A bunch of big machines for construction or dredging is all that's here. Zo must have caught an earlier ride. Rotten shame that." Donna pulled her iPhone from her coat pocket. "I was ready for some fine body-dumping Instagram shots. Would have been a big hit too and — uh-oh." Donna pointed down to the dock and the shadow of a man approaching. He aimed for the gangplank, the light catching an earring and reflecting off a dingy blond ponytail.

"I . . . I know him," I whispered.

"Lucky you."

"At least I think I know him. Hard to tell from this far away." I leaned out over the railing to get a better look as the guy stepped onboard. A whining motor sounded somewhere up front, cutting through the stillness of the night. The gangplank inched off the ground and Donna grabbed my hand. The plank rose higher, then higher still and slid neatly back onto the boat. The diesel engine revved and we slid gently away from the dock.

18

"Where have you been?" Mother gasped as I hobbled in the back door of the bike shop the next morning.

"You . . . cleaned?"

"I was worried sick, I had to do something. They found Paddy and wedding cake crumbs in the cart out by British Landing around dawn and there's some story about Zo's body in a refrigerator and . . . Dear God, Evie, I'll have to go back to Chicago for a vacation if you keep this up."

Mother put her arms around me and hugged. "You smell like . . ." She sniffed my hair. "Gasoline?"

"Evie?" Sutter stopped dead in the back doorway. "Where have you . . . I'm going to wring . . ." He pinched the bridge of his nose. "This is why cops drink."

"I got lost . . . we got lost."

"On an eight-mile island?"

"It happens," I said, all calm and cool just

like Irish Donna and I had practiced, huddled together in the back of the boat from hell. "You see, Donna and I did go looking for Zo in the refrigerator." I held up my hand to stop Sutter from blowing yet another gasket. He had to be running low on gaskets by now. "Then we decided that you were right and it was too dangerous and it was trespassing and that's against the law."

"Because that has stopped you so many times before," Sutter mumbled.

"So while we were out there in Donna's buggy, I told her that this was all for the best and I was tired of running into dead bodies because of this black cloud thing. And Donna said since we were all the way out here and the moon was aligned with Mars, she'd help me get rid of my cloud. She knows all about those Irish blessings and curses; wasn't that nice of her? So we hiked into the woods looking for water sprung new from the rocks to complete the ritual, and we got lost."

Sutter exchanged looks with Mother, and together they applauded. "Not bad," Sutter said. "I think the water sprung new needed some work, but with you and Donna as partners in crime there's no chance at the truth. Besides, we got other problems. Fiona's missing. She masterminded a jailbreak. Miraculously, as if the angels from heaven descended, the key to the cell materialized and Fiona walked out of her cell, then crawled out a back window."

"No!" I gasped, putting my hand to my heart. "Maybe she's free because she's not the killer and those angels knew it."

"I locked Fiona up to keep her safe. The real killer's after her."

"Real killer?"

"You were right, Fiona would never threaten the cats." Sutter paced. "He's pinning these murders on her, and he doesn't care if she's alive or dead. Fact is, dead is better because Fiona won't be able to defend herself. He can make her demise look like an accident and she's out of the picture."

"And it didn't occur to you to tell me this when you hauled Fiona, my best friend, off to jail last night?" I could barely get the words out.

"You running around like a lunatic to find her innocent had to make the killer believe all the more that his plan of framing Fiona was working."

"You used me!"

"It happens." Sutter headed for the door. "I've got to get back to British Landing and see if we can find that fridge and Zo and the blasted phone that started all this. I came here to get a piece of your clothing for the tracking dogs. Next round of drinks at the Stang is on you, Chicago. Everyone was out beating the bushes to find you; even those mystery groups from up at the Grand got in on the hunt. They're like mosquitoes, they're everywhere."

Sutter grabbed my last Hello Kitty Post-it off the counter. "This is the number out at the landing if you can't get me on my cell. Call me if you see Fiona, but do not go after her on your own. Think about it; you'll lead the killer right to her."

The door closed behind Sutter, and he walked past the back window with Bambino and Cleveland napping on the sill. Sutter's footsteps faded across the wood deck and I gave Mother a wide-eyed look. "Holy crap, we have to get Fiona back in jail! Did I really just say that? She's been passing herself off as a maid up at the Grand, and I can do the same thing so I don't lead the killer to her. I know she's there trying to find out what Penelope is up to because Fiona thinks she's the killer. What if she is? Fiona could be in a world of trouble."

Mother gave me a kiss on the cheek. "I'll head to the hotel for high tea. No one really knows me at the Grand, and I'll see what I can find out. If I don't hear from you, I'll meet you behind the grand piano at three." Mother took my hand. "A ritual in the woods? Really, dear? That's the best you could come up with?"

"It was either that or stuck on a work trawler, winding up in Mackinaw City, escaping down a gangplank in the middle of the night and catching a ferry back here."

Mother laughed. "You're right. No one would believe that one."

Cal rolled in at ten thirty fresh from his morning ritual of cannon blasting the island into a new day. I fed him the lost-in-the-woods story that he didn't buy for a minute, grabbed a bike that hadn't been painted yet and looked really blah, then took off for the Grand. I needed to travel incognito. The employee parking lot was packed with delivery drays . . . UPS Mackinac style. Employees hurried about unloading and I parked my no-name bike in the employee rack. I picked up a box big enough to cover most of my face off a dray, then followed the line of other boxes into the hotel.

"That one goes to Annex 2," a thin lanky man in the official maroon Grand Hotel blazer said to me, checking something on a clipboard. He pointed up the steps behind him, then paused. His brows knit together as he took me in. "Where's your uniform? You don't work around here without being in uniform, you know that. What kind of people is HR hiring these days?"

"I was unloading" — *think, Evie, think* — "water bottles for the employee room; they keep a stack there, and one leaked all over me."

"Get a uniform from the front desk; you can't go around looking like you just walked in off the street. Tell them Hank said it was okay. We need all the help we can get today, and no one goes home unless they're bleeding from their eyes. Hurry it up!"

I hurried up the steps, turned for Annex 2 and opened the door to Operation Gift Basket. The room was loaded with flowers, bottles of champagne, ribbons, gifts of every sort, rolls of cellophane, bows, tulle and long tables with workers stuffing everything together.

"Put the box over there." A lady with wild gray hair and scary eyes pointed to a table. She shoved a huge white basket with champagne, two crystal flutes, a dozen gorgeous roses and a box of delish chocolates at me. "This goes to the Jane Seymour room."

"But —"

"No buts, this place is booked solid and we're swamped here with gift baskets. This one's a romance basket, so deliver it with a little pizzazz, will you, not like a sack of old potatoes tossed in a grocery cart."

She shrugged out of her white apron and flung it at me. "What happened to your uniform?" She held up her hand. "I don't care what happened to it, just put this on." She wound my hair on top of my head and stuck a purple lilac stem through it to hold it in place. She thrust another basket with a robe, bath salts, candles and wine at one of the bellhops and spouted more orders.

I put on the white apron with a ruffled top that covered my front and more ruffles on the skirt. This wasn't part of my great game plan to find Fiona or the killer, but it was a good cover. I asked one of the maids in the hallway for directions to the Seymour room and headed off to the service elevator; at least I knew where that was located.

"First day?" asked a waiter propelling a room service cart into the cramped area.

"First five minutes."

"Remember, no tips like they do in other places. You get caught taking a tip for any service and you are out the door. Good luck."

I got off on the third floor and stopped in front of the door with *Jane Seymour* scripted on a plaque. The Grand Hotel was big on scripted signage. I had no idea about the pizzazz thing. Throw petals, sing a song, balance a ball on my nose? The door opened. "Luka?"

"Evie?" We stood there for a beat, staring at each other, till Molly came to the door draped in a pretty pink robe and yanked me inside.

"What are you doing here?" Okay, I'd asked some pretty stupid questions in my life, but this was probably top of the list.

Molly slapped her palm to her forehead. "We're trying to be alone. Living on this island is like living in a goldfish bowl. Do you know what it's like to get some privacy without every move being discussed at the VI the next day?"

"Or bet on in a pool?"

"And now you show up? What are you doing in a hotel uniform?" Molly scowled. "Did my mother send you to spy on me? My dad? Father Phillip at Saint Ann's?"

"I bet it was Angelo." Luka shook his head. "He'll think I seduced Molly; he loves Molly like a daughter. I'm dead meat. *Sleeping with the fishes* isn't just a line from some movie, you know."

I held up my hands in surrender. "No one sent me. I'm looking for Fiona." I sat the basket on the dresser. "I never saw you here and you never saw me here. No seeing of any kind occurred in this hotel, okay?"

I backed to the door, then stopped and turned to Luka. "So, how did you score this great room? The hotel is full, has been for months."

Luka raked back his black hair. "*The family* has their ways of doing things. We know how to get what they want."

"Threats?"

"That's old school and gets really messy. I talked to a manager and he made it happen. Trust me, for enough money anything can happen, even here at the Grand Hotel."

I stepped into the hall and Luka closed the door, as my brain scrambled to figure out what Luka meant and how the money angle played into this.

"There you are." I spun around to another maid stomping my way. "HR said they were sending a new girl to help me, and it's about time. They didn't tell me it was a new girl with a bad uniform." She shoved a cart in my direction. "The Tiffany Room called for a spruce; their grandkids trashed the place last night, and then we got the whole second floor to do. Everyone's behind. Don't just stand there, get a move on and follow me unless you want security to usher you out the back door on your first day on the job."

Security ushering was not an option. I'd never find Fiona or the killer or figure out this room thing if I got booted. "Well?" the maid barked. "This isn't a vacation, at least for you it's not. Here's the card to get in the rooms. Remember to knock and call out *housekeeping.* You better do a good job. Now move it."

By four I was tired in places I didn't know could get tired. I told the maid drill sergeant I needed a bathroom break before I drowned, then snuck down to the first floor.

"You're over an hour late," Mother whispered as I pulled up beside her at the grand piano. "Where have you been? Nate's here looking for Fiona; he's asked me twice where you were, and they still haven't located Zo in the refrigerator."

"The maid uniform thing kind of backfired. So far I've made beds, cleaned bathrooms, vacuumed, dusted and polished fixtures and hauled linens to the laundry and not gotten paid one cent for it."

We scooted behind a fern and I sagged against the wall. The flower in my hair was long gone, my once-crisp white apron wilted. "Did you find anything?" I asked Mother.

"Madonna is giving the managers all kinds of grief over not finding Zo, the mystery weekend people are eating it up with a spoon, and Idle Summers bought enough Hello Kitty merchandise at the gift shop to start her own gift shop. She has a Hello Kitty obsession worse than you do. I think it started when you were about —"

"On my eighth birthday," I said, trying to make sense of things. "Best party ever. My friends talked about it in reverent tones for years. Idle has a child. That's why she turned her life around and why Fiona is helping her. Best I can tell the little girl is staying with someone while Idle works, and she's probably trying to protect her daughter if things go south."

"Do you think Fiona would help Idle enough that they'd do in Peep? Idle pushes him off the porch and Fiona clobbers him?"

"Maybe . . . I hope not." I did the *I don't know* shrug. "Why are things so complicated? But right now we've got something else to think about. How would you like to get a room here at the Grand Hotel?"

A grin tripped across Mother's lips. "You and Sutter have plans? Finally something good is happening today. My daughter the little sexpot. I knew I should have gotten the day after the wedding in that pool."

I held out my arms. "Mother, seriously, do I look like a sexpot? More like stew pot, chicken pot, soup pot that's been cooking all day." I hitched my chin toward the desk. "Talk to Penelope or her manager playmate. Say you want a room and you're willing to pay whatever to get it. See what happens."

"They'll laugh, that's what'll happen. I don't think you can get a room at the Grand during the Lilac Festival no matter what. Look at this place." Mother waved her hand over the crowded lobby. "I heard people making reservations now for next year."

"Say that price is no object. Somehow Penelope and lover-boy are making a lot of money on rooms, I think. I just can't figure out how they're doing it."

Mother smoothed her blue linen skirt and hiked her expensive taupe purse up onto her shoulder. "American Express, here I come. Time to start chalking up sky miles."

Staying hidden, I watched Mother cross the lobby and approach the desk. She smiled, she laughed, she waved her black AmEx card in the air. Penelope got her manager honey and he clicked away on the computer. Then he smiled and he laughed and he took Mother's card. He swiped the card through at the desk, then left for a minute. When he came back he handed Mother the credit card, the room card and some papers.

Mother strolled back my way and ducked around the piano. "Room three fourteen. I could have gotten one of those signature rooms but I would have had to sell our home in Chicago to afford it. The room I got was expensive enough. There was some kind of surcharge that cost as much as the room because it's the Lilac Festival."

I studied the two papers Mother had in her hand. "There are two separate charges." I looked at one paper. "This receipt is from the Grand Hotel." I flipped over to the second sheet. "This receipt is from the Grand Hotel Michigan and it has the last four digits of your credit card written by hand."

Mother arched her left brow. "I got a feeling the Grand Hotel Michigan is Penelope and lover-boy's little nest egg. You got to give the devil his due; this is brilliant. One charge for the Grand Hotel and one for them. They run the second charge through on one of those mobile credit card readers and credit their own personal account. That's what the manager did when he walked off for a few seconds. He has pre-printed receipts; that's why the credit card number is handwritten."

"But what about the room? How do they get the extra rooms available? Like you said, the place is packed, probably has been for months."

Mother studied her credit card for a second. "They double-book the people who make early reservations. When you reserve a room it's by name and credit card. Our two entrepreneurs book two rooms knowing they can sell the second one with that surcharge scheme later on when rooms are hard to get. They cancel the original credit card and the fake name that held the reservation and run through the new card and name and add their surcharge, explaining it's for the special weekend."

"Or they peddle a room upgrade for an extra charge. Peep realized what they were doing when they suggested an upgrade to him for a lot more money."

"It takes devious to catch devious."

"There she is." The maid drill sergeant pointed a bony finger at me and did her storm trooper march across the lobby. The gal from gift basket central marched beside her along with the guy off the loading dock, and there were two big guys in navy Polos looking more security guard than hotel guest.

"HR never hired her, I knew it right away," the sergeant continued as she drew up next to me. "She's horrible at cleaning;

she left a ring around the tub and ate the pillow mints. She's a fake."

Penelope came over. She looked from me to Mother to the papers in our hands. She didn't recognize Mother but she knew me, that Fiona and I were friends and that I was involved with Peep. And there was the dropped bagel incident in the employee room where she and the manager were talking. She knew that I knew the two of them were in cahoots over something. I could almost hear the little gears churning in her brain, her eyes slowly widening as she put it all together.

"And they're both dangerous," Penelope said, pointing to Mother and me. "In fact, Officer Sutter was around here in the hotel looking for them. He asked at the desk if I'd seen either one, and here they are right in front of us. Evie was pretending to be a maid, so that proves she was up to something. You know, I think she's the one who killed that Peep guy; she's been involved in all this since the beginning. She was out in the gardens when they found his body."

"Why would Evie kill Peep?" Mother asked. "She didn't even know him."

"Says you." Penelope folded her arms, looking smug. "I bet she knew him really well; she and that Fiona girl were in it together in knocking off Peep and maybe knocking off Zo too."

The Corpse Crusaders hurried over; Gabi was shaking her head and pulling out her notebook. "Evie's not on my suspect list anywhere. This makes no sense. If Evie were the killer, I'd have notes, some evidence."

She turned to Penelope. "In fact, you're the one who is on our who-done-it list. You're one of the top two murder suspects."

Manager lover-boy came out and said to the security guard, "You can take these two in the back room until we find Officer Sutter." He faced the crowd, held up his hands winner style and smiled. "Isn't this murder mystery weekend fantastic, folks?"

Everyone applauded.

"This is ridiculous!" I waved the receipts at the security guards. "Penelope and this manager are the guilty ones, and they are guilty for real. They've been scamming the customers and the Grand. They're adding a surcharge that's bogus, and it goes to them and not the hotel."

One security guard held my arm, and one grabbed Mother. Red flashed before my eyes, it really did. No one touched Mother. "You leave her alone!" I tried to wrench free, and out of the corner of my eye I noticed Penelope and the manager making a beeline for the front door.

"They're getting away! Do something," I screamed at the guards.

"You're not getting anywhere," the taller guard growled. "You're going to jail."

"I had no idea," one of the Murder Marauders said to me. "You're a much better actor than I thought. You might just get an SH after all. That's a Sherlock Holmes," she explained to the growing crowd. "It's an award for the best actors in this murder mystery weekend." She pointed to a board across the lobby. "You can cast your votes right over there. We're having trophies and everything."

Mother leaned my way and whispered, "Run."

"What?"

"They're getting away. On three. One, two, three."

Mother fell to the floor like a sack of those potatoes I was warned about earlier, the guards lunged to catch her and I pulled free, darting into the surging crowd, something a big burly guard had no chance of doing.

I tore for the front door, yanking off my apron as I went. I could hear the guard bellowing for me to stop, but in true mystery weekend fun and excitement, more crowds cheered my escape across the front porch. I galloped down the red-carpeted steps, grabbed a bike from in front of Sadie's Ice Cream Parlor and pedaled as fast as I could down Cadotte, getting lost in the shadows of a lovely evening on Mackinac Island.

19

Cadotte was downhill all the way, and I was flying like a bat out of hell. The bad news was I had no idea where I was going. How would Penelope and lover-boy escape off the island? A plane was not a quick exit; their own boat at night was playing Russian roulette with takers out there on the lake, but the ferries ran like clockwork, there were a lot of them and Penelope and the manager could have persuaded a Grand Hotel carriage to take them to the docks. Like Luka said, with enough money you can get anything you want.

One long blast came from Shepler's, meaning a ferry was headed out. That was it! Penelope and lover-boy were headed for the ferry and once they got to the mainland they'd disappear, I was sure of it. I skidded around the corner onto Main, darted around carriages, bikes and pedestrians and fishtailed onto the docks, where riding bikes was strictly forbidden.

"Hey, you! Stop!" one of the dockhands yelled.

"Get out of my way!" I flew on past, heading down the dimly light concrete pier full tilt. There were just a few fudgies left to board, and the two right ahead of me were running. Penelope and the manager? I wasn't the police and the ferry wouldn't stay in port because I said so. I had to get them before they got on the boat.

Neck-and-neck I pulled beside Penelope and hit the brakes to knock her off balance except . . . except there were no brakes! I grabbed Penelope to slow down, then grabbed the next nearest person for the same reason, but nothing worked and Penelope, Nate Sutter and I sailed off the end of the pier into thin air and landed in Lake Huron.

Cold black water closed over me, my shoes and clothes weighing me down, down, down. I thrashed around like a wild woman to swim, as someone grabbed my shirt and dragged me to the surface.

"Take this!" a guy in an orange vest with a blinking light shouted, shoving a buoy ring under my right arm. I was instantly hauled onto the pier, Sutter sprawled out on one side of me like a landed fish, Penelope on the other and all three of us hacking and choking.

"Penelope. The manager," I managed between coughs that sounded like I was bringing up a lung. "Bilking the hotel."

Sutter pushed himself to a sitting position and wiped water from his face. It started to sink in that Sutter was here on the dock at this time of night and that a dockhand of considerable proportion had the manager by the scruff. How? Why? "Mother called you?" I wheezed.

"I ran a check on Grand Hotel Michigan." Someone tossed a blanket over my shoulders, then Sutter's. He took a deep breath. "If I put it together right, you and Carman were causing all kinds of hell up there at the Grand, and Penelope was on the run. The ferry is the best way out of town."

A dockhand peered down at me. "Didn't we fish you out of the lake last year?"

"Not my fault, it's a black cloud thing." I pulled my blanket tight over my shoulders and tried to stop shaking. Wobbling to my feet, I looked down at Penelope. "You two killed Peep so he wouldn't blackmail you, and then you got rid of Zo to make Fiona look guilty?"

Teeth chattering, Penelope shook her head, her wet hair slapping against her cheeks. "I didn't kill Peep; *we* didn't kill Peep. He was a dirty rotten louse and deserved what he got, but we didn't do him in, and I have no idea what happened to that Zo girl, I swear it. All of a sudden she was just gone."

"Gone because she knew what you and your boyfriend here were up to. You stuffed her in the fridge out back of the hotel," I insisted. "She knew what Peep knew, that you were double-charging people for rooms. You got rid of her and planted the turtle bracelet that you stole to frame Fiona for the deed. Getting into Zo's room was a snap with the manager passkey."

"We didn't do any of that, and we didn't kill anyone," the manager added. "We are not murderers. We were both working the night Peep was killed, but we didn't do it. If we did kill Peep, we'd have that blasted phone and be gone by now. You can search our condo; we don't have it."

Sutter raked back his hair. "My guess is that Zo had the phone all along, threatened to blackmail you two, and you tossed Zo and the phone in the fridge."

Penelope sniffed. "We're thieves, not killers."

"That's what they all say." Sutter stood beside me and tweaked my nose. He

344

brushed hair from my face. "Nice job, Chicago. Except for the header in the lake. Thought you had better bikes. No brakes is bad for business."

I looked over the edge of the pier down into the water. "It's not a Rudy's Rides bike, and that part is good for business."

Sutter laughed, then gave me one of his lopsided grins. "I got a ton of paperwork, we're still waiting to see where that fridge is and I got to get these two locked up."

"But not in the good cell."

"Nope, not in the good cell."

"I'm off to find Fiona. She can actually sleep in her own bed tonight. She's a free woman, finally." I took a deep breath. "I can't believe this is actually over." I glanced back at Penelope and the manager. "I . . . I should have figured out what they were up to before this, and then maybe Zo would still be alive. I feel bad about that. She wasn't my favorite person, but she deserved better than a refrigerator coffin in a recycle yard."

Chilled to the bone, I walked home. I took a hot shower, then swore to do laundry as I hunted for a pair of not-so-dirty jeans and pilfered Mother's yellow fleece. I grabbed Nancy Drew and a KitKat from the blue shoebox under the workbench with *Rudy only, stay out, this means you* scrawled on the top. I headed for the Grand. I was dead tired, and every pedal of the bike was pure torture. As soon as I told Fiona that her troubles were over, I could go to bed and sleep for a week, or at least until ten when the cannon blasted and the bike shop opened.

With my fleece not exactly fitting in with the after-dinner fancy crowd at the hotel, I parked around back. I darted up the back steps and slunk behind potted palms and wingback chairs to avoid staff and guests still talking about Penelope and the manager. I blended in with a family trotting up the main stairway and headed for the second floor. Idle and Fiona would be busting out the champagne about now or . . . or maybe not. We still hadn't found the blasted phone, and that meant that anyone who had it could start the blackmail thing up again.

The phone could be in the fridge with Zo like Sutter said, but when I was trapped under the desk in the *Employees Only* room, Penelope told her manager lover-boy they had to find the phone. That meant neither of them had it then, and tonight on the pier neither of them knew where it was. It sure would be nice if I could find the phone and drop it in the lake, and then Idle and

346

Fiona's troubles would be over for sure.

I took the service elevator to the second floor and headed down the hall to the cheap seats. A maid's cart sat off at the far end, and since I'd been a maid — a free maid — I knew some of the maids stored their master cards on their carts instead of having them on a tether that got tangled or got in their way. I hunted for a few minutes and retrieved the card. I'd replace it when I was done, but now I took off for Zo's room.

Yellow crime scene tape crisscrossed the entrance. I reached around, slid in the card, and opened the door to the total mess I'd seen before. Actually it looked even worse than before, if that was possible. And the window was — open? And . . . and holy cow, someone was lying on the floor.

"Fiona!" I gently turned her over.

"Like, don't worry," came a voice from above me. "She's, like, still alive."

"Just not for long," Madonna added. "And the same goes for you."

I stood and looked from Zo to Madonna, just a few feet away. "Together . . . you're in this together?" I did a mental head-slap. "Of course you are. *You* both killed Peep. You pushed him over the railing," I said to Madonna. "And you clobbered him with the olive oil bottle you found where Fiona

347

lost it," I said to Zo.

"That was a bonus," Madonna said with a chuckle. "We hadn't counted on Fiona being in such a state that she'd leave her yellow bag behind, but there it was right in the lobby. I handed it off to Zo, and she used the olive oil bottle, the perfect frame for Fiona. We planned on using a rock and leaving Fiona's hat behind. We had one from her L.A. days, but the green olive oil bottle was a much better idea."

"But why kill Peep at all? I mean, he's a no-good jerk, but the wife and the mistress teaming up to do him in?"

"Peep had chickie number three lined up and he was planning on ditching me and Zo. When I told Zo what was going on, we decided to ditch Peep first and frame Fiona for it. All we had to do was get Peep out here to Mackinac."

"That was, like, my idea," Zo said, holding up her hand. "I, like, sent him threatening notes, and he thought someone was after him, the poor baby. I knew he wanted Fiona back as editor on the paper, and I talked him into running off to this place."

"And then you framed Fiona."

"She hated him, everyone knew that. Peep threatened to tell her parents what scummy things she did to get the stories she did, but

348

when Idle came on the scene and they bonded over her brat kid and Idle turning her life around to start fresh, Fiona left and got Idle here too. Blackmailing Penelope and that manager was just a bonus for Peep. He was always playing the angles."

"And this time we, like, played him. Madonna would inherit the paper and I, like, knew how to run it. It was our turn to cash in and make a bundle."

"So you two staged all the fights, and Madonna and I trapped in Annex 1 was a warning?"

"I wasn't supposed to be in on that," Madonna said. "But if I didn't go, you weren't going to go. You needed to be scared and back off. You were snooping around all the time. When I faxed my legal stuff to L.A., I saw the fuse box, so killing the lights was easy enough and added to the drama. You got to have drama. When you mentioned that Penelope and the manager could have done the murder together, Zo and I were afraid you'd start putting us together. So we got rid of one of us, and Zo got the short straw."

"I've been, like, hiding out in Madonna's room forever. But we had to come here and find that cell phone. It has stuff on us that we don't want out there, just like everyone else. And where else could Peep hide the thing but here?"

"You came back for one more look, and so did Fiona, and so did I."

"We were going to have Fiona take a flying leap to her death, making it look like she was guilty all along." Madonna took a pink lipstick from the top of the dresser, pulled off the cap and scrawled *I'm sorry* across the mirror. "Hard to do handwriting analysis on a mirror with lipstick. Fiona's body on the service road far below will certainly smack of suicide. It has to be done. Fiona saw Zo here, she put it all together, she has to go."

"And, like, so do you."

"Over my dead body!"

"Like, that can be arranged."

"Arrange what?" Fiona garbled, pushing herself up. "Are there more wedding plans?"

Zo pulled a gun from her pocket and aimed it at me.

"Like, now we shoot you, make it look like Fiona did it and toss her out the window. One of those murder-suicide things. Murder 'cause you knew too much and suicide because poor Fiona here couldn't live with herself. Madonna and I don't live in Hollywood for nothing." Zo flashed Madonna a big toothy smile, and they did a high five.

Zo aimed the gun and —

"Jeez Louise!" Gabi yelped as she and the Corpse Crusaders barged into the room, crime scene tape draped over them as they tried to brush it off. "I tell you that phone has got to be in here and . . ."

The Crusaders stared, mouths open, eyes bugged. "You're . . . you're alive?" Gabi gasped.

"Like, you bet I am," Zo said, a big smile plastered on her face. "And Fiona here was the killer all along. Just look at her and . . . and now Madonna and I are going to go get the police and you all win! You stay right here with Fiona and —"

"No way!" I yelled. I'd had enough of the Zo/Madonna production of *The Mystery Hour.* I lunged for Zo and the gun.

Well, dang. This looked so easy in the movies, but Zo was scrappy and a lot stronger than she looked. I grabbed her hand as she backed me toward the open window, inch by inch getting closer. I tripped over a pillow, Zo gave a final shove and I tumbled out the window, catching a chunk of red geranium drape as I dangled over the service road below . . . far below. I could feel the material tearing under my weight. It was all those Nutty Buddies and KitKats, not to mention wedding cake. I was fat and I was going to die and it was all my fault and a hand grabbed my wrist as Sutter peered over the windowsill at me.

"I got you." He reached down, grabbing my other wrist, and pulled me up, with my gut balanced on the sill and my butt sticking up in the air. Sutter tugged on my jeans and we both tumbled into the room. Gasping for air, I rested my head on his chest; his heart was pounding.

"I thought I was a goner."

"Ditto."

"Zo? Madonna? We got to —"

"They already have." I looked over to Zo and Madonna in handcuffs at Molly's side, surrounded by the Crusaders. The Murder Marauders in purple shirts streamed in the door with the Body Baggers right behind them.

"They still think . . ."

"Yeah, they do, and no matter what the papers say or the courts do, it will always play as a murder weekend at the Grand. I think I'm up for an SH."

"What about when they go to prison?"

"They'll get fan mail."

"How did you know?"

"They found the fridge and there was no body or phone. Peep had his life on that phone; he wouldn't have let it out of his sight. If it wasn't in this room, it would be on him." Sutter pulled the silver phone from his pocket and made it do a little dance in the air. "He hid it in his three-inch lifts. The man was smart, sleazy but smart."

I took the phone from Sutter's fingers and tossed it out the open window over our heads. "That thing has caused enough problems. From this high up it'll be in a bazillion pieces when it hits the ground."

Sutter kissed me on the head. "You owe me a dance."

"Now?"

He kissed me again, this time full on the mouth. "I can't think of a better time to dance."